Family Affairs

Family Affairs

Jane Watkins

Harper & Row, Publishers
New York, Hagerstown, San Francisco, London

FIRST EDITION

Designed by Gloria Adelson

Library of Congress Cataloging in Publication Data

Watkins, Jane.
   Family affairs.
   I. Title.
PZ4.W3347Fam [PS3573.A842]   813'.5'4   77–3807
ISBN 0–06–014574–9

77 78 79 80 10 9 8 7 6 5 4 3 2 1

"My hat it has three corners,
Three corners has my hat,
And had it not three corners,
It would not be my hat."

Watkins, Cushman, Massar

Part One

Chapter 1

———··❦··———

IT WASN'T SOMETHING THAT Alma Thomas wanted to do. If the idea was unsettling, what would the visit be like? What she longed for was twenty minutes just to look at her founder. That's all she needed and all he wanted. That first gaze would be, always was, a profound moment of love between them. But she knew she would never get away with it. Alma and her father would both have to go through the motions of wanting her to stay. She felt she had no choice but to go. Her father's birthday could hardly be forgotten, nor could she send a card or an English ivy plant the way her sister Mary could. Alma still lived too close to her father not to visit, and besides, no matter how far away she lived, she would have to go this time. He would expect her in his new home. Another hello that always seemed like goodbye. If she didn't look at him, she knew she would not be able to stand the burden of such bad behavior. And sometimes, as she thought about it, she realized that her normal adult self-possession vanished when it came to the old man. She simply slipped back into childhood, judging and being judged.

She felt she had said goodbye to him four or five months ago in February, the day she dismantled his library just before he moved from the house on Pembroke Avenue. The Hughes house it was known as, even she thought of it that way, and in the leaving of her father, the last of the family to move out, she realized that Thomas and Margaret, Mary and Alma, were being divided, auctioned off, discarded along with the grand piano, the highboy, the pots and pans, the garden tools. Mr. and Mrs. Hughes and the two girls on Pembroke Avenue belonged to the past. The whole neighborhood came by in ones and twos to remark on the sadness. The day she said goodbye was not the last time she saw him in their house or stood in the hall the day of the closing, still part and parcel owner for a few more hours. It was the day some time before, the day she spent almost eight hours on a stepping stool, removing, sorting, throwing out his whole life while he sat across from her, leaning out of his chair into the console television set, special hearing aid adjusted, volume turned up so high that in the end she heard nothing at all, she was so enveloped in noise. He never took his eyes from the screen, not even to drink or eat his lunch from a tray. He was tended by his second wife, Bess. Alma did not think of her as her stepmother. They were both too old for that, and it wouldn't have worked at any age. Alma missed her mother that day. It seemed she should be there alive, not dead, ashes in an urn in the ground. As the afternoon went on, and the packing and moving began, Alma had to climb over the electric cord, arms loaded with books, to leave the room. Even at that he ignored her until she took to walking across in front of the picture. With that he waved an impatient hand at her as if to push her aside. She snatched his gold traveling clock off the desk and stuffed it in her pocket, but sleight of hand didn't matter to him now either.

He must feel something, she thought. Surely it was a shattering experience, one that could kill. But to look at him she knew he was composed, whatever emotions he might normally feel long since severed and left to drift, unanchored, in his mind. When she was done, the boxes sealed, the discards stacked in the garage for the college book sale, she rested against the doorsill. The room looked sacked, the specially built walnut cabinets and shelves empty and dirty. She felt as though she had

4

murdered him, but he refused to die. He was beyond this library that had been so precious to him. Way back where he was, he didn't read books. How far did he have to go before he moved into the here and now? She wanted to swing out and touch him, slap him, belt him, and have him smack her back, both of them like angry children, his withdrawal from her to hurt her, and her instinctive demand was for something more solid to remember than this vacuum called old age. She thought of how disgusting he had been when he ate Sunday supper at the kitchen table while she was growing up. It seemed more real than this.

She kissed him goodbye. He patted her on the cheek as she leaned over him, his eyes still on the television. "You're a good little girl," he said, "now run along."

She began the trip home, walking, running down the back side of the hill to the river road, the tears clouding her vision dripping from her chin. She licked them in. At the bridge, she stopped, exhausted, and realized it was cold. She buttoned up her winter jacket and pulled her gloves from the pocket. The dirty snow was crusted along the curb. The river was a slow-moving mass of slush, deceptive and dangerous. Beneath the surface the water ran swift and cold; a newsworthy death, foolhardy, they would say. Thoughtful, she looked at the river with new respect. And then she marched; not a funeral march, not a death march, but a march to do battle. Why did she always care? Still. For forty years.

The two miles home took half the usual time. The chill in her face froze her tears until they hurt. When she came through the front door of her house, she went directly up the stairs. On the landing she passed her daughter, Polly—"What's the matter, Ma?"—but she strode on up. She fell into her husband's arms where he sat in the big high-backed chair before his desk. James held her as she sobbed and stroked her frowzy hair and grimy neck the way a parent soothes a wounded child. He'd been primed for these days, this season of the destruction of Alma's past, and she knew he hoped blindly through those funny-looking specs of his for some rebirth. It was a bad time for her, the autopsy before the death. He didn't always come through for her, or for himself, she knew, but as she lay across his familiar chest she never stopped to suppose he would fail her now, or even that he would succeed. She was too taken up with herself to think of him.

Eventually she stopped her crying and looked up into his face. "It was awful, James. Right in front of his eyes and he never saw me. I wrecked forty years of his building in one day. I love him and I hate him. I never want to see him again."

In early June Alma wrote to her father appropriately to say she was taking a day off from work, and she and James would visit to honor the old man's age. Eighty-seven is a lot of adding up, and Alma had some admiration for the sheer gall of such longevity. In her letter she stressed that there be no fuss, no bother about lunch. To eat with her father had long since become an agony for her. She was only protecting herself. By return post she received a carefully typed note. "Dear Alma, delighted to greet you and James on June 21, my eighty-seventh birthday. Be sure to note that it is a Friday. You will have to take time off from work. Luncheon will be served at 12:30." Paragraphs about alternative routes. What to do at the Big Bunny supermarket, a sharp left. Straight along the main street until you pass the Union Hardware Company, where you bear right. Up past the airport. On and on. Love, and in the most tenuous hand signed "Pa," above the typed full names, Thomas Hamer Hughes. Four spaces, flush left-hand margin. Mrs. James J. Thomas. The old man's present wife had been his secretary for thirty years.

On receiving one of these communiqués, Alma felt so totally her father's incapacity for the personal touch, for love, that she would go around for days, fifteen, thirty-five, forty years old, longing for her daddy, knowing it wasn't the one she really had.

James and Alma accepted the ordeal of lunch and she set the subject way back in the cold cellar of her mind, where things are frozen in total disorder, in hopes they will get lost. The evening before the trip, she felt edgy and began to talk about early start, gassing up, trip to the florist. James paid no heed. They both knew that whatever time they arrived, it would be too early, that lunch would be at least an hour late, what with the hysteria involved in overcooking the meal.

On the Friday morning, Alma lost her calm and called into the emptiness of the kitchen where she knew James was lurking, like a cat hiding to avoid being jammed into an animal carrier before a long trip. "We're already fifteen minutes late," she said, "we'd better go." From behind the bathroom door came an abusive sentence amounting to up yours and leave me alone, I'm on the john.

James was angry enough to go up two flights of stairs to his study to get his briefcase. This meant the "togetherness" of the journey would be replaced by Alma's driving while James buried his understandable but unlovable angers and doubts about the duties of the day in some unreadable book about the comparative uses of the word for testicle or the dirty passages in Catullus. Much more fun than the personal communication between them that so often ground to a monologue, Alma dead center stage.

James was a scholar, and like most scholars he had his dried-up side. Alma suspected that overdoing it wasn't just being better than anyone else but finding peaceful escape from the living in the words, ideas, historical societies and individuals that didn't talk back. Alma talked back.

James was sexy and funny and gentle. Alma liked his hair and his hands, and this was one day when she could have used his support.

"Hey, talk to me."

"Sure," he said, turning the open book upside down on his lap.

"I feel like hell. I'm bored, I'm already tired." She wanted to pull over to the side of the highway and ask him to hold her, but she was afraid to be a child, his child. "I'm scared and I need you badly."

"What's there to be scared of?"

"You should ask?" Alma said angrily. "Same thing you're so

7

uptight about. Seeing him. So old, so out of it. In a new place. Why do you think you exploded this morning?"

"Everything with you is a big drama, Alma. I exploded because you hand on all your own doubts to me. You think marriage is falling apart on someone."

"For Christ's sake," she said. "I read your learned papers, wash your underwear, write your mother, hang onto your balls at night, and right now all I am is someone who dumps on you."

"Okay, Alma, okay." He went back to his book.

I never have learned to ask for something, Alma thought. Right now I feel about five years old.

She drove fast, miserably alone, in the past, the present and the future. By the time she had maneuvered all the turns, she almost ran Bess down in her care to keep her eyes on what was coming next. Bess was out by the mailbox right on the road, pretending to clip the tall grasses around the base of the post. Bess wore a pair of well-fitting pants and a gay shirt, her hair brushed back from her face becomingly. And the pathos and guilt hit Alma simultaneously. Here was this poor woman, sixtyish, anticipating the arrival of one of her next to least favorite people in the world with pleasure, hope, a mark of the loneliness she must have always felt as housekeeper/hospital attendant to Alma's antisocial father. Even in the city no one was encouraged to visit. God, how she must resent those ancient dreams of loving, touching, caring. Of seduction. In the months since the old man and Bess had made this move, she must have mowed and pruned and weeded and transplanted hundreds of hours away. What would winter bring?

They greeted each other, James especially gracious, leaving Alma with a few hateful thoughts to get stashed away in a hurry. James and Alma admired the house, the gardens, the wonderful rock-filled fields. Bess was pleased. "Oh, do you really think so, Alma? You do like it. I'm so glad. I've always loved the place, but it's just a farmhouse." Just a farmhouse, Alma thought. With everyone rushing to lay down pioneer stakes, Bess had quite a bit of just a farm, and she'd had her anxious moments about pleasing Alma. Why? Alma could only decide that in her desperation, Bess had forgotten how much of Alma's mother and father lay between them, Bess and Alma, and Bess did deserve some kind of purple heart. She'd had all the declining years of a superego. Not the best.

"They're here," Bess called. No answer.

They approached through the kitchen, the center of the house. To the left Alma saw the old part, every inch she could take in filled with a chair, a table, chest of drawers, braided rug, a mirror, pair of candlesticks, and yet another desk. Speckled wallpaper, one room blue rosettes, another in pink, and so on. It gave a dizziness of no continuity.

Alma heard her father before she saw him.

"Bess, where are my socks?"

She stepped into the living room to her left, moving toward the familiar voice.

"Right there by the bed, Thomas." Bess raised her voice. "Wait a minute, I'll put them on for you."

"You say they're here."

"Yes, they took the turnpike."

"Did they take the turnpike?"

When Alma realized that the old man was going to emerge through that narrow doorway, skirting the several objects between herself and him, like the face of a pinball machine, up and down the lanes to winning position, she stepped forward to the door of his room. He was just getting started, crutch tucked under his arm. He looked up at her from the hollow eyes of the elderly, that both beg and don't see. His head was large and smooth, almost ludicrous on top of his frail body. Some months before, Alma had come upon him in the dusk, asleep in his hospital bed, then planted indelicately in the Pembroke Avenue drawing room. He was scrunched down in the bed, his backside uncovered, his huge head lying cheek down on his small folded hands. He had always been proud of those hands. Some private vanity. And at that time Alma knew he would die soon. He looked like a six-month-old baby, napping. Six months old, that's how far back he had gone. Not much more to travel. Now she saw it again, but this time she had to move. She squeezed his brittle shoulders and kissed his lips, child's lips, unable to form the kiss back.

"Sensible to take the turnpike, Alma. You would have gotten lost the other way."

"I'm glad to see you, Daddy." She was. He must have felt the tears on his bald head.

The old man extended a gentlemanly hand to James, who was poised over the back of a wing chair, as if he and it must share the only standing space in the room.

Alma walked backward, facing the old man, through the living room, over the tread to the narrow kitchen. At that point he looked up and saw her fearing for him. He stopped his slow, unsteady progress until she turned her back on him to continue through the pantry into the "study," his room, dominated by his life machine, the video box. The room was jammed with bad pictures of himself being important. Before a microphone—the Council address; with colleagues at an international congress. But there was also one handsome old portrait familiar to Alma. It came from a drawer in the highboy that once dominated the entry hall of Pembroke Avenue. It was nailed now at the side of the pantry door, far from the old man's fading sight. It was a picture of his piano teacher. How far back was that?

The old man arrived with some majesty and lowered himself onto the sofa. Bess took James and Alma through yet another door into the latest addition to the house. The old man hollered after them about the competency, the craftsmanship of the carpenter, fine man. Reminded him of his boyhood, real farmhouse, local artisans, pride in their work. Bess said the carpenter couldn't nail up a curtain rod, and in his wildest dreams Alma knew this house could never be compared to the cottage house of the old man's youth. But then maybe old people learn not to face reality. Clearly her father had never seen the new room. It was an oddly shaped, narrow space, an old garage originally, big enough for a 1930s Ford. The room was almost windowless, partly paneled in fake walnut. The typing table was squeezed next to a wardrobe, beneath a tiny window. Here Bess had chosen to place the symbol of her special skill. Lightless, cramped, one wall away from the roar of the television, it was not for privacy or reverie, rather the most pathetic piece of a room of one's own that Alma had ever seen. Why, in a house with half a dozen front rooms? Some new form of self-abnegation. Bess's life was a chronicle of punishments.

Beyond the new room, at the same level, they walked directly into the hazy light onto a deck made of red cedar to clash garishly with the bright red of the lovely clapboards. Alma recognized an old porch chair from Pembroke Avenue, the first of many recognitions, this one certainly not painful. She hoped the others were as easy. Here Bess hoped the old man would sit in the sun and look over the apple orchards, perhaps mastermind her gardening. The stage was all set; it was a dream all built that would never come true. He would never sit in the heat again, never notice another apple tree or trellised vine, planted to soften the naked newness of this bower on stilts. James and Alma commented on the practicality of her plan and the arresting view. They returned to the study, where the old man sat before a tray with many tall glasses, each one with a different decal of an old period car, a special at the Amoco station with a new set of tires. There was tonic water, gin and ice, already melting. He was itchy to get on with it. "Hanging on the ropes," he used to call it.

"Make me a drink."

Bess hurried. "We have gin and tonic, that's what your father always has, but perhaps . . ."

"My drink, Margaret." James and Alma exchanged glances. The perpetual mixing of names. It was Margaret, Alma's mother, whom he knew as his wife, his only wife. He was way back again. And it was just noon, just one hour to the dot later than his normal "midday" drink. Waiting made him testy and forgetful.

Drinking at this hour made Alma giddy, foolish, restless, sleepy, in that order. But not one of them would question the need for all that at this moment. Besides, there was the ritual of it. Years ago it was Scotch at 1 P.M. After the old man broke his hip a while back, and Alma told the examining doctor defensively that at seventy-eight her father had a right to drink what he wanted, the doctor agreed calmly, only to point out that eight to ten ounces of alcohol a day over an adulthood left a body unreceptive—politely put—to surgery. "Oh," was all Alma had to say. And in the course of that operation, near death and recovery, a regular regime of drinking was worked out between medicine man and believer, seal of approval, so that the old man had never felt another moment of guilt. The slip on the stair carpeting and subsequent bone-breaking one evening nine years ago, while eavesdropping on Bess's telephone conversation, did more to restore his health than any number of antacids or carbohydrate diets.

"James will want a real drink, Margaret," the old man turning to James. His statement was more self-revealing than Alma would have expected. "I only have two of these gin and tonic now; I used to have more." He knew his own losses.

James stepped into the pantry, where the makings were ready. Bess was on her second gin and tonic, drinking privately, tensing up in her effort to relax. Did Bess mind being extinguished? Did she mind being called Margaret? Alma watched her through the pantry door. She felt sorry for her, but that was all. James mixed two chilly martinis, his served in a fragile stemmed glass in contrast to the gas station ware. He poured Alma's drink into a cut-glass openware piece, which her father filled amply with ice, since he controlled the supply. They settled to drinking. The old man criticized the missing lemon peel. Bess leaped to the kitchen, scolded child. He was definitely on a return trip to Pembroke Avenue evenings, where the first round opened with the ritual of Margaret Hughes raising her eyes to the ceiling while he rubbed the rind of a lemon round and round the rim of the glasses.

The old man patted the cushion next to him. Sign to sit like a loving daughter.

"I'm glad you took the turnpike, Alma."

"It makes me happy to see you looking so well, Daddy. The children send their love."

Alma gave him a kiss and he shoved her away with his tiny

hand. She sat in an accompanying armchair. Business. Call the gas company in the city; we don't owe them a thing. But it says right here on the slip it's a credit, Daddy. Just tell them we won't pay; we don't owe a thing on Pembroke Avenue. Bess, find the cards from the library; we don't have those books. Pretty soon Alma found herself making a list. Bess was rummaging through the house looking for lost stubs. Alma left the room to pace off some of the discomfort, urging James to move into the seat of honor. The old man liked the lower pitch of a man's voice. In fact, Alma suspected, he had some matey fantasy about the importance of man to man. Alma settled in the doorway, unnoticed. Could she stand it? She wanted both of them and they had each other.

"See that picture up there by the door? That's my old piano teacher. Good name, too. David Williams."

Alma watched James move politely to view the picture, which he must have seen ten times before.

The old man felt unusually expansive. "I was good at the piano. Voice, too. I used to sing while my mother played. My sister and I, we performed at the Welsh Society every Sunday night until I moved away from home."

Alma wondered why so much all at once. Not for years had he such energy. Did he feel the pressure of time running out on him? James and Alma listened attentively.

"My father wanted me to be a minister. A minister. He cleared peanuts in a mill and I made fifty thousand dollars a year at the bank. It all began with the safety razor. That's a good laugh."

He began to sing. "Dropping, dropping, dropping"—his tenor voice grew wondrously strong—"hear the pennies fall. Every one for Jesus, he will get them all." He stopped, one verse was enough.

He's way back now: six years old, Sunday school. It's frightening, Alma thought, frightening to travel with him. All three of them were silent. Neither James nor Alma dared to speak.

"It's a fortunate thing your name is Thomas. Thomas Hamer Hughes. The best. That's mine. James Thomas. I like you,

James." A nudge of an elbow so frail it couldn't quite make it. "It's the pureness of background that counts. At least your father had Welsh ancestors back there somewhere, James."

Alma lingered in the pantry, squeezing gin and ice water from the bottom of the mixing glass. She wanted to hear the purity of line theme that she knew was coming. Why subject myself? she wondered. Just to be one hundred percent right? It was a mistake.

"Did I ever tell you about the couple in Cardiff?" James said. "They were at the university. His name was Hughes and her name was Thomas."

"That's a good one, James. Alma Hughes. Now, that's purebred, my seed."

She'd heard it. That's me. A human being, not his pure anything. How can anyone be pure something? It always hurt. The hardest thing she had ever had to face in forty years was that her father was an emotional coward. No room in his scheme of things for a separate entity. Possession. Ownership. The hard work for her of making him look good. In all those years of trying, she knew now, her assignment had been no more than to relieve his own self-doubts, but she didn't know it then, and of course she could not do so, and thus she always failed. The life inside her, nurtured by his neglect, abuse, desire, grew long and thin like a single meadow flower shrouded by a thicket of weeds and brambles, struggling against darkness and death to finally reach the light and bloom. Long ago, she imagined, he gave up loving and settled for success. She had been his sacrificial offering. The credo rang out: Alma plus what he cared to bestow on her—his money, his prestige—equaled acceptance for herself—and him. He was downright small, way back when, she thought. What woman, what girl—for she had recognized the truth young—wanted to know that her father was small? And how did he get that way? She had never been able to face it. It made loving him now both angry and sad.

She moved into the kitchen, where she noticed two lovely T-bone steaks laid out on the table. When had she last seen that, and the pity of the overcooking? Bess passed her going the other way, a stack of papers in her hand. I don't need to be there when the lost library cards don't show up, Alma thought. She moved on into the first or side parlor. It was a journey she knew she must take, but she had been unsure for days how it would feel.

In the months before Alma's father sold the house on Pembroke Avenue and made the final move to assure comfortable, one-level living while waiting for death, she had spent many hours dismantling the lives of two or three generations of family from full attic on the fourth floor down to the stone cellar. The mutilation began in the attic, filled with signs of spent life— papers, letters, outmoded and elegant outfits carefully wrapped years before in tissue, shredded and torn with age—without the breath of a living human being, except hers. It gave her a terrible feeling of voyeurism, not into some parlor scene heady with sexual excitement, but back into the secret alleys of lives she had known well in other contexts. The tearing apart moved down the stairs, through familiar rooms and their familiar trappings, now recalling scenes of her past, as often as not bringing only numbness. By the time she reached the basement, her perspective regained, no villains in the family, no saints, she had felt as if her beginnings, her childhood, had been wrenched from her and lynched. Only the physical fatigue of steady work made the task possible. She was at it unceasingly.

The family possessions were divided. Almost all were associated with only one of her parents, her mother. A tail for you, an ear for me. And here in the Bournesville side parlor Alma wandered, searching out some of the pieces, objects that had been chosen by Bess to tide the old man over. She could hardly accommodate her old thoughts with familiar chairs and tables in these new surroundings. It must have troubled Bess, because she came from the kitchen, smoke pouring from the electric broiler, to hover, to explain, to apologize.

"You'll see that the two bedroom chairs just fit in there behind you. Look through the door into your father's room."

Alma turned. An unmade bed. After all, he had left it with her coming. The accouterments of his old age. Surgical socks, bladder bags. The chairs were squeezed in before his bed.

"He rather likes to see them, you know. You didn't want them?"

"They must remind him of his old bedroom." Alma spoke. "Forty-some years is a long time. I'm glad he sees them." She inspected the worn and unclean covers; green they were. And the only thing she would see was the sight of him sitting in one of these ordinary chairs, bent double, his head almost on the rug. Wheezing to death, reaching out for the syringe that she put into his hand. Then she remembered watching while he shot up his leg to relieve the asthma. Why did he want to lie in his deathbed and see that? Perhaps he saw his wife across from him. In those years, twenty and more ago, Margaret Hughes had sat in the accompanying chair and reached out to hold his hand, her face pinched, waiting for the rasp that would be the end. How many times had she administered? Each night; no, only a few times a week. And she had known that it seldom happened outside their home. Did she suspect that something about the discomfort of their lives joined together might trigger these attacks? Psychosomatic medicine. Not then. It would just have been a dull unformed ache in Margaret Hughes's mind. It must have been a terrific bond between them, one they both hated and feared.

Enough. Alma moved on to find a snake-legged table, the Hepplewhite armchair covered in raw silk, yellow, the one that Mary had so much coveted. Now it was placed in the crowded room behind chintz curtains. The handsome American eagle mirror that she and Mary had been cautioned about each day. "Not before that mirror." No ballet fantasies, no great choral conducting, no mime faces, for fear it would drop from the wall and smatter. Here it hung, diluted red and gold, against the rose-petal wallpaper that made it almost unnoticeable. A desk, another mirror. Alma's mother's favorite friends, her loving family, her possessions, spoke to no one that mattered now. Alma could have told her that in the end love was something else. I guess I did often enough, she told herself. Critical, arrogant. I used to make her cry.

"Doesn't that mirror look nice there," Bess said. "If I'd known what it was worth, I should have given it to you, but it was always my favorite piece of your mother's things."

Ironic. After all those years of careful tutelage, these things mean nothing to me, and Bess, who owns them, thinks of them as someone else's. "I'm glad you have it," Alma said simply. Bess kissed Alma for what she thought was dignity, generosity maybe, and was only a dismissal.

"Let me show you the attic."

"I think Daddy is hungry, Bess."

Bess flew from her moment of friendship. The meat burned, the smoke to cause the old man to cough. Frenetically she tried to cover up her neglect, her pleasure. She called them to lunch. The slow progression began from study to kitchen, where the table was laid. Three of them stood until the old man was seated, almost sideways on the hard wooden kitchen chair, no cushion to shield brittle bones where flesh once had sufficed. He leaned on an elbow to hang over the table. The tiredness showed in his eyes, and the familiar irritation in his voice.

"No salad. You know that." He pushed the bowl aside.

"Your father wanted sliced tomatoes—his teeth, you know—but I thought you'd like this corn." Bess scraped the kernels off the cob into a small dish and placed it in front of the old man. He shoved it away and reached out his fork to the serving board to stab a thin slice of meat, which he flung down on his plate. The rest of them carefully offered food and hospitality around the small table.

The discomfort of the meal made Bess apologetic and expansive. "I'm sorry, the steak is overdone. I'm not much of a cook, you know. Your father likes his meat rare. He finds it hard to chew."

The old man looked at her as if for the first time, and he did not like what he saw. She fumbled nervously for her napkin, mopped her lips.

"You know, James, those berries you see over there on the counter came from the farm. Early bearing, they call them.

There's a wonderful bakery in town, Alma. You might want to stop. They have scones."

When Bess handed Alma a local map, downtown Bournesville, Alma heard her father ask, "Are they leaving now?" Years ago he would have addressed Alma directly: "Beat it."

Alma knew he was in a hurry to be rid of them, but she was too slow-witted to know why. She just filled up with the same old resentment. She was stuffing in strawberry shortcake. A flat hard cake from the local baker, some squishy berries, not enough of them, and that stiff white shaving cream that is commercial whipped cream. Comes out of a spray can in a thick twirl. She didn't want any of it but it was easier to say yes than fight the protests.

Her father was still pushing his cholesterol-low margarine around on his cold potato. Alma's indifference to everything vanished. Just to see him eat did it. His hand shook so badly he couldn't find his mouth. She watched him, and because of his age she was touched, but she remembered back in the beginning when he couldn't find his mouth because he was drunk. Drunk before supper, during the meal. She used to stare at him and be revolted. And of course, he would have had to be drunk to crawl into her childhood bed at night. Instantly the memory was vivid and detailed, and with it the dream of punishment she used to spin out to silently hex him. And now, just for a moment, she had the same wonderful fantasy, after more than twenty years. In fact, it was better. She was excited. It grew because she had a new setting, not the old house on Pembroke Avenue.

She wanted to tell him she had come to make love with a big black Israeli, oh, God, that there should be such a thing just for her. Maybe make the old man an unwanted grandson, right there in his new old country house, in the next room on the sofa where the old man sat habitually, eight hours of soap opera and sports on the TV.

The reverie died. There was her husband, James, sitting right beside her, perishing for a beer, and it wouldn't work anyway. Now her father was too old to hear the ecstasy, the sighs, the moans, the little cries she had saved up for him, too old to hear the rock of the sofa through the gaps in the old farmhouse wallboards, age-thin, the rock, rock as the rhythm quickened. Then, when it was easy not to love him, she did not have the courage to unnerve him. Fifteen, sloppy, overeducated and undersophisticated, she was nobody who could make her parents' way up into "right" society, neither horsy enough on the one hand, nor fragile enough on the other, despite the right schools, despite rich and well-born connections, whom she took to be her friends rather than stepping stones, and despite the natural endowment of too much nose and prominent cheekbones. Very well bred, if you didn't know better.

Well, if she had had the nerve to play out a very modified version of the gorgeous fantasy, say bring home something that didn't wear a button-down oxford-cloth shirt, she might have gotten through his soused brain cells to the motor control that set off the expletives, through to the soft center of his mind, where fear governed his total intolerance of everything he could not control. He controlled Alma, all right, for the first twenty years of her life, and now when she had all the courage of this fierce freedom that a woman finds and then continually fights to keep, as if there were something unreal and ephemeral about it, the freedom, now it was too late. He was deaf and pathetic, well along on his journey backward. And besides, now she loved him. Same old gyp, just a new form.

So she didn't try out the old black-Israeli bit on him, because she was forty and he was eighty-seven that very day. She studied him, his fingers resting heavily on the tabletop. He pushed the blood from the tips. He's impatient. She pushed back her chair, just slightly. "You going?" he asked in a hurry. She shouted, "Not yet, Pa. We're not going yet. We're just going up through the hayfield. I bet you have a lovely view." They both knew the sky was overcast. He looked up, a blank gaze, and nodded his head back down to his plate like one of those purposeless wooden penguins that tilts its nose into a glass of water if you give it a gentle shove.

James and Alma, barely through the kitchen screen door, heard, the nation heard, the roar of the TV. "Jesus," Alma said, "that's it. That's why he wants to get rid of us. Our birthday visit interrupted his television schedule." *The Right to Life, The Edge of Darkness.* Filled with the real people that mattered to him, and in livid color. Alma's flesh was pale compared to Janet Anderson's shocking-pink arms, her daughter Marcia's yellow-red hair, and Marcia's lover, Bill, in rosy sports shirt. It was continuously amazing to Alma that a man who could hardly hobble ten steps with the aid of his metal crutch to greet his favorite child, could get from the kitchen table to the television set swift as a bird of prey.

Chapter 2

————··◦≪◯≫◦··————

JAMES AND ALMA WALKED along the veranda of the house to the front steps, adorned with a hideous wrought-iron handrail, new, twisted in the current American old style with a crooked-necked handle, shiny black enamel paint. It hollered out good-naturedly against the mockery of anything so modern, stable, there to hold up the leaning wooden steps and the footsteps of an old man, both about two centuries gone by.

They crossed the dirt road—the main road—five paces, and entered the hayfield. The fence was down, and as they began their walk, James noted the slovenliness of the local farmer, who had mowed down too early a swath of the field and left the rest seemingly to lie forever until season rot ruined the soil. James knew about these things. Through the stubble Alma still wore her blue sandals, thirty dollars' worth, with heels, done up for the day, but as they came upon knee-high growth she snapped the buckle and took them off, to carry them dangling by the thin straps from her thumbs. The dew would wet and ruin them, and the wonderful feeling of freedom, her wide childlike feet, flat-foot tough. She felt she had much to be free of this day.

More talk about the upkeep of farmland and rotating crops. James cared. His city shoes would get crusty from the wet, and his suit trousers, misty damp, might lose their press. It didn't matter. He had a lot of gentle talk, too. Notice the cow vetch. He handed her a stalk, perfectly rectangular, sharp-sided, with the spear-pointed series of purple bluebell drops opening in her hand. The field was wild with daisies, the choice of flower Alma had made at the florist's to celebrate the old man's day, a wonderful juxtaposition of natured and denatured. There was always some trick on her; the old man liked it that way.

At the rise of the field they saw the stone wall that marked the property's edge, lined with oak trees, unusual in this part of New England, where the maple prevails. And looking back down the valley, there was enough light to see the patches of clearing outlined by further stone walls, hundreds of years old, darting diagonally, perpendicular, just plain crooked across the fields and in and out of the woods, each a barrier signaling privacy and possession. It was a beautiful sight, the meaning so clear, and for a moment Alma forgot her turmoil and felt nothing painful. Peace. To the left, up the field, she could see the silo at the outskirts of the farmer's work buildings. It was weathered and in need of repair. By contrast, in the foreground, there was a large and lush vegetable garden, the soil plowed up deep, rich brown. Not a vitamin would ever reach the old man's needy body, not unless Bird's Eye frozen. Rows of peas, string beans on a latticework of twine, pole beans. Tomatoes just reaching up to be staked. Feathery tops now above the ground. Lettuces —Boston, bibb, oak leaf; thirty feet of them. Cabbages already grown to head. Broccoli flowers forming, and greens, maybe spinach, chard, beet tops. To the far side, down the slope of the hill, the familiar potato bushes and squash vines growing together in a high road/low road mass of disorder, to be sorted out later in the fall.

Such a garden was a pleasure to Alma as well as to James, and always brought her romantic notions of tender care and harvest, straw hat and broad shallow basket over her arm. Perhaps she was wearing a denim skirt and espadrilles. A kind of variation on the Marie Antoinette theme, in silk brocade puffed up with crinoline skirt and dainty sleeves, cream-colored satin slippers. It was a fantasy that got Alma through all those roadside buttercups and black-eyed Susans. Of course, the Queen of France was cutting gladioli and peonies and pinks, and it would ruin Alma's image of her as her nation's freest, gayest, cruelest irresistible if she were out there digging onion bulbs or dusting cutworms. Besides, surely she didn't eat; only candied violets. But then again, she came to a bad end.

Everyone has her memories, as the queen must have had in her bad times. But Alma remembered all those bugs on the potato plants and who picked them off. And the endless crop of beans, two months, enough for twenty mouths a week, pushing them down twice a day, the three or four of them at home. The old man had had a gardening phase, and it came to him wisely when he had what he referred to lovingly as a pint-sized labor force that couldn't say no. Protest, sure. The thrust down of a shoulder, the broken leg, the severe brain tumor. But quit—out of the question. Amazing the number of dirty jobs a kid of eight or nine could pack in while the agricultural architect kept the broader view in mind. But Alma was sometimes blessed in that he left town every now and then. Always on Tuesdays. On those Tuesday evenings, Alma's mother ceremoniously dumped the coarse beans down this right-up-to-the-minute in disposal, a built-in incinerator that burned one floor below in the cellar. The next day Alma's mother marketed for fresh vegetables.

James and Alma stood at the garden fence. "God, think of the potato bugs," Alma said. I'm getting crabby, she thought.

James didn't hear her anyway. She could see that he was beginning to itch to get personal with each of the plants. This would surely bring out the farmer for one of those "ayah" and "well" conversations that men always have while their feet are planted on earth. Alma didn't need any more people; it was all she could do to cope with those she had. She turned away from the garden fence and walked along the edge of the stone wall to stand above the house that cupper her ancestor. Even from up here she knew that Janet Anderson's husband, Robert, in red pin-stripe, perhaps, had come into screen view. "Oh, Bob, thank God you've come. Marcia is there with Bill."

Alma sat down on one of those flat stones with tiny pinnacles of growth right where she settled her tailpiece. She tried several times to find the pillow-soft surface. She put her knees up, her head between the palms of her hands, and settled into a long winter's tale. James looked the other way and eventually climbed the low wall to cross into the next field.

She looked down at the house, a perfect clapboard, painted barn red, a funny elongation of life, each room built too small, one off the other, over generations of expansion, contraction, escape. There was a shapeless barn and chicken coop to the right of the house, added by some high-powered woman; only women can cope with the chicken shit. It was the childhood home of Bess, and indeed, she owned the property. They called it the Carmody place, after her family, and the airfield and housing development moving in was enough to release her physical strength and mental anguish to revengeful, redundant petitions and telephone calls to the town fathers, who were all for tearing up her land to bring money into the languishing economy.

When they sold Alma's house, the family homestead—the old man's achievement to right-street living, solid red brick, newly pointed, ten rooms, best neighborhood, the porch advertised as a patio—when they sold the house Alma heard Bess cry. Bess said in her family people didn't sell home and land. Difference between city and country? Going up or coming down? Which way was the old man moving? Lord, Alma didn't know, but she liked Bess for crying over Alma's house, for saying all that right out.

Bess didn't much like Alma, and she despised Alma's sister Mary due to a falling out over a dozen dinner plates. But then Alma and Mary were not supposed to like Bess, the two girls and the mistress. Bess married the old man at the nadir in all their lives. She had been the flame that kept ablaze a long-termed, painful and testy marriage—Bess stashed away where all knew about her. And at her mother's dying, the old man was, for the first time Alma knew him, adrift. The flame was flickering low from neglect, useless. The regret and fear were enough to keep him totally condemned to his pain; he bought a new car two days before she died and had a lengthy, detailed monologue about horsepower and leg room over the feet of the drowsy woman, sleepful the way death tells you it is coming.

"And, Margaret, it's black. Four-door. You always wanted a black car. We'll have it washed regularly so the dirt won't show. Pretty soon you'll be driving it down the hill to do your marketing."

For the old man nothing about Margaret Hughes's dying had anything to do with Bess. Good thing, too, because if Mary and Alma had known too much more, in their guilt, perplexity, negligence, indeed the shame Alma felt for her own physical strength—had they suddenly been called upon to understand that life with Bess as well as the death before them, they would have questioned the natural compassion they could only begin to recognize for this woman their mother, suddenly a person, whom Alma would have gladly offered a week's holiday from the business of dying, but it doesn't work that way.

In the midst of all this Margaret Hughes died, sure that at last her husband was attentive, that she was beyond enduring pain, that her family was always there at the wrong moments, that her bowels moved irregularly, that her bed jackets were improperly laundered in the hospital. Her shrunken body was black and blue, her cheeks those of a young girl, flushed dead with blood and hope. The memory was twelve years old, and it had never left Alma.

Still squatted on the stone wall, Alma looked from the farmhouse below, her memory distracted for a moment by the rustling in the woods far back behind her. She noticed the sky was heavy with rain clouds. The longest day of the calendar year, and no daylight. She waited for the movement behind her to take form. It couldn't be James, not all that noise. And she turned her head to see Bess's young collie dog come pushing through the skirt of the trees, in smooth, successive leaps, almost mechanical, as if the animal would never know physical frailty. The dog halted at Alma's back, slobbering on her neck. She had seen this creature jump at her father to snap the twigs, the thigh bones, that formed his lap. She shoved the dog aside, and remembered the brutality of her childhood behavior, often out of just such affection as this dumb animal's. And then, of course, she thought of her own children, Ned and Polly. Young, strong, self-absorbed, abusive, the slightest discomfort or pain —a splintered finger, a day in bed with cramps—a mark of the world's ill will toward each one's push for acceptance.

She heard thunder. Thunder. That's right, they used to call me Thundercloud. Cute. She couldn't like herself, an exposed child. Her thoughts were not nice. Why was she never a nice child? She heard the thunder again and realized that she sat on the stone wall looking down at the old man's new home.

Alma put her face into her open palms and dug her feet into the crevices in the stone wall until her toes hurt. How can I be so mixed-up-kid at my age? What about all that dignity of growth, the rising above, the understanding? How can the old man still get me? He keeps coming back at me.

And in the foreground came the swell of the organ music signaling the end of episode three million on his life box.

It drizzled. The rain felt soft and the field smelled ripe. James stood poised. Balboa discovering a new ocean. His shoes were wet. Maybe he'll discover me and cure me and take me away from it all. I could use a little fairy tale in my life, Alma thought. I feel bereft, grieving for something. Me.

"It's going to pour," James said.

"Let it," Alma said sulkily.

He went on. "The dark is moving right over the house; we'll be heading into it."

"So what."

"Come on, Alma, let's get it over with." He took her by the hand, a tiny tugging against the limp resistance of a reluctant kid. She let herself fall forward off the stone wall onto her feet, scraping her bare toes on the rocks. They walked slowly down the field into the black storm cloud that now burst over the house before them. The Wizard of Oz, Alma thought. The twisting storm, the horrible laugh of the witch. But no yellow brick road, no magic red shoes. Going into the storm, the house, the rain now blowing up the hill into her face, down the front of her blouse, across her bare legs, it wasn't that she was afraid she would never get out of the house. She was afraid she would never get rid of him, the old man. She would be stuck with him for the rest of her life. His coldness and her need. And then there was this business of time. Was there time to bury the ghost before the body?

At the edge of the porch the sob of the television was audible again, counterpoint to the storm. Alma and James entered by the kitchen door.

"Your father's watching television." Bess spoke without hope. She was spraying oven cleaner on the surface of the stove and burning her unprotected fingertips as she scoured.

"I suppose it'll rain all night. Usually does when it comes like this," she said. "It always sounds so lonely."

Alma and James entered the study. The station break was on. James moved across the screen to stand at the back of the room. Alma perched on the edge of a side chair. Her father waved his tiny hand at her without following her with his eyes.

The three of them sat in silence through the series of advertisement monologues. Alma signaled across at James, and they gathered themselves to stand before the old man, his frail legs stretched out, sticks, his ankles crossed like a flamingo's, one foot rakishly at right angles to the other. "We'll have to go now," Alma said. He didn't look up. "We've got to get home to the children." On the screen there was commotion and sadness now. Closed doors, a nurse carrying a tray. Illness. A quick flash to the bedside. The dying woman dozing comfortably. Alma knelt to put her face in front of her father's. He saw her briefly and smiled. He was crying.

James drove home. On the expressway it poured so hard the windshield wipers could not fight back the rain. Alma sat inside the car, protected against the wet, the tears flowing down her face, into her mouth, her ears, down her neck into the collar of her shirt.

"Was he crying for me?" she asked. "To see me come or go?

For his sister Alma? For his dead wife, for the woman on the television screen? For himself? Why did all those others get the good of him before me, before I was born, so that it was used up by the time I got there? By the time I was ready to be his darling, a little girl astride his knee, his dog at his side, his dreaming was over, and he was too tired out by it to love."

"Horse shit, Alma, he's an old man. He's your father. Leave him alone."

"Leave him alone!" she screamed at James. "Me leave *him* alone. Jesus, James, that's what he always did, leave me alone, especially when I wanted him."

"I know, Alma, but it's all over now."

"It's never over, James. That's where you're stupid. It's never over until it's understood. You have to go back before you can go forward."

James backed the car into the driveway. "Not me, Alma, but you're a charter member of the postanalytic school. Never mind, it won't be so hard the next time."

She buried her nose in the soft crotch of his pants. The faint smell of sweat. She wanted to make love right there, right now, before she expired.

She lifted her head, her arms and shoulders, to lean across his legs.

"There won't be a next time, James," she said into the door handle of the car.

He slipped his hand down into the pocket of his jacket. "Here, blow your nose on this," he said, handing her a dirty handkerchief.

Chapter 3

———··❦··———

ALMA AND JAMES HAD rented an eight-room semidetached
house in Prichett Circle, on the wrong side of a thin real estate
line, for ten years now. It suited Alma's reversed snobbery and
their academic pocketbook. The stucco was cracking, the wallpaper, painted over five or six times in the last twenty years,
peeled at the corners along the molding, behind the doors at
the seams of the walls, where Alma tacked it back in place and
then painted again. The garden was large and shaggy, an open-
air playpen, for it was what Alma and James had always shared,
in good times and bad. The yard was shaded about by ailanthus
trees that smelled saccharine when Alma hacked off the shoots
that continually appeared at the base, and there was one maple
at the far fence. But close to the house, where the sun moved
in, she grew zinnias and bordered the tomatoes with marigolds
to keep off the bugs. He tried strawberries, raspberries, fruit
trees, was jubilant with a crop of three berries, worried at each
failure.

The kitchen of the house was oblong and tiny, somehow allowing for a kind of familial confusion that brought parents and
the two children frequently together. At times, a few years
back, it seemed the warmest kind of exchange, bringing a closeness that Alma worked on very hard—protective, admiring

mother, paterfamilias, sitting squeezed in between drop-leaf table and sink. Then the children, little, needy, responsive, gathered with them while Alma cooked spaghetti or meat loaf. Children's food. She kissed her children often, tucked them into bed, fixed their bicycles, searched the bushes for lost kittens. Every night James sang them a song. It was the perfect reversal of Alma's own beginnings, and she was proud of her good mothering. If it was boring and demanding, she tried to stifle the feeling of demeaning. It was the price she paid for being better. It mattered to her that she be better.

Now in adolescence, Polly and Ned seemed to fill the tiny kitchen, the small house, with their grown bodies, squeezing Alma and James into the corners. The children ate strange things, seemingly purposefully unappetizing. Cottage cheese with catsup. They read that dishonest Presidents ate it, and ridiculed their mother's attempts to rationalize her disdain. A steak between two pieces of Bond bread, toasted. They drank root beer for breakfast and orange juice at night.

It disturbed Alma now that she found them tiresome and hard to love. Their demands were louder than hers, and she often had the feeling that to give in because it was easier was somehow betraying herself. Growing children depressed James. He missed what he called domesticity, the family together, and was hurt when neither child would hang around long enough to listen him out.

When he heard from the children about other parents, how oppressive they were, he felt better. But then there was hate and respect, and he suspected that his children felt neither for him. His speech style became more and more long and lingering when he was with them, as if he could lull them into relaxation and attention. He always lost, and Alma could see that the smallest shred of closeness, achieved now and then, with one or the other brought a nostalgic comfort to James that was always brutally shattered.

So that while he missed something past, Alma longed to go forward, sometimes to the point, she knew, where her own behavior was adolescent in itself. Impatient, experimental, me first, always returning to abuse the known. And it occurred to her often that adolescence was a perpetually returning state. It was the experimental stage, always painful, unsure, self-absorbing, self-doubting, which led to change.

Now, the birthday visit finally over, still in the front seat of the car drawn up before the house, Alma remained stretched across her husband's lap, blowing into the handkerchief he had just handed her. She felt the intense exhaustion of too many pains. The day, the children, the evening to come, the realization that she was haunted by her past, dissatisfied with her present, afraid of her own future. How many times had this trinity seeped through to her consciousness to hurt her?

She flopped back down on James and longed to make him her lover again. Did he feel it? Was he pleased? She wondered at his extreme patience. He hated to sit in a motionless car. Stolen minutes. He stroked her hair in a way she had almost forgotten. She relaxed against his thigh, drowsy.

"I love you when you're like this, James." Now who was going back? She was, wallowing in the comfort of touching.

They were silent for a long while. It was a moment of peace. He spoke gently. "I realize it's been a long hard day for both of us, particularly for you, baby."

The truth made Alma challenge him. "Hard. What was hard about it?"

"Come on, baby. You said so yourself."

Even the endearment was right, and in a kind of rage at her own dependency she turned on him. "A poor doubting Thomas. Two life-thirsty kids and a regressing wife."

He stopped caressing her. Immediately she regretted talking down to her protector. She had denied herself what she loved most. His soothing hand at the back of her neck. "Alma," he said, "first you doubt yourself and then you doubt me. Sometimes it's hard to feel as if I stand anywhere with you. You're always like this before the storm. I hope we survive this one."

She was numbed by his word "survive." He was offended? Doubt. Did it unsettle him so? Why? Why not? She was drowning in doubt, she was treading water to survive. And when he lifted up his knees so that she hunched onto hers rather than fall to the floor of the car, she felt threatened by his rejection.

She began to arrange herself in sitting position, proper adult again. At that he stepped from the car and in the abated rain, a drizzle now, he carefully inserted his key into the door to lock his side, as if to commit her within. But she could flee from the other side. She watched him go toward the house. Would he stick with her? Did she want him? Any of them? He had stroked her tenderly, or was that the final moment, the point of no return.

Jesus, she thought, that's all I need. Loss. Father, Son and Holy Ghost. Who was who in her life? The closest thing to a ghost was the old man. He was her loss now. "Man in three persons, blessed Trinity."

It took time to compose a façade. Open the mail, put the laundry in the dryer, start supper. Stay away from everything real. Smile. She followed James along the path, stepping bare-footed into each puddle as she approached the rotting house. Inside, in the hall, the water collecting at her feet on the worn Afghan from Pembroke Avenue before the front door, she watched him retreating up the stairs.

James felt Alma's stare lancing his back, right beneath his neck. At the second-floor landing he knew he was out of sight. He took the last flight of stairs two at a time, light-footed and alone. When he reached his study he shoved open the door with a lively kick that left a faint black mark from the wet leather of his shoe on the white semigloss paint.

For once he did not resent the overflow of Alma's past, the moving cartons from Pembroke Avenue stored behind the door. What she didn't have stashed away in their bedroom for him to sleep with, she had dumped in his study for him to work around. While he loved her especially because she was in touch with her feelings, each of her dramas was full-length. A little Shakespeare, a little Restoration, a lot of Tennessee Williams or maybe Eugene O'Neill. And right now he felt a little light-hearted lyricism along with his anger, exhaustion, even jealousy. One thing he could say about Alma—she didn't hold anything back. In the end she always felt the sweet relief, he realized. And now he recognized the signs. She was finally moving through Act I; the unfolding was beginning. God alone knew what Act II would bring, but at least the culmination would come, and she would be sane again, and his. He was tired of waiting for her and eager to have her back.

From the top of one of the boxes he snatched a garden-party hat, torn chiffon, off-white, on muslin made stiff by circles and circles of wire. The apricot-colored ribbon hung limp to one side now. Silly-looking thing, he thought. Margaret Hughes's gracious hostess helmet. He moved around the boxes to stand before a long gilt-edged mirror. It was propped up against his bookcases. How did the mirror feel in the natural disorder that was of his own making? No Pembroke Avenue elegance; he was firm. Not in my study.

He stuck his tongue out at the mirror and saw himself. It's okay, he thought, better-looking at forty-two than at twenty-two. He knew more and it showed in the pockets of roughness in his face. Strong, medium height, summer blue suit and shirt, silky brown hair that Alma said she liked so much, small hands, aristocratic, which did the touching. One of them held the foolish hat. He plopped it on his head, and made a *moue* into the mirror, just as his mother-in-law, handsome in the same hat, had passed on to him at his marriage to her headstrong daughter, the old man's spitting image. How Alma refused to believe it!

"She's often cross in the mornings," Margaret Hughes had told him confidentially. "Be gentle with her at first." How had this woman believed that he didn't know her daughter, morning, noon and night. In bed and out. Sometimes right there in her own elegant cold house. Margaret Hughes remained naïve to the end.

He tossed the hat aside. It landed on Alma's piggyback plant on the reading table. And suddenly it all depressed him. The exhaustion of Alma's pain, the best behavior of the day, the evening to come with the children. Sometimes he longed to have them back in his lap. They frightened him and he knew they saw it. He tried not to let the hurt in—he was a rational man—but it did, and he made it worse by not being able to let go of them.

To hell with classes; he hated the summer session. He still had a couple of weeks to prepare. He picked up a John D. Mac-Donald, *The Lady in Pink*. On the paperback cover she didn't wear panties under her shift. She looked over her shoulder to invite him in. He hoped the book was loaded with cheap sex. He stretched out on his mangy day bed, his one remaining relic of cheap living, when he was a graduate student and Alma some sort of research analyst. It was simple fun then. Dirty rooms, cheap sherry, and ugly throws from the five and ten everywhere, covering the holes in the upholstery but not the springs that stabbed you before they conquered you by forcing you to sit or lie around them.

They had fish for dinner, breaded and slightly overcooked. Alma actually didn't like fish much, but James did. She had it in the back of her mind to placate him. Angry? Miffed was what he was. Because she had loved him for a moment, pleased him, and then doubted herself and him, too. While she cooked he had holed up in his study, exhausted from too much day, she supposed. And she understood in the think part of her head. But when he withdrew she needed him desperately. When he was there she was often impatient with his carefulness. She remembered his touch and her whole body flashed warm. When he touched her she liked it; at least she was sure of that.

She drank several martinis while confronting the stove. Hardly gracious living. The whole idea of drinking was supposed to be the delight of "putting your feet up" at the end of the day. That's what her doctor told her. And he had also suggested that a glass of ginger ale in such peaceful conditions would do just as well. It was the relaxation that mattered, or the idea of it, or the illusion. And the doctor was positively sure that alcohol was just something we had all been educated to believe was sophisticated. Sometimes she wondered about him. While he was there to palpate her breasts and take her blood pressure, and he was often so humane she felt she should take care of him, he seemed to know little about heads, at least her head. He had once talked expansively about the kinds of people who drank too much. Ambitious, insecure, lonely. Ad men, professors, priests. Certainly not a mum. Busy life, work and family, surrounded by love and the wonderful untruth that she was needed. Odd that so many people in the world, Alma's world —and not all men, to be fair—never questioned the personal desires, the ambitions of a woman turned mother. Ladies' Lib was for the discontent, they said, and a firm commitment to the local political scene or the drug program at the high school was just what the doctor ordered for the recurring identity crisis. But why did it recur, this identity crisis? Never mind. Bandage up the wound and hope it heals from the inside out.

On the last gulp of gin, Alma called the family to dinner, laid out on the maple drop-leaf table in the tiny kitchen. Informality. The children ate with them this evening. Hominess. And when they did it was almost never peaceful. For a few brief moments, Alma could admire her family. Handsome. Two blond females, two brunet males. Strong chins, silky hair, Polly's beautiful young bust highly visible in her brother's undershirt. She resembled her mother, but in every way she was bigger than Alma. Her stature, her power, her beauty, her independence of mind at sixteen, her abuse of her parents; things that Alma was proud of in theory. At close quarters all was not nice between them. Polly was the only person Alma would not confront.

The men were medium height, the younger was taller, and at eighteen Ned had the wide even-fingered hands of his father, and James's hands mattered to Alma. They did the stroking and much of the love-making. She laughed at herself nervously. Incest is best. The kids joked all the time.

"Butter."

"Is there any tartar sauce?"

"Milk or beer, James?"

"Beer."

35

"How was Granddaddy?" someone asked at last.

"Fine," said James.

"How was he, Ma?"

Alma looked at James. Yes, he looked hurt. Here again someone had doubted him, the spitting image of herself. But Polly knew too much to accept his answer.

"He was the same," Alma said. "Okay. It was terrible. It was like seeing someone you know very well for the first time. It was ghostly. It made me feel like a child all over again."

"Was he drunk?"

"No."

"Were you?"

"Goddammit no, Polly. Don't be so uncivil."

They ate in silence. Alma and James feigned quiet dignity, taking their time. Ned and Polly shoveled it down, forks, fingers, haste and much waste. The beans were stringy.

"What's the house like?" Ned addressed his father. Alma knew that because her first-born loved her so assuredly he had a kind of compassion for this man he hardly knew anymore, who was rarely available to him in his first manhood.

James was clearly pleased. He enjoyed the expectation he assumed to be on all three faces as he prepared to answer the question, and at length; they all knew that.

"It's a nice old house, built about 1800, I'd say, the original part. It's been added on to some. It sits at the edge of a field. The farmer doesn't take very good care of the crops."

Polly picked up her half-empty plate and full glass of milk and moved toward the sink.

James looked directly into the face of his son now. "There's too much furniture in the house, but your mother found some of the things from her house on Pembroke Avenue."

The water ran hard down the drain.

"Your grandfather seemed perfectly comfortable and I had a nice talk with him."

The door to the dishwasher slammed shut.

James slowed down even more. "I took a walk through the oak woods. Curious they should be oak."

Chair legs scraped along the vinyl. Ned cleared his empty dishes. "Sure, Dad."

Dismissal. James talked on slowly, in reveries, avoiding the awful fact of desertion.

Why the hell do we go through this? Alma thought. This family-together stuff. "Suffer ye little children." She was reminded of how contemptuously she had behaved, how hurt she had felt, when on visiting her mother in the Pembroke Avenue house years ago now, in her own young adulthood, she had discovered a short attention span to the details of her own life. Her mother seemed both pleased to see her and uninterested in her. It was easy for Alma to understand now. Children so consistently expect to be the center of their parents' lives, even in the long search for some center in their own lives. She recognized with some chagrin some of the same feelings lingering in herself. Witness this very afternoon.

Ned stood at the sink now. Polly squeezed between chair and stove to leave the room, only to return immediately, posted at the pantry door. She put one dirty-sneakered foot on the chair seat where she had sat. Alma and James continued genteel eating, both acutely aware of her further intrusion and their own struggle to ignore it. Alma recognized the staginess. Some announcement to come.

"I'm going to New Hampshire this weekend, to a concert."

"Are you asking or telling?" said Alma.

"Okay, Ma. May I go to New Hampshire this weekend to a concert?"

"Who with, where will you stay, how will you get there?" Alma asked wearily. Why the same old litany? Why couldn't Polly just do it the easy way. Yes, I know, Alma thought. Rebellion. Growth. All those super new concepts that were as old as language itself.

Polly's face clouded with resentment. "With some kids from school. We'll stay at Anne's house. Ned is driving us."

Alma looked at Ned. Blank-faced. All innocence. How could she kid herself about his priceless pure love for her? Collusion.

They always set it up this way. Why so devious? Because it works.

"I don't know," said James. "The last time you went off like that Ned got picked up for going through a red light."

"Fuck it, Dad, that was once." The verbal abuse, the all-powerful weapon of the revolutionaries, the ones on the way up. Another form of the black Israeli, but at least in her day she kept it silent. Out of consideration? No, out of fear.

"I don't like being spoken to that way, Ned." James put his fork down. Who could eat through this?

"I don't know either," said Alma, ill will welling up in her. "As I remember it, you also came home at one in the morning, and I was sitting on the front stairs wondering what the hell had happened to you, and powerless to know or help. A ten-o'clock deadline. My God, I was scared and angry and all Polly could say was that you didn't pass a phone booth. It's been going on for years and I don't want all that abuse."

"You're an ass, Ma. You're cruel." Spitting image again.

"I thought you were pretty cruel yourself on that occasion," said Alma calmly. Polly slammed the pantry door. The truth again, thought Alma with some pleasure. Ned, cool and disdainful, quietly followed his sister. The pattern never changes. Demand, attack, until you get what you want. Thwarted, then abuse. In a few hours all would be sweetness. Another try. The only two who were devastated were the parents. Repeat, repeat.

James sat silent while Alma cleared the dishes and cleaned up the kitchen. It was hard to know what he felt, but in her own need to be listened to and accepted, she felt empathetic. It was one of the nicest things they had between them, this ability to find comfort in their own silence with each other.

Later they went together up the stairs to the top floor of the house, he carrying his briefcase, back to the study, back to his own comforts, she following, distributing clean underwear and blue jeans before the closed doors of the children's rooms. It was a kind of journey, a retreat to their own world, fortressed by a flight of stairs and an all-pervading, accepted sense of privacy.

It wasn't often that they made this trip together, but unspokenly, perhaps, this had been a day which would best end in a reaffirmation to each other, and at least Alma, for one, was considering, indeed hoping for the long, lingering kind of love-making, exploratory, thorough, explosive and finally restful. No nasty fantasies out to get someone, but real and acceptable. And when the loving was good for both of them, she felt that her capacity to love prevailed in the ambivalent human being that was herself. James, she realized, did not often fight the demons inside him. He existed, longing for peace. To make good love made him feel good, she knew, and she was glad to contribute to that peace, and to what was always for him a good night's sleep.

At the head of the stairs he turned right into his study. Leave him be, Alma thought, there's time enough.

The bedroom reminded Alma of a miniature warehouse, the boxes piled almost to the ceiling in rows behind the bureau, the love seat, and along the wall by the bed. She and James had bedded down in this impermanency for months now, ever since Alma had moved her family papers, photographs, shreds and relics from Pembroke Avenue into this unsuitable storage room. Once stacked, the boxes were a continuing reminder to her of her own inability to let go of the past, until she understood it, she said. Standing in the doorway now, she felt her indecision more keenly than usual. The room perfectly mirrored the wearisome day, personal fact and fiction walling her in, waiting to be unpacked, discarded or tucked away. For the first time since she had hidden her ancestors in these boxes, she felt the urgency to rediscover and be done. In fact, she felt there wasn't much time.

In a desultory way, to hide her timidity, Alma peeled the sealing tape from the first box at hand. Books, spine up. *The Thurber Carnival* next to *The Value of the Peso, 1921. The Federal Reserve System, 1933, '34* through *'39.* A complete set of Robert Louis Stevenson, tattered leather. No, not complete. *Kidnapped* was missing. Why? *The Power of Investment Abroad.* She closed the four folds of the box lid, corners in, to set the problem aside. Photographs and portraits, hundreds and hundreds, loose and in albums identified in white ink on black paper. Her mother and father young. Her grandparents, both pairs, holding the first-born. That would be Mary. Already Thomas and Margaret Hughes were into middle age, years childless. Mary must have been the most photographed child in the world. Snowsuit, on the swing, feeding the ducks. Dozens of prints of each that never reached the distant aunts and cousins. A set of documentary photographs detailing the building of the house on Pembroke Avenue. The year was 1933, after the great crash. The building site on the crest of a rise overlooking fields and marsh. Nineteenth-century clapboard houses on either side. They made the top of the hill even when moneyed families were pinched. How did Thomas Hughes pay for it? The safety razor, he said.

Thomas Hughes walking across the boards that covered the foundation. The first of three chimneys, eight fireplaces in all. The stability of red brick, the pillared front doorway, colonial Georgian. The spindly maples and pines that grew to be like the hundred-acre wood.

And all for me, Alma thought, all to house the next baby to be born. She closed the box and carried it into the hall, where she dropped it noisily. Permanent home in the basement. Could she burden another generation? Sure. Polly and Ned wouldn't even recognize these people. They could dispose unknowing.

At the sound of moving, James came from his study, carrying the pink-colored paperback, to see what was happening. He saw the small disruption of boxes and knew that chaos must follow chaos. Alma was unearthing from the bottom of a deep chest, throwing clothes about their bedroom, a kind of disrobing like the seven veils. The floor, the bed, every surface was draped.

"Where are we going to sleep?" he asked.

She paid him no attention but stripped off her own clothes quickly, dropping them where she stood, polyester skirt, cotton knit blouse, nylon bra and underpants to lie with chiffon, silk, lace and soft wool. She paused for an instant while he looked at her naked body. Then she stooped to grab a mauve dress from the floor. When she stood and reached up her arms to slither into it, the fringe covering her head, she wiggled her torso at him. Her skin was already summer tanned, her small breasts crowned by erect nipples, the flesh along her rib cage taut. When the bottom of the fringe reached her waist, left uncovered were ample hips, her protrudent pubic bone covered in brown hair, comfortable thighs. Her blond head, then her face emerged, and she put her uncovered arms down. The dress hung loose to midhip, 1920s, showing every curve. The fringe rested at her knees, kid's knees, round. Her lower legs had always been good.

"My God," James said. "Is it twenty years or are you the same shape you were when we used to make love in your parents' basement on that couch thing from the set of porch furniture?"

"My waist is thicker. Don't you always look?" In that business-like way James recognized when Alma was stifling some pain that often as not would well up to hit her, and him. Alma tried on the soft wool suit, piped with grosgrain ribbons, she told him. She could not hook up the skirt. Then an unbecoming violet outfit, with pink panels and a train or cape thing. It must have been Margaret Hughes in her club days. A stunning velvet evening dress, styled in the 1900s. Alma said she remembered it. It was a costume especially made for her mother to wear to the opera. She would have been five or six, maybe, before the war clothed her mother in Red Cross uniform.

"Keep that," James said. "You look swell in it."

She set it aside from the discard pile.

And the off-white dress. Layers of stiffening under the chiffon, apricot girdle to set off the handsome woman's still tiny waist. Pretty, frail and tough, even at sixty, James thought. That was the woman he had known. Her youngest daughter had had the energy of a team of draft horses, or Margaret Hughes might have had her way. What was a poor student from no place, New Jersey? No money, no family income; to be a teacher. James Thomas. She had been dauntless about his lacks, and Alma was just stubborn enough to fight. If Alma had married him to spite her mother, she was crazy enough to love him, too.

"There's a hat that goes with this."

James went back to his room and closed the door.

In the corner of the bedroom was a pyramid of white boxes, special ones, tied with white ribbons. Naked again, Alma prepared to assemble the outfit on the love seat by the open window. The air smelled sweet and fresh after the rain. The boxes had not been opened in twenty years, she knew.

The white satin slippers, the white hoop skirt, the piece of old lace from Grandmother MacNeil made into a virgin's cap with orange blossoms over the ears. The tulle veil was torn. Alma opened the largest box. Her wedding dress. Under the tissue she saw unfamiliar cream-colored something. As she unfolded the gown she knew it was her mother's; she had the official marriage picture on the wall by her bureau. Tenderly she laid it down. Once again the feeling of snooping. She knew nothing about that wedding between her mother and father—it had never been mentioned—and she had made peace with her mother long before her death. In the years since, time had left only love in Alma's memory. She looked back into the box. The next layer of tissue revealed the white satin of her own gown, or rather her mother's choice for her. When she drew it out, miles of train, she found the shoe box underneath. "Jordan Marsh," it was labeled, "Better Shoes." Tied with brittle string, there was a note attached. Alma carried the box to the light on her bureau. She saw her nakedness in the mirror and felt foolish for a moment. She struggled to read the card. The handwriting was firm but faint. "Dear Thomas," she read, "Please destroy these yourself. Lovingly, Margaret." Alma placed it hastily on top of the cream-colored dress. Enough digging.

Instead she grabbed her own wedding dress and trailed it into James's study. Standing before him, she put it on. Fully aware, he read carefully to the end of the page, then watched her, head bowed, as she looped the millions of buttons first down the long sleeves, then from the navel to cleavage. The waist gaped open.

She moved to the gilt-edged mirror. "I'm thicker in the waist."

He looked at her reflection and got up from the day bed. "That fits you like one of those foundation girdles in the newspaper ads. No stomach, no ass, no nothing. You're sexier with your gut hanging out."

He stood behind her looking into the mirror, she looking back at him. He lifted first one foot, then the other, to untie his shoes, strip off his socks. He stepped out of his pants and underdrawers, lifted his half-buttoned shirt by the back of the collar over his head. She saw his silky hair fall across his face. She did not move.

He came around in front of her and began the long business of unlooping buttons. With each one he touched the nakedness beneath. She watched his back in the mirror as he labored. "This isn't why Mother had a house full of mirrors," she said, pleased. He tore the loops at the sleeve.

"What if Polly wants this?"

"Not like your mother, Alma."

"It's pretty, James."

"If Polly ever consents to live married, she'll make it legal in her blue jeans."

"Why do men undress women when they want to make love but never dress them afterward?"

James looked up at her for a moment. She's teasing me.

"Yes, I know why," she said. "I was only teasing."

He threw the dress from her shoulders, kissing her face, her mouth, her neck. Alma watched him in the mirror. Why do all men have red bumps on their bottoms? He sucked each breast noisily, as if he were eating a particularly ripe pear, she thought. His hands moved across her belly and down her legs as he knelt to put his head between her legs.

Gently she pushed him away. "How can people do it surrounded by mirrors? It's fascinating. That's you and me, but I'm too busy looking to feel."

They lay on the floor of his study. She stroked his hair, his head across her bosom now. They had come together. She thrust her pelvis forward to feel again the push of his penis somewhere inside her abdomen. He closed his arms around her.

He would sleep as deeply as they had loved, she knew, and she lay with him for a few more minutes. As she moved from beneath him, the opaque semen traveled slowly down her upper thigh to form a puddle on the skirt of their marriage dress. She watched the viscous fluid seep into the satin to stain it. It made her laugh out loud.

She did not try to wake James, but covered him with a light blanket. When he came into the bedroom, stretching against the hardness of the floor, he saw her sitting naked on the rug, bedside lamp pulled down beside her. She was reading letters from a shoe box.

Part Two

1916

Chapter 4

THOMAS HUGHES SAT before the writing desk in the attic room
of his sister Alma's house. He had classes to prepare and papers
to correct, but all the evening the words didn't seem much
more than black marks on a white page. The fire was down in
the grate, the coal bucket empty; it was a cold winter, but he
was unable to force himself down the stairs to the bin at the
back of the house. The clay pipe lay packed full, unsmoked. For
a time here, he had been at peace. He had done the things he
had to do, and wanted no more than his books, his pipe and the
warmth of Alma and her husband, Caerwyn.

But he wanted more again. The compulsion was not new to
him, and he expected to have what he wanted. He looked at the
crumpled balls of letter paper that he had thrown to the floor
and resolved to try again.

> Dear Miss MacNeil:
>
> It is Saturday night and you will not receive this until school
> reconvenes Monday morning, but I shall deliver it by hand to
> make sure it reaches the young and talented Principal herself.
>
> A few hours ago you said you'd been troubled and doing a lot
> of thinking. I will not have you suffer on my account nor on your
> own. I like you too much.
>
> You said, too, that if I said *that* (you know what) to many

persons, perhaps someone would believe me. You put it pretty straight, and it hurt, but, of course, you were right. I should not say those things, and I will not again, never, never, so help me by my patron Saint Dennis.

Now I'm going to tell you the truth. It's no use my being a hypocrite about it. I've said *that* before—just once in my life; and I thought I meant it but I found out that I did not. That is more than anyone knows about me, except one person. Perhaps you will believe what you say, that I'm some sort of Don Juan—a poor one—but whatever you think, I'm not going to give you the chance to say that stuff again. I want to be the best friend to you that I know how to be.

If you worry or torment yourself, why the sooner you wash your hands of me the better for your peace of mind.

Sincerely,
THH

They met the following Saturday afternoon. It was their custom now. He always waited for her at the corner of Hope and Cypress streets, where he knew she would have to pass on her way home. He allowed her to continue to pretend that her meetings with him were just accidental, to ignore the conflict of allegiance and affection already within her. And while he had not heard from her all week, he knew she would expect to see him.

School was dismissed early on Saturdays, and Margaret MacNeil's parents were pleased that she was always so conscientious as to use the extra hours to complete her administrative duties. Although Margaret and Thomas had met in class week, a year and a half ago, he the university graduating speaker, she president of her college class, his interest in her was recent. Thomas suspected Margaret's sister Mary knew about it; the two sisters were close in an odd way. He could see that. Yes, he had met Margaret's family. Mother, father, sister, aunts Florence and Polly. Her father ran a shoe store in downtown Providence, and they lived in a big red house, barn red, he'd call it, clapboard, near College Hill. It was considered a nice district, one Thomas suspected Mr. MacNeil could ill afford. Thomas knew very little more about Margaret as yet, except the college degree, rare in a woman, and that she was naïve, physically frail and had the long slender nose and high cheekbones of natural good breeding.

But Margaret MacNeil's mother was to be a formidable adversary. She did not care for Thomas Hughes, that he knew. Country boy with country connections, and a sketchy personal history he did not care to fill in for her and she had not pressed him as yet. He was laden with university honors and acclaim, but not money or "good" family. But the elder Margaret MacNeil, Mrs. MacNeil, did not realize that the same ambition that gained her daughter the position as principal of the Hope Street Technical School at the age of twenty-two, to bring pride and prestige to Mrs. MacNeil and her family, this same willfulness would teach the Miss MacNeil to thwart her mother in time. He knew Margaret was strongly attracted to him, and she recognized he was on the way up. Thomas Hughes was confident he would win.

He watched her come down the school steps, a stage entrance. She had told him that she had done amateur theatricals in college and at the church. Books in her arms, carefully putting one foot in front of the other so that the skirts of her coat and dress swayed with each step, showing the toe and heel of her black button boots. She wore a small feathered hat, very dear, he could tell by the looks of it. It was perched on the top of her hair, rolled back from her face to form a blond crown, the better to show her sharp, prominent features. She walked slowly, in some majestic fantasy.

He knew she knew he watched her. It was a fine performance, and he wanted to run to her, but stood his ground. She approached him now, brown eyes, half-lidded, piercing through him. He took her elbow and felt the thinness of her coat. The cape of his greatcoat fell around her arm. Neither greeted the other. He took the books from her. They walked down Hope Street some few blocks.

"You're cold," he said. "You should have heavy tweeds for February." She turned to face him now. She was almost his

49

height. They stopped together, she looking into his eyes, he back into hers. She smiled broadly, the same childlike smile she always gave him when she intended to surprise and shock.

"I wear a great many petticoats. It makes my mother think I am heavier than I am. I borrow some from Mary so Mother will not think the number of mine unusually large when she counts the laundry. She is very particular about laundry. Each vest and petticoat must be starched. They keep me warm as well as make me look plumper than I am, and I can comfortably wear a lighter cashmere coat, more stylish than ugly bulky weaves. Sometimes when I am walking, the swing of so many skirts makes me feel like a lady in a brocade gown, a lady in a stage play."

She had rarely been so expansive. He put his arm around her and hugged her.

"Not on Hope Street." She was alarmed.

He withdrew his arm unwillingly.

"I admire your elegant hat."

"Oh, my aunts make my hats. They have a shop on North Main Street, right in the fashionable blocks. They make hats for all the ladies on the Hill."

"Your aunts run a shop? Alone? What an extraordinary family of women."

"Aunt Florence makes the hats. Aunt Polly does the book entries after English classes at the Girls' Normal School. She is a very distinguished teacher."

He laughed at her out loud. "You're so serious. 'She is a very distinguished teacher,' " he mocked her, "just like her most distinguished niece Miss Margaret MacNeil. Do you have any middle names?"

"Isabella."

"Miss Margaret Isabella MacNeil. That will do very nicely. A very distinguished name."

She liked the fuss.

At the next corner they crossed the street and took the trolley car to the end of the line. It was to become their natural habit. In the park they walked along the creek, a culvert now, snow on ice that formed sharp-cornered prismatic patterns where small boys had thrown stones to break through and rest in the cold waters. Thomas stooped to search out a stone and toss it into the creek.

He talked about his English classes at the university, she about hers. She would only become principal, she had said, if she was allowed to continue her teaching. It was only her second year.

Each had taught the Romantic poets last term, but he was preparing Shakespeare now. Aunt Polly taught Shakespeare. Pity he couldn't discuss it with her. Oh, she wouldn't mind; in fact, she'd like it. Only . . . better not now.

He said he was sorry, and then he told her that he was just finishing his master's program in history, economic history; he found it fascinating. A change from English. He had been teaching English for eight years now.

"Eight years!" Margaret exclaimed. "How old are you?" She blushed. "Forgive me."

"I want you to know about me. I'm twenty-eight, twenty-nine next June. I taught English in my town, and after a time I left and went to South America. I taught in Puerto Rico, too, before I came to Providence to the university. I've been teaching ever since I got here, more than four years now."

"South America. I knew you were old and experienced, but I won't tell. It would just upset my mama further."

"I'm not that old; she need not worry. I have a future. I will take a doctorate with the money I have saved, and then I will have a handsome teaching job in Worcester or maybe even New Jersey. I always come out ahead. You tell her that."

At the broadening of the stream two young boys slid across the bumpy ice. "I used to do that. Ever skated?" Thomas asked. Margaret demurred and Thomas threw down her books, scooped her light body up in his arms to carry Miss Margaret Isabella MacNeil over snow-stiff meadow grass and set her down on the ice.

"Come on, I'll pull you," but she hung back like a mule. They toppled together to the ice. Her hat skimmed across the surface.

He had overstepped. But when he was on his feet, ready to right her, he saw that she lay rocking on her back, powdery ice clinging to her coat and gloves, mouth wide open in formless foolish giggles.

He lifted her up. "I'm sorry." She fell against him in her laughter and began to slip again.

"Steady."

She doubled over. "It's all right, it's all right." She wouldn't stop laughing.

"Wait until I take you to the Berkshires. I'll teach you to skate on the pond above the waterfall. It is beautiful clear ice, perfect, but you must promise to be careful to stay away from the mouth of the spring, and the ice will crack if you go near the falls."

He was flushed, full of expectation. She dusted off her gloves, her coat. Her shoes were damp.

"I'll never go to your mountains. I should like to, but I have my teaching and my school. You know it would be improper and unwise. Your mother would not like it any better than mine."

"If you were mine—I should not say *that* again, I promised I would not—but if you were to be my wife, you would be most welcome."

"I must go home," was all she said.

"My sister Alma would like to serve you tea."

"That is kind of her, but you know I cannot. They will be expecting me at home. Mary is singing in the church this evening. I cannot be late."

In March the snow fell heavy and Thomas and Margaret could not navigate the uncleared paths in the wilderness of the park. But the sun was higher and hot, and Thomas felt giddy about everything in life. Margaret MacNeil had consented to come to his sister's house for tea, and the meeting had been entirely successful. What's more, Margaret had told her mother of the visit because she would not continue to see him behind her mother's back. She said she felt quite informed on proper behavior. After all, she was the principal of the Hope Street

Technical School. Margaret told him that her mother had cried, something Margaret had rarely seen. It might seem cruel, Margaret said, but she enjoyed the feeling of personal power over her mother. It was new to her, and Thomas felt the weaning of Margaret away from her family had come more rapidly than he could have hoped. Thomas Hughes was pleased.

Thomas and Margaret spent their time together walking the town, exploring everything. It was a long tramp from the Mac-Neil house at the foot of College Hill, along the river and over the bridge to East Providence, with its slums and promise of low life. But despite the chill of a late March day, Margaret wanted to see forbidden parts, and Thomas welcomed the time with her.

On the bridge she put her hand at his elbow, a signal, and he waited. It was a long time before she asked.

"Tell me—I think I want to know, I think it's time. Who did you think you loved; who was it you said that to?"

"It's a long time ago now. It's really a family tale. Are you sure?"

"Tell me it."

"The girl—woman now—is Elizabeth Roberts. She's the daughter of our minister. Mr. Roberts is a special man, much respected in the town. And in her way Elizabeth is special to my family. She's cheerful, warm, a big farmhand of a girl. She sings well and plays the organ at Chapel with rigor, and some skill, I'm told."

Thomas was silent. Perhaps he had said enough to get by. He took Margaret's hand from his elbow, spreading his fingers between hers, and held it against his thigh.

But it was not enough. "And why did you think you loved her?"

"It goes way back. You must understand that when my parents left Wales it was a terrible sad thing for them. They were from farming people, north midlands, Llanidloes and Newtown. Some eighteen miles it was for my father to travel to do his courting. When the crops failed, they left behind the family and the land to move south, and my father went into the mines. It was ambition made him do it. He wanted more. I was born and when the mines failed, too, my parents brought us to this country. All they had was the clothes on their back, and they had the Bible. Or so they tell it."

"Funny names in your country."

"This is my country. I'm a naturalized citizen. But some of the Welsh names are hard for those unfamiliar. Llanidloes. It's like a purr. You should hear my mother roll it off her tongue."

The wind blew strong across the water, burning their faces, sending columns of snowflakes up into the sky. Thomas moved behind Margaret to take the river side of the bridge, turning the back of his head into the cold. They walked quickly and in silence, Thomas, for once, distracted from the presence of Margaret by the winter, by the memory of the graveside in the heavy snow, where he stood in the dusk with his arms around Elizabeth Roberts and told her he loved her for the last time. It was just before his leaving.

Across the river Margaret and Thomas, relieved from the bitter blow, raised their bent heads simultaneously and looked into each other's faces.

"Why did you tell her you loved her?"

"My parents wanted me to go into the ministry, though I preferred to teach. It would have particularly pleased my father, the ministry, and Mr. Roberts was a powerful influence on us all. He was strongly in favor. It was somehow understood that Elizabeth would someday be the minister's wife. There were few encouragements *not* to think I loved her. The whole family expected it."

"I've never heard about your family; you never talk about them. Are there more of you?"

"My parents, and you've met Alma. Then there's Dorothy and John. There was a sister named Margaret, but she died young." He shook his head too vigorously.

"Is that why you like me? Do I remind you of your sister Margaret?"

"You know that's not so. It's a bad memory, that's all."

"How did she come to die?"

"Diphtheria. They wouldn't let me in the house. Elizabeth Roberts wrote me at the seminary. I came right home. But I had to stay at the Roberts' house, along with the others."

"I'm sorry she died."

"It's a long time ago, but it's still bitter in me. She strayed into the hearts of a middle-aged couple who didn't expect her and perhaps wouldn't have asked for her, and just as she got their whole world running about her as the center, she went out of it.

"I couldn't stand it, all that bunch of cantering phrases that Mr. Roberts spoke in the miserable cold on the hillside. Nothing but to-high-heaven imbecility and hypocrisy. How could words fill up the hollow that death brought in my poor parents? I left the seminary."

"But your father, you just hurt him more."

"Perhaps, but when I took the post to teach English in Buenos Aires, he came to the station with me alone. He looked filled with loss, but he told me I was right to go if I could not believe."

Margaret stopped walking, pulling Thomas back to her. She placed her gloved hands on his cheeks and waited for the pain and anger to go out of him. "Sometimes it's hard to know what to believe, but he sounds like a nice man, your father."

"You'll like him, Margaret," Thomas said simply, "and he'll be daft about you."

Since Thomas Hughes had become an acknowledged figure at the MacNeil home—he had been there several times of late for tea in the garden, tea with a sliver of lemon: what kind of a drink was that for a man?—he found that he saw less of Margaret and more of her mother. Pressed into his Chapel suit, his Phi Beta Kappa key and his grandfather's gold lion's head ring prominent across his vest, he had been presented now to the immediate family and a "few" friends. They were not Margaret's friends, but rather Mrs. MacNeil's core of women, who seemed to behave more like a selection committee at a church or school, screening him, themselves screened behind paper-thin cups so inadequate that he could not comfortably manage one, even with his small, perfect hands.

Mrs. MacNeil and her allies were always plumed and draped in shimmery, icy fabrics and carefully constructed bonnets, each one the special work of Aunt Florence. In the sometimes oppressive stillness of early-summer city heat, he wondered that they could remain rigid and brisk in so much adornment. He had thought of his own mother's simple black dress, which looked cool in summer and warm in winter. Except for Chapel, he never could remember her without a clean white apron tied round her waist. And she was always in motion, even over her tea in the kitchen. Only Margaret's aunts seemed ill at ease at the series of inquisitions, and as if to indicate openness of mind if not approval to his cause, they wore simple dark dresses, and without hats.

All the women—they had come in twos and threes—were unnaturally attentive and boldly curious. He wondered at their manners. It had always begun with where was he from? A country boy. A moment's vagueness, blank expressions. Already the damage done? How could he tell? Who was his mother? His father? How interesting. British. Oh, I see, Welsh. Hard-working people, yes. South America? Puerto Rico? To teach English to those dirty, dark-skinned souls. How curious after considering the ministry. Applied for a teaching position at Princeton, in New Jersey. So far away. Economics. A new study, you say. And when you were doing so well in literature, nothing fly-by-night, newfangled.

His answers were often cursory, he knew, but he felt his examiners were narrow-minded and supercilious, and he was offended. He tried to shield himself behind what he hoped would seem a businesslike manner, with just enough arrogance. Sometimes he would easily have exchanged the warmth of the wriggly brown children, barefoot and half-clothed, in the hut that served as school, dispensary, orphanage, his home, for these crews of matrons. He had considered the cheerful acquiescence of fifteen-year-old Maria, who cared for him in San Juan, placing a bowl full of hot beans before him, folding his clothes while he lay in the bed, slipping loose the lacing at the neck of her shapeless wrap, which she wore in his bed and out of it, her knees and legs visible below the hem, while with his eyes he had openly followed Margaret, in stiff white folds and enough buttons to discourage further speculation. He saw the ladies notice his interest with approval. He laughed at himself and them. Despite their questions they were incurable romantics, longing for love, which they may have seen, known, but never recognized, and few would be able to return. They saw youth and love. He sought affection, adornment, intelligence, the enhancements to complement the ambitious triumphs he would have from life. He looked at Margaret and her sister and thought they resembled the vestal virgins.

When Margaret's father would come through the garden gate promptly at six to receive his hot tea with milk like a man, before he made his amenities, Thomas envied him with all the little boy in himself he could remember. Mr. MacNeil, affable and distant, Mrs. MacNeil's unspoken disgrace, was allowed to escape into the kitchen, teacup still in hand. He read the newspaper at the table. Thomas would see him through the open door.

A familiarity with Margaret's family, indeed a companionship that grew between himself and the distinguished English teacher, Aunt Polly—there was a woman he could talk with—left him disgruntled, fragmented, angry with Margaret for letting so much of her family come between them and for the suspicion that she enjoyed his discomfort at the hands of these women she had known most of her life. He knew she had bridled at the same kind of interrogation. He would have wished to see care, distress, even pity for him in her face. Instead he saw the impish smile. He could not tell what it revealed, or more to the point, what it did not reveal. But when she walked with him to the corner, her skirt swinging against his leg, her hand just touching his arm, her whole body alive again, she would smile up into his face as if to tell she was glad to be back from a long journey. She lingered, often unwilling to let him go. There was more to Margaret than he had thought, and while he was made miserable by her seeming aloofness sometimes, he chose to attribute it to her discomfort within the family: child, yes, but college graduate, financial contributor, too much a man's responsibilities for a woman. She was so different from the others, in looks, in grace, in intelligence; she was superior —he could spot it. Perhaps what seemed disdain for him was rather for them. He wondered at his own self-doubt. He was not accustomed to such uneasy self-appraisal. But the complexity of Margaret excited him. He hoped, he counted upon, some hidden warmth reserved for him alone. And with this expectation uppermost, he felt something that was more exciting than desire. He felt possession. He knew he was winning.

Thomas Hughes could hardly refuse the invitation to dinner when Mrs. MacNeil had extended it a week ago. It wasn't something that he wanted to do. Dinner at the MacNeils', while an indication of Mrs. MacNeil's crumbling bulwark against his suit for her daughter, did not constitute her acceptance of him, he was sure, and the prospect of extended family visiting from Chicago only meant more questions and doubts.

As he lay lazy in bed on this fine morning, he knew there had been times in the past few months when his pursuit hardly seemed worth it. But despite it all, he still wanted Margaret MacNeil, and on just such a close June day as this one, Friday, the end of the week, the end of term, a walk in the park, an ice from the ice cream parlor, to be alone with Margaret and reaffirm their specialness to each other with a kiss and an embrace, that was what Thomas wanted to accomplish before he left Providence tomorrow.

When they met in the afternoon, from the moment of greeting, Thomas knew there was something amiss. As they rode the trolley down the street toward the park, he listened to Margaret intently now. Her behavior perplexed him. It was totally unlike the reflective and well-mannered young lady, the Margaret he knew was hiding there, the woman he wanted, to be so needlessly chattering, on and on about Aunt Mabel and Cousin Charles. He already disliked them. He tried to elicit from her some word, some gesture to take with him, but something had happened, something to turn this self-possessed, educated woman into a witless child.

"What is it, Margaret, what is the matter?" he asked, but at that moment the swaying of the trolley stopped. She moved lightly to the wooden steps at the rear of the car, flicking her hands at him as if to shoo off a flock of messing chickens.

They walked the familiar paths in the park where on that day in February she had been freer with him and he closer to her than on most of the occasions they had shared together since. As they grew to know each other, it sometimes felt like a game of war, offense and defense; they alternated sides. He understood it was the busyness of love, and regretted it. Now he looked down at the unkempt swamp grass, fresh green shoots everywhere among the brittle brown straw of last year's growth. From birth and strength to rot. They stopped beside the border of the stream.

"I'm leaving tomorrow," he said simply.

"I know. Dinner will be good; Aunt Florence will make the pies." She twirled before him, charming, indifferent, infuriating.

"I want you to miss me, Margaret. I want to hear from you."

"Oh, I'll write sometime. I hope the good weather holds." She lifted her arms, her face and neck to the sun as if to receive another's warm embrace.

He grasped her forearm roughly. Beneath the thin cotton, in the full sleeve of her blouse where she usually stored her handkerchief, he felt the crinkle of something stiff. It took him a moment to understand. Paper.

"What's that? Is it for me?"

She tensed and looked at him for a long time, thoughtful, on the verge of telling him something, he was sure. When at last she spoke—"You're hurting me"—she tried to peel his fingers from her arm.

"Margaret, you're hiding something from me, something you shouldn't. You once told me very directly that I was not to tamper with your feelings. You have no reason to do so with mine now. But the more I want you, the more nonsense I endure at your mother's hand. You're playing with me; you enjoy both my love and my discomfort. Now, when I wish I could hold you, you make fun of me."

"Never mind Mother."

"Never mind, never mind your mother. It is you who do not mind. You recognize my accomplishments, you see my future, and I like to think you care for me. A hundred of your mother would not make the woman you are. What happened to that lovely woman, that serious schoolteacher who learned to want more? Was that one of your theatrics, too?"

Her face collapsed. "I forbid you to talk about my mother that way."

He had gone too far.

Margaret did not speak on the ride back into town. Instead she twisted the ends of her long blond hair, loose from the crown of her head to follow the curve of her neck to shoulders and back. He thought of the willow trees along the river. Weeping. Who was weeping? Margaret? She was off in some unsettling daydream. Was he weeping? Thomas gave up trying to reach her. He had rarely felt such defeat. He sat with his hands on his knees, legs slightly apart, body a little forward, as if to spring. He studied her. She looks like a child, arrogant, sulky, withdrawn. Challenging, tiresome, needy. She's moody. I don't understand her.

He did not escort her to the steps of the house. She seemed to pull ahead at the corner of the street. He left her, but she called out to him. "Be prompt." He turned to watch her. To his amazement, her head was cast down, her body hung on a pin at the back of her neck. She dragged herself along like a fettered pony, away from him and into that stable of mares that was her home and family.

He did not look forward to the evening to come.

Margaret MacNeil did not stop in the hallway of the house, but went directly up the stairs to the room she shared with

Mary. As she reached the second-floor landing she heard her mother call out to her: "Margaret, we were just talking about you." "You always are," she muttered, but she did not stop. She closed the door of the bedroom as silently as if she were not really there, then looked around. Thank heaven, Mary was not curled up on her bed with her music manuscripts, filling the space with her interminable under-the-breath humming. From the sleeve of her dress she took the letter. All afternoon she had willed herself to show it to Thomas, to tell him what had happened, to ask his help. But some piece of her would not release the woman in love. Indeed, she had not been supportive to him in the face of all those silly ladies like Miss Fowler and Mrs. Woods. When she was with Thomas she felt the security of her own accomplishments and his will to have her angered her, but when he left her she missed his voice, his look, his hands, and she longed for the moment when he would embrace her.

Thinking about kissing, his lips on hers, was both frightening and exciting. She remembered the same feeling when she was a child. When she was twelve she and Mary had been declared old enough to see death. They had been taken to the funeral home to see Uncle William laid out. It was required that they kiss him on the forehead. Neither one of them had ever liked kissing Uncle William. They held each other's hand in their terror. She went first, of course; she always did. She found it was like touching her lips to the worn leather of her father's smoking chair, cool, just the slightest roughness. Even as she kissed him she was amazed at her ability to question herself. "Go on, Mary." She had pushed her sister boldly. "Margaret," her mother had scolded, "mind yourself." It was an odd comparison, she knew, but it posed the same unknown. She had been sheltered from a man's love as carefully as she had been protected earlier from death, maybe more so. She hoped the kiss of love lived up to her expectations. She had been disappointed in her first encounter with death. Uncle William did not look different, grander, in death. He looked fat and angry. But she remembered that the stillness chilled her. Now the thought of love made her shiver, and on reflection—there was more to making love than kissing—she was not altogether sure she wanted more right now. And so when she settled into the rocker by the window to reread the letter from Aunt Polly, she forgot the ache of Thomas's leaving tomorrow, and for the first time since she had found the letter on her pillow last night, it gave her comfort. The choices were hers, and she must consider her obligations to others as well as to herself.

My dear Margaret:

When you came into the shop yesterday afternoon and I spoke with you, I little realized that any word from Aunt Polly could call forth such a look of dislike—and for me. I release you from the promise you may feel obliged to honor—the promise to reconsider your attachment to Mr. Hughes and remember your own abilities. Believe me when I tell you that at the time I asked you to make that promise I fully knew, as I know now, no one has a right to dictate to you in a matter which seems already to have gone so far. Two weeks ago I watched you walk to the corner with your young man. I saw something in your face which led me to ask you as I did. No one has a legal right over you; are there any moral obligations?

You are not the first to be placed in a position of this kind—I feel like saying "history repeats itself." I spoke to you from bitter experience yesterday. The same call came to me three years later in life than it has come to you. Everything for the future looked rosy *for me.* The man was also a college graduate and he, too, held the correct key—a teacher with a salary of $800. I fought with myself and rebelled against others. I asked for two years, which were given. Two years later he came, holding an even higher position.

Meantime I saw in how many ways my mother, sister and brother gave up things for themselves to educate me.

I gave him up, knowing that he was, and is now, nearer to me in one way than anyone else can be.

So when I hear myself styled "old maid," I wonder and think of the sacrifices made for me in my girlhood, and I know way down deep in my heart that any loss I may feel has only given me a chance in my time to give my family some trifling comforts. To give up on my part was all for the best.

When I tell you, Margaret, that you are the first one in the world to know this poor story of mine, you will understand me when I tell you that this letter is written for *no* other eyes than yours. This subject will never again be taken up by me without your permission.

If I have presumed too much out of my feeling for you and your future, I ask you to remember that I have only thought of your good.

Hoping I still may be to you lovingly

Aunt Polly

The letter left Margaret thoughtful. This time on reading it she felt her own power again, and liked it. Poor Aunt Polly, so much goodness. But on going through it yet another time—how many now, and how many different feelings: anger, loss, challenge, pity—she wondered at her aunt, the woman she herself had always wanted to be like. Aunt Polly was the only one who actually engaged Thomas in conversation. She was capable of recognizing his fine achievements, and even deferred to his opinions and admired his abounding intellectual curiosity of mind. Only she could appreciate the meaning of being on the way up. She understood the prestige that would accompany his appointment at Princeton, should it come through.

The door opened. Margaret slid the letter under the seat cushion.

"What's that?" Mary asked.

"Nothing."

"It's not nothing; it's a letter. Don't you think I can see? From your Terrible Thomas, I suppose. Now you have secrets with him from me. What a hornet's nest you've stirred up with your university man. I can't even play the piano. They sit all day in the parlor and carry on about you."

"They have always talked about me."

Mary cried out. "Why is it always you? Why do I go on picnics with the Fulton twins while you walk with your Mr. Hughes? And against Mama's wishes, like one of those girls from across the river. You've no shame with your Mr. Hughes."

She collapsed in Margaret's lap and burrowed her face into the folds of the skirt. Margaret stroked her older sister's hair.

Gentle, dumb Mary. Mouse-brown hair. Clerk in an insurance company.

"I'm sorry, Margaret," muffled by Margaret's thighs. "I want for you only what you want."

And Margaret felt the power once more. Could she really reach in to upset the lives of these people she had loved all her life? Now it frightened her. Aunt Polly was right. She owed her family some comfort—and the money. But for herself? Why did a woman have to choose? No man was forced to decide between his head and his heart. In fact, there would be something wrong with him if he were not grandly ambitious for himself and his family. Look at her sweet, broken father, with his dwindling business and his sips of rum. Could she have Thomas and teach, too? She knew Thomas would not allow it, and he was right; she wanted to belong to him, to a man, and be cherished and cared for as she had never been.

"Oh, Lord," she said out loud, "either way I lose something I want."

"What?" from Mary.

"Never mind," Margaret said.

Tonight, she thought, after dinner, I will ask Thomas for two years.

Chapter 5

───────···❦···───────

WHILE THOMAS HAD ALWAYS considered Margaret naïve and therefore malleable, it was clear to him throughout the dinner party that her silence marked a grim inner evaluation of him, perhaps, and of herself. Watching her, so different this evening from the unfamiliar child of the afternoon, he found the distance she put between herself and him tonight frightening rather than irritating. She appeared shrewd, judgmental. She answered when addressed, helped out when it was expected, offered nothing more, neither grace nor intelligence. She seemed to him powerful and cold. And he was bewildered by the many Margarets he kept meeting. It was as if within her family she was a stranger from them and from him. During the course of the evening his own sense of dejection and confusion made him remote, he realized, but the rest of the MacNeil women were so busy with each other that he received relatively little attention and no one seemed to notice his withdrawal or hers.

He had come with the good news. He saw it as an offering, his dowry, in a manner. He wanted to present it to Margaret, dazzle her with the security and status he could give her, seduce her with his goodbye embrace, kiss her at last and hear her tell him that she loved him. Despite an earlier ambivalence and the strangeness of the afternoon, he knew this was his winning card. He had it all planned.

In the entry hall of the house he held her back, reaching out to grab her arm. "It came, Margaret." He whispered to promote intimacy. "The letter. Good news from Princeton."

"Good for you." She barely heard him out and did not linger alone with him. He followed her up the stairs and into the parlor.

Ironically it was her mother who was pleased. "Oh, Mr. Hughes, how distinguished. Margaret's Aunt Polly tells me to go to Princeton is a great tribute, a sure sign of your continuing success. Nothing will stop you now, eh, Mr. Hughes. You will have a fine salary. Did you hear that, Mabel? Margaret's Mr. Hughes will go to teach at Princeton, in New Jersey. Polly, come here. Mr. Hughes was worthy of the position, just as you said." She strutted Thomas before her sister Mabel. Her pride in him made him uncomfortable. Too much the pride of lawful claim. It was he who had expected to be feeling pride of ownership. And what of Aunt Polly, who had been so attentive, interested in his new work in the study of economics?

"Congratulations, Mr. Hughes. New Jersey is a long journey away from Providence. You will be able to build new friendships."

Was everyone to behave so out of character? Or was his own judgment of these people so very wrong?

While the older women retired to the kitchen and Margaret and her sister set the table in the dining room beyond the parlor archway, Thomas sat uneasily on a straight-backed chair across from Mr. MacNeil and Cousin Charles. After introductions and pleasantries, the three of them fell into a miserable silence, the two older unaccustomed to each other, to being thrust together without the women to give them welcome anonymity with all their talk. From time to time Mr. MacNeil sipped from a small blue glass; his digestive, he called it. And he hadn't even eaten yet, Thomas thought. The door to the smoking cabinet beside his leather chair, in which he habitually sat, was partially open. Copper-lined, it was the gift of Margaret and Mary. Against the polish of the sides Thomas saw the bottle. Dark rum, he knew. Another of Mr. MacNeil's failings. It worried Margaret, and in telling Thomas some months ago, she had felt ashamed of her father. She had said so, and she had never spoken of it since. Mr. MacNeil's drinking mortified his wife. It was the only thing he did that stirred her from her indifference toward him. In company she remained silent, but she let the whole world know with her look. Now when she came into the dining room to oversee some detail of the table, she scowled at him. Thomas watched carefully. Mr. MacNeil looked his wife full in the face and smiled stupidly. Thomas could imagine the upbraiding, the withdrawal, when they were alone.

That's something I'll never do, drag myself down with the drink. The thought disgusted Thomas.

The gathering was called to dinner around the circular table. There was no head of the family, as he was accustomed to think of his own father. Margaret contrived to sit between her sister and her father, physically removed from him. He saw that her behavior did not bespeak indifference but rather some turmoil, for he noticed that she shrugged off Aunt Polly's hand from her shoulder. What was between them? Following the grace, Margaret rose to preside over the serving of the meal from the lowboy as naturally as if she had been carving like a man all her life. It bothered Thomas.

Pink corned beef, carrots, potatoes with parsley, hot breads, sweet butter, fruit pies. At least this family ate a man's meal. Could Margaret cook?

The talk was with the women.

"The corned beef would melt in your mouth, Mabel. It's so good to have you back with us."

"You could travel the whole country, the corned beef is not the same elsewhere. Only Egan's down on Prospect Street knows how to make the brine strong."

"Delicious, Florence. Flaky and sweet."

"It's the sweet cherries, have to be naturally sweet. And the shortening. Never skimp on the shortening."

67

Aunt Polly worried the dangerous cost of ribbons to push the price of hats up. Thomas mentioned the concept of supply and demand, Aunt Polly would be interested, but even she did not listen.

"I must have some new hats before I go back West. Everybody comments."

"Yes, I'll style you some new ones, Mabel. I've been treasuring a strip of satin for you. Rich dark green."

And about the picnic after early Sunday services.

"There will be plenty of meat for the pies."

"I'll be needing help to bake tomorrow."

"Mary will help."

"Mama, it's Saturday. I must work."

"Ah, yes, but Mr. Hughes will be leaving, Margaret can help. Good practice, Margaret."

Margaret looked down at her half-eaten pie and Thomas saw that she bit the tip of her tongue until it bled. Her face was flushed. And suddenly he knew it was not worth the uncertainty she prompted in him to marry this mercurial, unpredictable Margaret MacNeil: gracious, quick-witted, intelligent on the one hand; disdainful, angry, aloof on the other.

And again he thought of the loyalty of Elizabeth Roberts, the warmth of Maria. Did he have to give up being cared for to overcome his simple beginnings and gain respect and comfortable circumstances? For he would succeed.

Thomas broke up the evening. He said he must get an early start in the morning. Mrs. MacNeil warmly ushered him out of the parlor, and Margaret after him. She followed him down the stairs to the entry hall. She stood close to him now, confusing him yet again. Unthinking, he turned to embrace her; unexpectedly she came to meet him. He drew away, mindful of his resolve not to want her. But she would not be rebuffed. Her hand on his arm again, she walked with him to the street corner. They stopped and were silent, a kind of unspoken impasse between them. She looked back to the windows of her house. He followed her gaze. No shadows behind the lace curtains this

time. He had noticed them before. She leaned against his side
lazily.

"I want to talk with you, Thomas. It's important."

He drew away from her. "Judging from your behavior today,
no one would guess it."

She would be contrite. "I don't blame you for being cross with
me, Thomas, really I don't. I get all mixed up in my feelings. But
believe me, I've wanted to talk with you all day."

This back and forth. Did she think she could twist him so
easily around her little finger? He would be purposely un-
friendly.

"You had plenty of opportunity to say anything you wanted
this afternoon."

"I just couldn't."

"What do you mean, you couldn't? I longed to have you back
the way you used to be. In fact, it's been a long time since I felt
your affection for me."

He's angry with me, and he has a right to be. But the truth
only made her petulant. She did not like to be wrong. She
planted her feet apart, arms akimbo. Her sudden movement
unloosed her hairpins. The plait of blond hair on top of her head
fell to one side over her ear. She stopped awkwardly to retrieve
a pin and fumbled to right the braid.

"Oh, believe me"—rising upright—"I did want to talk to you.
I needed you"—through a mouthful of bone. "But you would be
so demanding, always wanting to be serious, trying to make me
promise, as if you meant to own me. Those looks of yours.
Begging." She let herself go to challenge him. "Don't you think
I have my own life to live? You forget, I am the principal of the
Hope Street Technical School. You don't care about me; you
only care about yourself."

Her hair askew, for a moment he loved her for her imperfec-
tions. "Oh, Margaret, forget your fight. You wear me out. What
is it you want?"

"Wear you out. How dare you? It is you who wear *me* out."
She stamped her foot like a spoiled child. The plait tumbled
from her head.

69

How could a woman be at once frail and beautiful, and childishly bellicose? "Your hair is a mess."

He's right, I'm a mess. The shame made her reckless. "You think you can bend me to your purposes. You need me to ease your way to the top, whatever you think that is. I'm to cover up your clumsiness, your country manners. Teach you to wear a three-piece suit and a decent hat like a gentleman. Entertain the important people you dream of knowing. Be your help-meet."

They squared off now; every low blow counted.

"You look like a fool. The distinguished Miss MacNeil." He mocked her. "Puts on airs. Thinks she's better than other people. Cold-blooded and bad-tempered."

"You're the fool. I was going to tell you before you left tomorrow that I would seriously think about your marriage proposal, despite my obligation to my profession and my family. I thought I needed two years to consider the wisdom of such a serious decision. It will not be necessary now."

"I would never agree to anything for you, not under any conditions, not for all the riches in the world. When I board that train for home tomorrow afternoon, I will be free of you, Margaret MacNeil. I will not be on trial for any old-maid schoolteacher."

She ran from him, as if to flee a flogging, her hair nesting untidily at her shoulders.

"Don't you call me an old-maid schoolteacher, you immigrant peasant." She hesitated. "Besides, you said you were leaving in the morning." She was crying.

"I only just said that to get away from you," he called after her. Serves her right, he thought. But he stayed to watch her go. The screen door slammed behind her. He realized he was bathed in sweat. The summer evening air suddenly left him chilled.

He wheeled about, a military maneuver. Brusque, disciplined. Control. He must get himself under control. He was a man soon to be twenty-nine, and he had behaved like a child.

He must not allow such lapses. No woman was the stepping stone to his success.

Margaret slammed the screen door hard and regretted it. It would only bring the attention, the questions, when she could not cope. She stood in the entry hall, attempting to rearrange her hair. Sniffling back her tears. She did not want the anger and dismay, the total disarray she felt, to show. She must appear self-possessed before the flock of family that waited to scrutinize her face, her every movement, for the clues that would signal which Margaret MacNeil would prevail—professional woman and spinster, or wife. She shook uncontrollably. When she commanded her body to be still, it would not. She wrapped her slim arms across her breast like twine, as if to bind herself in.

Had she precipitated such ugly words between Thomas and herself? Did she mean all the nasty things she said? Or worse, did he? Was he to go away and she would never see him again? Dear Lord, why did she listen to the Aunt Pollys of this world? In supplication to the God she no longer believed in, she cried out, "What have I done?"

"Margaret, is that you?" She heard her sister, and she moved into the shadowed light under the stairs. Her face and neck were wet and she knew the flesh around her eyes would be swollen red. They were not tears of release. The fear simply flowed from her like a wellspring, never to be abated.

Mary came down the stairs. Margaret watched her crouch down to peer through the banister at her. I'm hunted, an animal, she thought.

"Mama sent me to find you. They are all beginning to wonder what has happened to you. You'd better come out of there."

Margaret withdrew still further into the darkness, trapped. Mary stood before her. "What happened, Margaret?" She stretched out her arms to her sister, and for once Margaret accepted the comfort of Mary's gentle embrace. And with this acquiescence Mary's voice took on an unaccustomed strength.

"You're squeezed in, all shrunken up small. I have never

known you like this before. You'd better tell me what it's all about; it will help. I simply do not understand you. Sometimes you are like a child again, bossy and angry. I bet you still bite your tongue until it bleeds. This Thomas has you all upset, and just when it was going to come out all right." Mary held her sister tight to her bosom and rubbed the back of her neck and her shaking shoulders.

Margaret barely listened, she so much needed the touching. She began to feel herself coming back, her mind and body reunited. The shaking stopped. In all her life she had never felt so close to Mary. Now she felt emotionally impoverished, and she laid her head on Mary's breast, clinging to her, clasping her hands at the small of Mary's back.

"I fought with him, Mary. I called him names. I meant to hurt him." She raised her head, but could not see her sister's face in the dark. It allowed her to go on. "Sometimes I scare myself, Mary. Everything that comes about happens to me. You are sweet, gentle, you willingly look after Mama and Father, and someday you will lovingly marry and raise good children. But I am always torn in two. I must give up one thing for another." Her sister's arms closed more tightly. "Oh, Mary, how much I don't want to give up anything. I know you think they have given too much to make me their success, but sometimes I envy the easiness you have in the family and amongst our friends. They never push you. You are accepted for what you are. I must be something for all of them, a credit. I am told not to think of myself, and when they want to punish me, they speak of 'ought' and 'should.' How will I ever know what is right?" The tears of release at last, and the warmth of Mary's body. She felt bathed in protection. How could she have ever been so high and mighty as to think she was different, better?

"But, Margaret, you are someone special. We all know that. You are like Aunt Polly, and you can contribute your gifts to many more than family or husband. That's what Aunt Polly says."

The anger returned hot. "Who cares about Aunt Polly? She's an old-maid schoolteacher."

"Oh, Margaret, now you are being wicked. You must learn not to be so unloving."

"Aunt Polly and Mother, they would tear me in half, and Father just sits there with his stupid smile, behind his rum. He never helps me out. They will feed me to each other."

Mary dropped her arms. "Margaret, I will not let you be so unkind. Why, Mama was just saying how Mr. Hughes would be very successful, and it is all right to start out humble if he can better himself so well."

"Now she likes him. His salary, that's what she likes. She wants to see her daughter in a grand house and in fine clothes, and Aunt Polly doesn't want me to have any more than she had."

"If you say any more of those things I will tattle, I warn you."

Margaret pushed Mary aside and began to mount the stairs. "Go ahead and snitch on me, I don't care; you always do. Mama's little goody-goody. Everybody likes you, but I must make your way up, you and all the rest."

"You're too old to keep talking such nonsense. No wonder your Mr. Hughes is fed up with you."

"You just wait and see, I'm only just beginning. I'll speak my mind and for once they won't get me to take it back."

At the top of the stairs she barged through the doorway into the parlor with such force that at the sight of her, disheveled, red-faced, the family rose from the harmonious cluster of divan and chairs to face her, all except her father. She came at them like an intruder, to confront. She addressed her mother, but her eyes followed around the roomful of faces.

"I mean to marry him, Mama. If he will have me now."

Her mother broke from the circle to meet her. "Of course he will have you, you silly goose. You are socially above him, he needs you and he has been most attentive. I am convinced of his excellence. He will give you many comforts; you will help him on the way up. And he will care for your family as you do." She raised her hands in happy expectation. "And, my dear Margaret, you will have a fine gown, Aunt Florence will see to that. The marriage will be a credit to us all."

"Mama, it's me that counts to me; I don't care about credit," but her mother went right on.

"Mr. Hughes must ask your father for your hand, good and proper, like any gentleman." Mrs. MacNeil looked down at her husband, sipping from his blue glass. "But your father will know what to say."

"I've fought with Thomas, Mother, I fought hard. They were ugly words we said. And for weeks I have let you test him, stand him on trial. Now that you are sure of his success, you've changed your mind about him and his country origins."

"Margaret, that's no way to talk to me. I have always encouraged Mr. Hughes."

"Mama, you know that is not true."

"Now, my dear, it is quite natural to be upset at such a time, such a big decision made. And you must be sure of yourself, I know from bitter experience. But control yourself, Margaret, for Mr. Hughes will not have your evil tongue. I have tried all your life to chase it out of you. No man will put up with that, not even your father."

Mrs. MacNeil reached out for her daughter, tentatively, as she always did, afraid of this headstrong child grown independent woman. But Margaret eluded her mother, stepping backward onto Mary's toes. Aunt Polly was to the side. Boxed in. Margaret faced her aunt. "And now that *you* see that I mean to have a husband, you do not want me to have what you gave up." She saw the pain snuff out Aunt Polly's face, but it must be spoken once and for all. "You speak to me of moral obligations, sacrifices in exchange for trifling comforts given. But you still miss your love, you said so in your letter. You called it a poor story." Margaret cried out, "I don't want to miss him."

"The story was between us, Margaret. I have never seen the sweetness go out of you like this. You throw away your power like a child. But believe me, there is much satisfaction in professional position, a challenge in a man's world. And it is a woman's obligation to help others."

The tears ran down the faces of both women now.

"You said I owed you no promise, you said no one had a legal right over me. Oh, Aunt Polly." Margaret threw her arms around the older woman's shoulders. "I have always wanted to be like you, I have loved you specially. How can you speak against my feelings if you love me as you say you do?" Aunt Polly pulled away, to slip from the room. "He called me an old-maid schoolteacher." And then she screamed to those she loved most, mesmerized, her supporting cast at the denouement of such a drama.

"It's my life you tamper with. It's me that you gossip about all day. And in my confusion to do what you tell me I ought to do instead of what I want to do, I have driven him away. Tomorrow he will go. I may never see him again."

She sat exhausted on the piano bench. At last she had convinced herself that she wanted to marry him.

Unexpectedly, Mr. MacNeil rose, threading his way through the clutter of skirts to reach his daughter. He lifted her from the bench and took her small hand in his to hold it against his chest. She made no move to resist his gentle, protective touch, but fell upon his small body to weep into the bosom of his shirt as she had often done as a little girl. He stroked her frowzy hair, down from the crown, across her neck.

"He will be back, Margaret. He cares for you as I do in my helpless way. You are a remarkable young woman, and he will give you the things I could not. He will be proud of you as I am."

"But, Papa, he said he would be glad to be free of me."

"A lovers' quarrel. I've had them in my time. He will be back for you."

"And you will say the right thing?"

"I will say yes to your Thomas Hughes."

And early in the morning, her nightgown unlaced, her hair loose, her feet bare, she ran down the two flights of stairs, gawky like a fawn, to look beneath the entry door. It was there, the white paper just barely showing across the sill. She pulled the edge of the envelope. It was wedged between the wood too hard. She did not want to unlatch the heavy bolt; the noise would surely bring someone to the head of the stairs. She wanted to be alone with Thomas no matter what was in the letter. She worked it back and forth to free it, prying, gently slipping it toward her until she could grab hold and tug. The envelope tore. She ripped it open, to find the letter intact, and for a moment she was afraid to read.

20th June
4:00 Saturday morning

Margaret dear,

As I look at your picture it is hard for me to believe that we disagree so vehemently. Perhaps someday when we have got beyond all of these preliminaries and have had some time to recover from the nervousness that affects both of us, we may be able to laugh at the possibility of serious disagreement. But just now I cannot bear the thought of laughing.

No doubt you have wondered at me today. It is strange that twenty-four hours can bound so much misery. Perhaps tomorrow, when I am home, I shall wonder at myself. Just now, though, I can't help feeling what I have felt many times before—that although we love each other beyond question, our entire progress towards what I believe we have both longed for has been marked by pleading on my part and resistance on yours. I have tried to express that fairly, as I see it. How to explain it is what baffles me and shames me. I am ashamed to say to myself that from the first I have always been in the position of the suppliant when we have discussed the future between us. Yes, I am ashamed, but that is the truth.

I understand, of course, that there are circumstances that hold you back, but it is not possible that such an intelligent and sensitive woman as yourself does not understand the significance of what has passed between us. And you must feel as I do the tremendous sacrifice that has been made by us already to satisfy your people. We have put off too long the engagement that should never have been put off at all. Our duty to each other is unmistakable.

When I close my eyes and try to sleep in the small hours of the night, I can hear you crying as you fled from me and I long more than anything to feel your dear head on my shoulder. Oh, what a fool I was to say those things to you whom I love as my life. Please forget it, Margaret. I do hope that last evening won't become an ugly memory in your mind, but I fear it. God, how I fear it! I'd do anything if only I might undo it. But, dearest, I love you, I'm mad for you, and there are so many things in my love, so many sides to it, that I am bewildered. It drives me to acts, words, that in the abstract I can't imagine myself doing.

But, sweetheart, I'll find my feet if only you will truly forgive me and love me.

I mustn't talk about this anymore. It has kept me awake all night, quivering and cursing myself for shame. I will go to you now to slip this under your door. And I won't think about the things we said ever again, only please write me that you do really forgive me, dear, dear child. I love you and I am going to hope.

T.

"Aunt Florence, I must have my white dress by noon. Starch it for me; you always do it best."

"You've someplace to go, Margaret? I thought you were the one to help with the baking today." Aunt Florence rolled out the dough on the smooth wooden surface of the kitchen table.

"Oh, yes," Margaret cried out. "I've someplace to go—I can go anyplace. I must go to the station, Aunt Flo."

"Quiet, child, you'll wake the dead with your yelling. You know your mother needs her sleep on Saturdays. I dare say she's extra tired after last night. I thought you meant to weary us all with your scenes. Spoiled just like you were as a child." She folded up the thin dough in quarters. "So you want to go to the train station. I thought you said your Mr. Hughes would never want to see you again."

"He slipped me a letter through the door."

"That's why you're not the usual lazybones this morning. I bet you think you're the first in the world to find love." The older woman laughed. "You're still a girl, Margaret, for all your education. Remind me of your Aunt Polly. Run and fetch your dress. We'll see what we can do to smarten you up. While you're upstairs wake Mary; she'll be late for work—and put something on your feet, child."

Margaret twirled away from her aunt, a polka step.

"I'm not a child. Thomas loves me. It smells good in here,

Aunt Flo." She dropped open the oven door, then slammed it shut.

"Stop that. My cake will fall."

"It will taste lovely." Margaret kissed her as she waltzed by. "You'll do my hat, won't you?"

"You're a greedy child, kisses only when you want something." But her aunt smiled.

Margaret finished a two-step before the table where Aunt Florence had cut out stars and half-moons with metal cookie cutters, each one with a little hat of a handle.

"You will teach me to bake and sew and mend so he will love me more?" She poked her finger through a crescent-shaped piece of dough.

"You. Cook and sew. You with your nose in a book all day. Your Mr. Hughes has addled your head, my dear. Who would ever think of you wanting to cook and sew? But at least you're happy again. You've been as morose as a preacher."

"I love you, Aunt Florence." She passed her flour-covered hand across her aunt's head. "I love everyone."

"Get on with your dressing. You've dirtied my hair with all your loving."

Thomas Hughes went early to the railroad station, eager to get moving, a little apprehensive, the fear of despair. For the first time, he would not let his sister Alma accompany him.

"The train does not leave till half-twelve."

"I've a lot of luggage."

"I'll help you on the trolley."

"No need, Alma."

"Of course, Thomas. I always go with you. It makes me feel in some way I'm going home, too."

"Not this time, Alma." He kissed her on the cheek and turned toward the coat rack.

She stood silent for a moment. Then: "It's different, isn't it? You won't be back, will you, Thomas?"

He put down the duffel of books he had hoisted to his shoulder. The doubt in her voice, the tone of regret . . . He almost could not leave her, for she had always nourished him. He held her the way a lover would hold the unapproachable suddenly in his arms, tentatively and tenderly, and then he embraced her hard.

"I don't know what will come, Alma. I'll be going to Princeton in some months anyway. I will miss you now as I will miss you then, but you have wished me well before. I want her, Alma. Do your praying so that I may have her."

She held him as she had when they were young. She felt him eternally vulnerable. Finally she rubbed her tears across his jacket and pushed him away. "Be off with your wanting. I hope she'll be decent to you in the end, Thomas."

"I just hope she'll have me."

Alma turned away from him. "You're a child of a man, naïve like a newborn. She means to have you."

"You're a witch sometimes, Alma. Come on with ye, wish me well."

"I wish thee well in everything you want. Now out of here before I lose my patience with your silliness."

She drew him down to kiss his neck and shoved him toward the door. "Take my love to them at home."

He partially lifted his laden arms in salute, without turning back.

The schedule read twelve-thirty for departure. He knew it by heart. The great clock set into the pebble-green marble wall of the station shed marked half after eleven. His ticket purchased, a laundry list of towns and cities that would mark his journey, he sat on one of the row of long wooden benches and studied the waffled lines of the slats that formed the contoured seats, the straight high backs. The outside light, dimmed through the dirty windows, the electric bulbs at the ticket counter, left the hall gloomy. The atmosphere was close, stuffy, it always was, and he felt again the impermanency that in the past had excited him as much as confused him because it meant he would soon be moving on, as often as not to home, to the people he understood best, the ones so like himself. But today he recognized the apprehension again. Growing. Some part of him expected Margaret to come, or why his early arrival at the station, alone, without Alma. It was Margaret's impulsiveness he was banking on. And yet his letter. He knew her pride, had felt her cruelty, and clearly he did not know Margaret MacNeil as fully as he'd like to think. She was always surprising him. Having written of supplication and shame, he worried about his own pride. Would he be found wanting? And he questioned still further his image in her eyes: brilliant, passionate, good-looking, or country-bumpkin, clumsy, crudely vain? Such self-doubt annoyed him. Only Margaret made him suffer it. He was at once excited by her power and angered by his own vulnerability.

He paced the station floor now, up and down the aisles between the benches, packing the tobacco down into the bowl of his brier to give a good draw. It was the first time he had smoked in a public place since he'd met Margaret. He was exhilarated; perhaps freed was the word. No, unleashed, that was how he felt. He imagined himself a distinguished judge or banker, with several three-piece suits, enough starched collars to change twice a day, a watch fob. Serious decisions to make now before his important business trip began. Here he was at the station considering the wisdom of his business move with Hamilton. Hamilton was an appropriate name for his colleague, an established name. "It's really a question of investing the principal in an up-and-coming product. I'm for backing the safety razor. Neat little gadget. You'll see, it will go a long way. . . . Yes, risky, I know, but railroads are through now, no big money to be made there anymore. It's all been done, Hamilton. . . . Yes, yes, I realize they are solid, dependable stocks, but we must take chances to make a show. I'm something of a frontier man, you know, dear fellow. Sometimes it's easier for me to see beyond. You're so much a man of establishment, of the past."

And soon Thomas found himself following the geometric pattern of the mosaics that bounded the edges of the vast station floor. He stood to look at the series of scenes played out in perfect symmetry across the open floor from the great entryway to the glass-paneled swinging doors that led to the train platform.

In one the figure of Pan danced dark blue on dirty gray, festooned about in ropes of vines. In another the head of a bull looked through ivy leaves. The rites of spring. He laughed now, enjoying himself at last, and followed on to the next. He stooped to stare into the face of a smiling nymph. He rested his elbow on his knee, for he planned to stay awhile with this coquette. He found her inviting, perhaps devious. A tease, surely, but worth it. And he wondered that he had never noticed her before.

He saw the toes of the white shoes. Dainty, laced in pink ribbon. His mouth went dry, the pipe stale. His knee began to vibrate so that he anchored his heel upon the stone all too hastily. He felt at once the same burst of glee, the way he had felt when he first beat his father pitching horseshoes—he'd won, with his skill and control he had won—but he also knew he was doomed to have her and she him. He remained crouched in the center of the station. If there were others anywhere about, he willed them away. This scene was his with Margaret.

Slowly he looked up the line of her body. Her foot was long, her ankles small. Beneath her full white skirt and tight bodice he saw her legs were long, thin, he'd judge, her body lithe, almost flat like a boy's. Her tiny hands, gloved as usual, just barely reached out from the deep ruffled cuff of the fitted sleeve. She wore her blond hair rolled back from her face to best show off her neck, her chin, her cheekbones. She looked down at him from under a large circular lace hat trimmed in matching pink.

She posed before him without moving while he studied her. She's costumed for the kill, he thought. She *is* an actress, and he recalled that descent from the school steps some months before, when they had first started walking out together. She knew exactly what she was doing, and he felt very much the suppliant, kneeling there before her. Before God—and he had long since thrown Him out of his life—he would only ask that she be as passionate a performer in his bed as she was artful and intelligent out of it.

He acted with deliberate slowness, removing the pipe stem from between his teeth, gently tapping out the ashes onto the face of the mosaic nymph he had minutes before worshipped like a pagan deity. He stood.

"Good of you to come with your goodbyes," he said.

"Poor doubting Thomas. I came to say I want to be your wife, if you will still have me."

He could not speak.

She laughed at him, breaking the porcelain pose, smiling broadly, teeth parted. Inviting.

And then she moved to embrace him with such unexpected suddenness that he was momentarily thrown off his stance, and only by grabbing her around the waist did he right himself.

He kissed her hair, both eyes, and watching her hold them shut, he sucked in her lips with his own. She swooned, of course, and held her hat. He hung on to her with his kiss.

When she finally withdrew her lips, he saw that she licked them thoughtfully as if to taste his kiss.

"It feels funny, soft, like sponge cake."

Again she had startled him. He felt he must be serious. "It is a very important decision to make, Margaret."

"I've made my choice, Thomas. I will cook and care for you and be your perfect wife."

"I will have to speak to your father first. You realize that."

"Oh, yes, Mama insists."

"She is right, Margaret."

"But he promises to say yes. And we will have to be properly engaged before family and friends."

The stationmaster called the twelve-thirty train to Pawtucket, Woonsocket, Northbridge, Grafton and Worcester.

Thomas drew back from her at last. Her face was relaxed, and his eyes were filled with tears. "And now I am leaving. It is the saddest moment of our love." He clung to her.

At the platform he unbuttoned his vest and slipped off the lion's head ring. "Keep this safe."

She hesitated, a little awestruck perhaps, something so much of himself. Then she received the ring into her hand and turned it so that the lion's head opened. Inside was the tiniest likeness of herself.

"Oh, Thomas," she called out in joy. "It's me in your grandfather's ring. I thought it was your mother and father."

"Tomorrow I will send you a picture of me to lie opposite the one of you. You must write and we will plan the engagement together."

He boarded the train, then ran down the steps to kiss her again. The conductor stood looking at his watch.

"Everything together now, Margaret."

She waved to him as the train moved, and then she began to run. "Happy birthday, Thomas," she called after him.

"My happiest. I love you, remember, I love you." And then she was only a slim figure elevated between the two pits that formed the railroad tracks.

Part
Three

Chapter 6

WHEN DAYLIGHT WOKE James Thomas, the signals in his brain
sent back the news that it was Saturday. He squeezed his eyes
tight so as to hang on to sleep and stretched out his foot to touch
Alma's. Indeed, he swung his leg across the bed to extend his
toes from under the light cover. He waited to hear the toilet
flush. Finally he hoisted himself up on one elbow and made the
effort to read the clock Alma had pinched from her father, the
face a pattern of lines like some damn ancient artifact. The
clock said five-twenty. The bedside lamp was missing. And then
he remembered. Pulling himself up to kneel on top of the
crumpled counterpane, he peered over the end of the high
fourposter bed, an elegant piece of Alma's childhood, which he
enjoyed for its enormity and antiquity and she still complained
about for the memories it forced on her.

Alma sat as he had left her, on the bedroom rug, the missing
lamp beside her. She faced away from him, and if she was aware
of him, she showed no signs. She had thrown a thin knit cardi-
gan over her shoulders; the empty sleeves hung limp like two
punctured balloons. Her waist and rump were bare and pink.
Her naked thighs stuck out to each side, topped by those kid's
knees of hers. She sat Indian style as if at a tribal peace negotia-
tion. Strewn around her on the rug, the floor, flung under the

bed, were the letters, bearing the frilled red two-cent stamp that he recognized as first-class postage way back before the First World War. On careful study, as usual, he could see order in her mess. The letters and cards were scattered in piles; the different handwritings and addresses were the clue. And the sight of her so completely absorbed in her work, like child's play, momentarily reduced the complicated feelings that grew between them. He always welcomed the simplicity of fact. He loved her.

"I love you," he whispered over the edge of the bed.

She barely noticed him. "Hmm."

"Hey, it's me, James. Remember? I'm the guy who holds you together."

She turned to look at him for the first time. "You look silly with your bare ass pointed up to the ceiling like some great camel rising from his sleep."

"One hump or two."

"Come on, James, I'm busy." She adjusted her cockeyed glasses.

"Well, you look pretty silly with nothing on except that sweater discreetly shielding your shoulder blades and those bluestocking glasses you wear to show how serious you are. You look like some turn-of-the-century don—Lady Margaret's Hall, shall we say—who just recently made it to the loony bin."

"You know, James, it's terrible what she had to give up."

"Who?"

"I've read through all these painful letters, and I've never felt so close to my mother in my life."

"A whole night with your mother. Boggles the mind."

"Oh, shut up. You're as bad about her as Daddy was about Grandmother MacNeil."

"Was she a grande dame, too? I'm doomed. Those things run in families like heart disease and fallen arches."

"Don't hurt, James, I'm being serious. Grandmother wasn't really very nice to either Mother or Daddy. I never knew that. She always seemed so proud of them in their big brick house. I used to feel she only liked me because I belonged to them. But now that I see how hard it was in the beginning, I feel sorry for both of them." She began to weep. "I really do, James."

James thoughtfully folded up his jocular criticisms of the ladies MacNeil and climbed down off the great vessel of a bed. He felt like Lord Nelson collapsing his telescope after careful scanning and descending from the poop deck. He leaned over Alma to unbutton the sweater at her neck and knelt behind her, his penis at her back, his arms tucked under hers so that each hand cupped a breast. She bent to sniffle against a hand. He nuzzled her sweet-smelling hair and felt the pleasure of an oncoming erection.

"And Great-Aunt Polly, the old spinster one, the one Mother loved so. Well, she wasn't very helpful either."

James rubbed against her back. "It's almost six in the morning, Alma. Come on to bed."

"It's sort of awful, James, to see into the lives of your parents way back."

"Hmm, I bet." He pinched her nipples. Immediately they hardened. It's just a question of time, he thought, her body's with me.

"It's like voyeurism—I feel somehow dirty. But then I don't stop. I want to know all about them."

"And I want to know all of you." He slipped one hand down her belly to the gap between her legs.

She dropped the letter she held and placed her hand on his, but she did not stop his fingers. Her head forward, the tears, heavy now, dripped from the pockets of her eyes, some to bathe the hand still on one breast, others to fall in a trickle down their arms, side by side, to run dry in the matting of little hairs on their forearms, hers blond, his dark. He lifted her up. She did not resist but tucked her feet under her as she rose so that she was standing, still against him. Gently he began to turn her to embrace her, but she hugged his head, neck, his back so hard he was momentarily thrown off balance. And then the force went from her.

She came easily to bed, allowing him to lay her out beneath the cover as if she were delicate, might break, the way he used to feel about the children when they were tiny babies. She held on to him beside her, her body pressed against every inch of his. The warmth of flesh became hot. He wanted her immediately, he didn't know if he could wait for her.

"I love you, James, do me a favor. Just slip it in and rock me to sleep."

My God, he thought. Out loud he said, "You sure? You usually don't like that."

"Just this once, James."

He slid across her and in the steady rhythm of his coming, he watched her face relax. The crying stopped. She closed her eyes, and she grinned up at him—a pumpkin grin—like a five-year-old.

"You look about five years old," he said.

When I was five, Alma thought, that means my father was fifty-one.

They were in the big high car. Four doors with long, crooked knobs to open them. Bumpy black top, rough, not shiny metal. The tires had big spokes, the spare pinioned to the rear above the bumper to give the back of the auto a kind of rear-view chic, like a woman's chignon. Her father drove, Alma sat in the front seat when she was alone with him. That meant it was Saturday. On other days Mother drove, Daddy sat beside Mother. Then he wore a dark suit and a large-brimmed soft gray fedora. The hatband was black. Alma sat in the back seat, lost like a package forgotten in the Christmas mail, never distributed, never received. Mother left Daddy off at the bank, and then Alma was finally delivered to the little red nursery school on Adams Street. Her sister Mary was so old she walked down the hill to her school all by herself. Alma knew that mother trusted Mary. Mary was good. Mary didn't go out in the car alone with Daddy. She stayed at home with Mother.

Alma struggled to stave off sleep. She wanted to remember.

Saturdays were the only days they were alone together, Alma and her father. They went to his empty office at the bank, where she swung in his desk chair or pushed her fingers through the numbered holes in the dial disk on the black telephone and pulled down, then watched the disk move around until it came back to starting position. Sometimes she squeezed her lips into the trumpet-shaped cone. She was not allowed to unhook the receiver that dangled like an elongated bell from a clip on the long black stem of the phone. The door of the office said "Mr. Thomas Hughes, Foreign Investment." She could not read it all. Daddy told her what it said.

But there were other Saturdays.

Suddenly Daddy stopped the car. He was wearing all white, puttees, blazer, golf cap. Her bobbed hair curved forward at her ears, the tips just showing. It was held in place with a bone-covered barrette. The sun was warm everywhere inside her and in the green countryside. The rhododendrons, lurid purple flowers ready to burst, were fenced onto the running board of the car, and twine was strung around the upper branches and through the handles of the car door to hold the bushes secure during the trip home from the tree nurseries. They were for the front of the house on Pembroke Avenue, the house her parents built when Alma was born. The shrub would grow to look grand, Daddy said, in front of the kitchen window, to look out at from inside and to shield the sight of the white sink from the neighbors. The restaurant where they had stopped was the same one they always went to in the spring. Alma minded that she must always have two soft-boiled eggs, although she had told him he should remember that she was five years old now. But she could drink Coca-Cola. Daddy said he had lots of money in Coca-Cola.

It was too much for Alma. She let go to sleep.

The French doors are closed. Alma knows she must not enter, and when she does the room is very dark, the blinds down, the draperies drawn at all of the six windows so that the red eye of the hideous green dragon curves out in full, stretched now to form the pattern on the yellow linen of the curtains, looks at her in evil, twelve times over, two side-view dragons to each pair.

Life is sealed out of the room, but everything is the same as in Alma's childhood. The grand piano that her father played all Sunday until Mother brought the cocktail tray into the living room at five, the china blue bowl on its rosewood stand. Alma passes between the Queen Anne chairs at either side of the fireplace and the rumpled velvet black sofa across from them. At the bay window she sees that the love seat is gone, the coffin in its place. The lid is off, and from where she stands she sees the bold forehead, his hairless dome above the rim of the box. She looks down at his frail shrunken body, his face skeletal, his tiny perfect hands, the skin crossed with veins like a blue cheese, folded across the familiar Viyella green plaid robe. How inappropriate, Alma thinks, all that he was to her and laid out in a sick man's clothes, or is it an old man's comfort?

And then he sits up to greet her. She draws back alarmed. But now he is small, her son Ned when he was four or five. He climbs down from the box, dangling his legs cautiously until his extended toes touch the rug. She holds him, his face buried in her stomach.

They hear the footsteps on the stairs outside the living room. Alma is suddenly his little child again, afraid. Mother will come into the room and catch them together. He leans down to pat her head reassuringly and steps back into place. He lies down. They are not caught. Alma is grown again, and he is her aged father, dead.

Alma woke miserably—and felt the relief of reality. She pushed the dream away, and moved up against the warmth of James's naked side to fall back into sleep.

Chapter 7

———————··⟨≫⟩··———————

IT WAS ALREADY nine o'clock, Saturday morning. His weekend begun yesterday with the turmoil and pleasure of Alma, who breathed heavily beside him, James was glad for the chance at a few extra hours of sleep. Now he wanted a good leisurely breakfast, in the peace and quiet of his own company, that meant alone, another of the extras of Saturdays and Sundays, sometimes, if he was lucky enough to get to the kitchen before some of the others. Weekday mornings were a kaleidoscope of ugliness, quick cups of last night's coffee, root beer spilled on the newspaper, the filling and emptying of the washing machine, the questions and demands, the slamming of doors.

He slipped furtively from the bed, then pulled back the covers on his wife. Everything about her dormant now, body, mind, voice, he rested in the rare calm of her and welcomed it. He wondered that the womanliness of her which never seemed to go fallow housed that childlike energy of hers which never seemed to mature. She lay on her side, fetus position, her knees drawn halfway up to her stomach. She cupped her head in her too small hands. Looking down on her, he admired her upper underthighs, the breasts which fell one into the other, askew across her chest, the power in her sturdy shoulders. She slept like a baby.

They'd had plenty of troubles in their time. Her obsessiveness drove him to mindlessness, threatening the very definition of his existence—teacher, scholar, thinker. Her need to discuss everything, live everything over and over, before, during, after, tore at his spleen, his bowels, his lungs, until once when the children were young and he was met every evening at the door with a tornado of abuse and complaint about her motherhood and his freedom from it, he had moved out of the house and into an empty guest room at the university. She had literally sucked him back into the fold with a barrage of telephone calls, every ten minutes, day and night, a technique to be emulated by any political campaigner. He had lived through her psychotherapy, every session totally recalled for his greater understanding. When at last she took a part-time job editing a collection of articles for a Pressing Political Issues group, which were outdated before they got into print, he was relieved that she made enough money to almost cover the baby-sitting costs. Her new life out of the house brought Bernard Miller into his hair— scientist, concerned citizen and, James suspected, local fancy fucker. Alma returned from whatever it was she did for this one —ostensibly rewriting and publicity for his worthy antiwar causes—to repeat to James each evening the words of the guru. When Dr. Miller moved his family and his genitals to harass the northern suburbs on the excuse that it would be better for his children, James was relieved.

Time had placed Alma in a small publishing house, where she read manuscripts and carried on her literary talk over endless mugs of black coffee, so that she often returned to the family nest shaking with vitality but mercifully talked out. James did not doubt her unusual intelligence, her skill with words, the fun of being with her. He was only glad that it was not all zeroed in on him now, for he could hardly keep full such a porous pot, beautiful like an Etruscan jug though she be, all by himself. Her life away from him had made their life together bearable at last. He knew why he loved her. Because the unharnessed intensity in her breathed life into him. And why did she love him? Because he was there for her, to slow her up, to give her peace.

He covered Alma and turned to look out the window at the roses she had planted last year, in an oval ring, right in the middle of the grass. They needed full sun, she had told him. Only Alma would plant bushes in the middle of a patch of city weeds, but it gave the scraggly backyard a kind of English-garden style. They bloomed their heads off, all the delicate colors she wasn't. Pink, white, yellow. Pungent-smelling. James stretched his arms and began to think of setting up his worktable in the hot sun beside them.

In the bathroom, he showered extensively, washing his hair, the nubs of his elbows, the nurd gathered like knitting wool from his belly button. He stooped to soap between each toe. Then he turned up the hot water until it scorched him. He let it flow and flow and flow. No one was going to yell, "Don't run the hot water," at him this of all glorious morns. When he was stinging with pain, could no longer stand it, he cut off the hot water and endured the agony of so much cold. It was a very secret ritual that he would never let anyone in on, especially Alma, who would tell him he thought he was in some Swedish movie, and indeed she would be right, all those hots and colds, and birch switches, and running naked through the snow after some big-assed woman.

Before the mirror, he wiped away the steam and brushed his teeth, examining the inside of his mouth like a horse merchant. No matter what he did about oral hygiene, he still had yellow teeth. All Greek gods have some fatal flaw. He debated shaving. To do or not to do . . . whether 'tis nobler, etc., to suffer. But then they were to go out to dinner this evening. Put off whatever you can for as long as you can, that was his motto.

At his closet he chose his dirty blue jeans, green T-shirt and clodhopper boots. His garbage man's outfit, Alma called it, although why, when his children wore Levi's with flowers on the behind or sometimes not, the hole just there. And he had heard Alma tell them that she had been born in a pair of blue jeans. She said she had worn them way back in the dark ages when not everybody did, before people lost all sense of individuality and personal identity. He smiled at the recollection. Polly had given Alma the business on that piece of snobbery. Good old Polly; there was much to be said for any girl child of his at once so vulgar and so beautiful. Somebody was going to get something out of her. He'd better not, James threatened. All too soon, he said back to himself ruefully.

He went cautiously down the stairs, past the bedroom doors where couched his progeny. In each case the laundry delivered last night lay where Alma had stashed it, stepped over, or on, perhaps, but never removed. In one case he noticed the door shut tight, sealed to keep in sleep until it was acceptable among his son's set to arise on a weekend morning. Never before noon. At which point the telephone began to ring. "Oh, nothing, I just got up," translated to mean: "Passed again the loyalty test by not stepping over into enemy—i.e., parental—ways of life." Then the plans for the day, always dependent on the testy cooperation of whichever parent could be conned. The car. "Dad, can I use the car?" Ned did not always prevail, depending on the strong mental health of both his parents, but out of self-defense James and Alma had taken up again the ancient and healthy art of walking, remarking to each other how much better they felt. This reminded him, and James reflected, puzzled, on what happened to the children's New Hampshire trip, which had promised to be a natural tug of war.

The other doors on the landing, bedroom and bathroom, were both ajar, unfortunately. This meant that possibly Polly was abroad and he might not have the kitchen all to himself. On the other hand, she was given of late to stepping out into the world at odd hours in a two-piece blue bag suit, complete with stripes and emblems, the chic variation of what he had worn in different context, in "halcyon," hated, schoolboy days, body-prowess days. The sweat suit—modest gray, his had been—the workout, the that-was-the-greatest-bomb-ever days, or that was the best pass you ever made, language applied to sports and sex interchangeably. James hadn't been much of a jock at either.

Polly was into health culture. It showed up in her diet. She had lately become a vegetarian and had gained five pounds on wheat germ and buttermilk. She was running this back down to normal weight and incidentally building muscles in her legs, which bulged like paper bags full of empty bottles. Once, when he had unexpectedly seen her rounding the corner, a small craft tilting against the wind, and on into a heavily traveled street, he was momentarily concerned that she would be run over. But he saw almost instantly that as she came down the middle of the four lanes of traffic, like Moses she commanded the cars to part, and the whole world watched his daughter's bosom jog by, a pick-me-up for any commuter, slumping his way, day in, day out, to the office. It only bothered James that she was his and he was powerless to shield her. Powerless, hell. It ripped him up that she required no paternal protection at all.

If fortune was smiling his way today, Polly would be off on some dirty pavement building calluses on her toes, and he could lay out everyman's breakfast to his heart's content. He gained the kitchen unobserved, and reached for the refrigerator door. Signs of Polly were everywhere, but he would ignore them. He drew out the bacon, the box of eggs, rummaged behind the cabbage head on the bottom shelf in hopes of finding English muffins. One left. Laden now, he turned to set down his stolen goods. The table was covered with sugar substitute and small curds of cottage cheese. Perhaps to maintain any elegance in his wider scheme of things, he would have to do a little mopping up first. He put everything back into the refrigerator and began to dig away at the sticky mess with a shredded sponge. Then the briefest brooming to eliminate the alarming crunch underfoot. Brought together in a neat pile in the middle of the kitchen floor James identified various forms of nuts and grains and fruits that went into granola, a specialty of Polly's. He stooped to sweep up a portion of the nation's billion-dollar food waste and dumped the contents of the dustpan into the wastebasket.

He surveyed the scene once more. Suitable for a sane man in his early forties to proceed with dignity and pleasure. He spread out his wares, searched further for a grapefruit, cleaned out the mold from the edge of the coffeepot and filled it with fresh cold water and the top with a fine mixture of Continental roast and ICA regular. While the coffee perked, filling his nose with good smell and his head with the irritability of waiting, he laid out four pieces of bacon—the forbidden number—in the cast-iron fry pan and mixed up two eggs. The coffee perked by now, he poured himself a bowl, with hot milk, and relived a moment in the south of France. He would breakfast out of doors. Now he had the stamina to cut out each section of the grapefruit half. The bacon draining on absorbent paper, the two halves of the muffin—parted with a fork, of course—toasting in bubbling sweet butter under the broiler, it was almost time for his scrambled eggs. He reached for a large wooden tray, sterling knife and fork, despite the eggs—that for a small nose-thumb at Alma, who was always eating eggs with anything at hand so as not to "stain" the silver—found the salt, the pepper mill, the marmalade. He returned to the eggs. A low flame, gently and continuously stirred to the light just-beyond-runny consistency that he liked and his family didn't. He chose a flowered pottery plate, which he heated in the oven. So prepared, he started for the door to the backyard, a country breakfast at the picnic table beneath the spreading maple tree.

"Hi, Dad. Eating breakfast outside?" The blue Valkyrie from the outer side of the screen door.

Shrewd observer, he thought. "Would you mind holding the screen door for me?"

"Sure." She snapped back the door with such thrust that it threatened to break loose from her and dash into his breakfast tray. The coffee spilled.

He walked onto the porch with majesty. "Thanks. Where's the newspaper?"

"Oh, I took it down to the riverbank. Must have left it there."

The screen door slammed behind her. James progressed to the picnic table and laid out his *petit déjeuner dans le jardin,* then sat down to serve himself.

Sometimes it's rather nice just to enjoy the food, the color of the sky, the flower beds, he thought. More often than not the newspaper brought alarming items, gorging up points of view and bouts of indigestion. Later he would walk to the corner store for another copy.

While James ate he watched the bees at work in the roses. Each morsel tasted and found superb, he and they would agree. He lifted his face directly into the sun and reflected on the wisdom of migrating south to steadier climates, New Orleans, maybe, and opening a restaurant. But there was something missing. Juice, a glass of juice. And the newspaper.

Leaving the dirty dishes to bake in the sun, he went back into the house to raise some money, journeying via the refrigerator. There he found a very large can with a very little bit of liquid in the bottom. Just right. He swizzled it around and emptied the can.

"Hey, you're drinking my V-8 juice."

"Righteo, Polly Peachum, I am. What's in the headlines today?"

"Polly Thomas's grandfather makes it to eighty-seven."

"I didn't know you cared."

"I don't, but Ma does. What was she doing on the floor, naked almost all over, with all that junk around her?"

"Later, kiddo. I'm off to replace the newspaper that I pay for and you lose." Today Polly was in a good mood, for a change, and James was equal to her and that felt right.

At the store James found the *New York Times* was out, of course. The other choices all read the same. June 22, 1974. War, corruption, the threat of peace. He supposed that was the news. He took the one that carried "Doonesbury," and "The Wizard of Id." Often he preferred this to the *Times,* since every newspaper he had ever come to know reported history with its own bias, and the *Times* was laborious. Besides, the kids liked the comics. So did he. As he passed to the checkout counter he saw the moisture collecting on the six-packs of beer through the glass door. At eleven in the morning it would drive Alma up the wall, and the very thought refreshed him. He wasn't at war with Alma, he reminded himself; it's just that since the birthday visit yesterday, she had some heavy thing going with her old man, clearly, and there was more to come. He would need reinforcements; better get the sixteen-ounce cans.

Back at the house, he added his books and papers for class

preparation to his collection and set up shop again at the picnic table. Moments later his little girl came out in a teeny bikini, all total one hundred and forty-four square inches of it bulging. She carried her baggage well, also a magazine, the suntan lotion and his large bath towel. She stretched out in the sun, her head close to his feet, and he was reminded with sadness of the time about three or four years ago when he was the man she loved, the Mecca of her universe. It made him want to take her in his arms now and touch the woman who lay before him. And he welcomed the built-in restraint of guilt. God, this business of seeing your children grow up was tiresome and tortuous all at once. No wonder Alma, with her feelies out all the time, said that middle age was just as agonizing as adolescence and that's why they came in the same package, enough for the whole family, finger-lickin' good.

James read the funny papers and then began his work. After he had chosen the translation for his first class of summer term, he reached for a beer. He pulled the flip top and enjoyed the release of air, like a satisfying fart. In the hot sun the taste of the first draw was like an unexpected caress, chilled and passionate.

"Can I have one of those?"

"You're illegal, in every way." He reached her a beer. "Here."

She whipped off the cap and threw it into Alma's roses.

"Come on now, your mother's roses are really something, and she won't like that piece of metal amongst the compost she'll have me spreading around as soon as she can come back to them, her latest babies."

"Okay, Daddy, but sometimes I think you do too much for Ma."

"Me, too, darling."

They settled to their separate business, together in the sun. James wandered through some Hittite texts, and he could see Polly was reading why women didn't have to have men anymore. The article was entitled "He Was a Male Sex Symbol." James felt he should be relieved. Maybe she would be a virgin forever. Was he kidding himself? What made him think it wasn't too late? It didn't trouble him today. He hadn't had so much love with Polly since he could remember.

"What *was* Ma doing up there with all those letters?"

"Oh, she was just going through some of the things from Pembroke Avenue."

"How come last night? That stuff's been up there for months. When she tells me what a pig I am, I want to tell her she's the same only she's got all the swill hidden in boxes. Doesn't it drive you crazy, Daddy, that you have to live with all that mess?"

"You're right, dear, I've had too much of it. But I think your mother is going through something very tough, and now she's going to take care of it."

"What d'you mean, 'Take care of it'? She's going to put it down in the cellar, out of the way, just like Grandmother Hughes. Ned and I are going to inherit the same old junk, piled up to the ceiling. What makes those women unable to get rid of anything?"

"Well, Polly, I think you're wrong about your mother. If you want to know what she was doing all last night, she was reading her way through a whole lot of letters that matter to her and not to me, and you know damn well she'll come out with some kind of answer."

"Answer to what? A whole lot of shrink explanation for everything she's ever done or is going to do."

"Well, honey, if it brings peace, why should we care?"

"Okay, Dad, but what she ought to do is get out and run some, like me. It would tone her up."

"Now, Polly, that's one thing I won't have you say. Your mother has the figure of a young girl."

"Oh, come on, Daddy, that's not what I meant. But she looks right in the right places for an old lady, and you like everything you can get your hands on."

"Polly, stop that. Sometimes you're not decent."

"What's decent about lecherous old you, Dad?"

James was wounded and crawled into his books. He loved Polly. She saw right through him and she was vulgar. And he loved Alma, and maybe she was aging. The patterns of the cuneiform seemed recognizable and comfortable. No affront, no sacrilege; just rituals. One goat, one jug of wine, a fire, and the king would be satisfied.

"Hey, Daddy, is the old man dying?"

"You mean your grandfather?"

"Yeah, Ma's problem parent."

"Your mother's problem parent—what makes you say that?"

"She's never quite sure if she loves him or not."

"Maybe not, but that doesn't seem very different from you and your brother."

"Sure, but we're supposed to be young and rebellious."

James was not responsive. Polly asked him again. "Is Ma's father dying?"

"He's awfully old, Polly. Pretty soon."

"What'll happen to Ma?"

"She'll take it, she always does. But it will hurt some."

"And she'll cry all over you."

"Why not, Polly? No matter how old you are, it's not easy to lose a parent."

"Are you afraid of when your parents will die?"

"I don't think about it much, they're young yet."

"Sometimes you make Ma do all the feeling, Daddy. She knows already how it will kill you when Granddaddy Jim or Grandma dies. She's ready to hold you until the pain leaves you."

"If you know that much, why don't you show her some sympathy?"

"You don't have to split your gut, Dad. I understand Ma better than you think. It's just that sometimes I think she acts like a baby."

James was shot in the *amour-propre*. Between defending himself against all this inside dope Polly had on him and defending his only ally, Alma, the vixen's very mother, he wished Polly would back off and be an impossible teen-ager again. At least she would be plausible. The shade on the window of the second floor over the garden went up like a missile. The twelve-o'clock whistle. Pretty soon his eldest would appear, perhaps he, too,

102

in some unexpected form of the love/hate that made up their close relationship. James looked longingly at the third-floor window, and began to wonder if Alma would ever appear to save him.

"Say, Ned must be awake. Whatever happened to your trip to New Hampshire?"

"We're not going."

"Why not?"

"Because I met this boy last night."

"Who's that?"

"Don Southland."

"You mean Donald Sourball? You've known him all your life. You gave him that awful name."

"Well, I just met him for real last night at Eliza's party."

"Where were you last night? When I went to bed you were in your room with the door closed."

"Yeah, well, it was late and I went up to ask you and Ma if Ned and I could go to this party, only you were asleep and she was all into this stuff on the floor. The letters."

"From her parents' lives before she was born."

"Are we going to get some more of her rich history?"

"I dare say, but your mother is a sensitive woman and she'll come to understand it. What were you up to?"

"We just went to this drunken party and Ned had to drive everybody home because he was the only one who was sober."

"He took the car?"

"Well, there it was. You weren't using it."

"And while Ned was driving all over town on my gas bill, where were you?"

"I told you. In the back seat with Don Southland."

Chapter 8

————— ·◦◦◦◦· —————

ALMA WOKE UP LATE, her skin prickly with the heat trapped beneath the covers, her head aching across the forehead, pulsing, like someone testing a ripe melon. She was the melon. She rolled over and tried to push away some unpleasant dream, then flattened out on her back, legs spread wide to touch the two footposts, and let whatever it was seep back into her every orifice. Not at all clear. Darkness, the draperies at Pembroke Avenue, those dragons, and death. Alma Hughes or Alma Thomas?

She remembered the letters, and the confusion of sides, and then the realization that she didn't have to take sides with one parent or the other. She leaned over the side of the big bed from her childhood, which James thought was such a gas, like sleeping in a tree house, and her mother used to tell her what a fine piece of furniture it was. She always felt she was leaning out of *The Spirit of St. Louis* or standing on the railing of the George Washington Bridge, and she was compelled to jump. At Polly's age she used to hang off the pinnacle of rocks in the Green Mountains to get closer to Lake Champlain. How come she couldn't look out of this bed at the mess on the floor without signing up for a three-month stay at a mental hospital?

At the window, she looked down at her roses. They were a

constant delight to her; she must not neglect them in the midst of whatever it was the other half of herself was putting her through. James had taken over the picnic table—books, dirty dishes encrusted with baked egg and the silver fork tarnishing from the yolk. His skin glistened with sweat—she had always thought that sexy—and oh, good God, he was entrenched in beer cans. Jesus, at twelve noon. By the time they got to the dinner party tonight he would be like a sponge. This is the distinguished forty-two-year-old Professor Thomas, youngest man in the world to ever make anything—tenure, a high school trollop, mushroom soup. Only, if you squeeze him too hard tonight he will leak foaming beer all over his hostess's rug, especially woven for her in Outer Mongolia. Alice Marshall was James's favorite student, in her fifteenth year of graduate school and immensely rich, because she was more clever than anyone thought a female academic could be in these times of HEW and affirmative action. She took her good looks and brains and married well, a-hundred-thousand-a-year well, modest estimate. Her husband adored her, she him, and she had pledged not to have a baby until she finished her thesis. She was safe.

Actually Alice *is* sweet, Alma thought, and I like her. Not the student's fault that her beloved teacher has this passion for beer in the hot sun, enough to drive anyone bananas, James Thomas and Noel Coward included. "He'd better behave himself," Alma said out loud. "All I need this weekend is a brilliant, indistinguishable drunk on my hands, speaking something resembling Chinese, a language he doesn't know when sober."

And Alma noticed Polly, naked to the sun except for some shred of a garment she got out of a Kleenex packet. They looked especially at peace with one another, father and daughter, a pleasant sight, and Alma felt at once an uneasy pride and envy. At this point, handsome, young-man-on-the-verge, Ned hove into sight, also pretty unclothed, his jeans pinioned from those hipbones that hung loose somewhere just above his pubic hair. He had bare feet, gorgeous broad shoulders, every rib visible and in place, the profile of a Greek god. That I should be so lucky, she thought. Father and son nodded at each other, son extracted the newspaper and loped back toward the kitchen. She lingered at the window for a moment, reminding herself how much she loved James, and then went on into the bathroom. The walls were awash, everything dripped. James had taken one of his secret showers, hot and cold all over the place. As she bathed, she traveled backward in her mind. She liked making love with James, anytime, anyplace, early this morning, even better last night on the famous, now defiled, wedding dress. In fact, she had always liked making love with James.

Things had not always been serene between them. They began life making love in the basement of Pembroke Avenue. It was a strong bond. As domestic crises grew in number and importance, his ability to recede from the arena meant that to be anything other than a seeming machine-gun barrage if she so much as opened her mouth, she had to truncate her personality drastically. While he may still have appeared to the world to be on the surface of life, it was only in sharp contrast to the hatchet job she had done on herself in order to play supporting officer to his dominant role. With the birth and raising of children, he even felt compelled to move out at one point, when things got a little rough. He holed up in an empty "guest" room at the university to steady his cool. There he drank beer with his "colleagues," whatever that term meant, to take up the lonely slack, while she bathed and diapered on twenty-four-hour duty, alone. She made a point of not contacting him except in dire emergency, and even then he regarded a phone call as a strafing mission. After some time without her to have and to hold, and to hear, he returned to the nest a needy man. Neglect was a tactic she would recommend to any woman with a message for her man. James had been unimpressed by her therapy, by her foray into the business world, and particularly by Bernie Miller, and with good reason. But now that she brought home some of the bacon, he had gained a certain respect for her brains, and he often talked with her at great length about his work and hers. She liked him for that. It made her feel he accepted their equality, and she felt free to live with no self-imposed restraints. Now their life together brought relief. She knew that she loved him because he had always had the right technique and equipment to subdue her crabby genes. And he loved her because she gave him life outside the card catalogue, library-stack permit of his mind.

When Alma reached the kitchen, the desolation reminded her of a burned-out house. Smoke rose from the empty frying pan on the stove. Of course, the flame was still on. She turned off the gas and studied her son, who sat plunk in the middle of the tiny room, completely absorbed in the newspaper, spread out before him to serve also as a table mat. The syrup on the heap of pancakes he ate from was spilling over onto the newsprint. The chipmunk cheeks of the President, doing nothing in particular about cover-up versus exposure, looked out at her through a thick, spreading ooze. I should look upon it as an improvement, she thought, and when my hand adheres to the paper, should it ever become my turn to read it, then I won't approach it with displeasure. Perhaps. Maybe.

She greeted Ned cheerfully. "Hi. How are you?"

"Okay."

"What did you do last night?"

"Nothing."

"What do you mean, nothing? I heard you roar off in the car in the middle of the night."

"Ma, I'm having breakfast."

"At noon, silence before breakfast is no longer sacred."

"Ma, I just got up."

"You're just like your father. You have to stoke the furnace before the motor runs and you can be civil."

"Who else should I be just like?"

"I guess you got me there," she said reflectively, and left him to his peace.

Opening the door of the refrigerator, she speculated on the nothing within. The empty white cavern looked like an advertisement for V-8 juice, the forty-six-ounce can front and center. She picked it up to pour herself a glass. The can was empty. A cabbage, the usual mashed-up, half-used stick of margarine, alongside the sweet butter that James liked, in the same condition. Eggs and one slice of bacon. Clearly she was off to the grocery store, a task only made bearable now, after all those happy years of providing for young mouths, by the fantasies that she drew upon with each chosen item. Fair enough with a whole sea bass. Tour d'Argent, set before her on a small Limoges platter, fish eye up. White wine sauce, truffles. Not so easy with a pint of skim-milk cottage cheese. In a family where each member had different tastes and plenty of culinary know-how, it was still the little red hen's job to get the goods close enough to the dieter's mouth or the chef's hand to make it all possible. Often she resented spending her Saturdays amongst her fellow sufferers at the supermarket. Everyone had an air of having-to-do, a society of martyrs giving up hours of floor-washing, ironing, or perhaps vacuuming to stock up: a community of women who suffered the indignity of failing the Ann Landers happiness test by working Monday through Friday for money rather than to bolster self-esteem. And Alma reflected on the tragedy of Ann Landers's life, or Dear Abby, or Dear Beth, and wondered what their lives were really all about. Everybody looks pretty good on the outside.

In sharp contrast to this cellblock of women she passed each shopping day over the pork chops or the kitty litter were the male basket-pushers, on holiday from the office, or the eternal purgatory, boredom, that comes with retirement. Often accompanied by their "women," these role-players, godfathers all for an hour or so before they returned to the dreariness of a whole weekend with the family, or no family, sauntered down the aisles as if on the boardwalk at a carnival. They, too, lived a fantasy, over a tin of sardines, a package of frozen *pommes soufflées* that would be mealy and heavy to melt in the mouth at dinnertime. Alma wanted to journey with one of these men. Where did they go? How did they travel? Light or heavy? Steamship or air? Looking into their faces, their shopping carts, she would be glad to accompany any one of them back to Sicily, Armenia—not what it once was—or off to newly formed Israel, maiden voyage. How about Southwest Texas—black-eyed peas

—or Philadelphia, even, but she hadn't seen a can of scrapple in years.

And then, of course, there was the single man, middle-aged, gray in his sideburns, a carefully styled matting of thinning hair over the bald spot at the back of his head. A glance at his basket told of years of being cared for by a former mate. Milk, eggs, butter forgotten. A can of mock-turtle soup, two packages of macaroni and cheese, chocolate ice cream with lady fingers, *à deux* for dinner tonight. A lemon for the martinis, tomato juice for tomorrow's bloody Marys. Alma experienced a welling up of the familiar mothering, latent now for some years, but ten or fifteen years ago it operated automatically. The urge to stoop and tie a dangling lace on one man's tennis shoes, tuck in the unironed shirt of another. And she mourned their divorces, their living purgatory, their faces blank with miscomprehension and pain as if to say, How did I get here?

Everything was compassion and death with her today. Goddammit.

Alma poured coffee and hot milk simultaneously into a mug, and took the *café au lait* out into the garden to join James and their together, all-too-together, female offspring. Alma moved quietly, a sense of spoiling something making her feel not quite welcome. The intruder.

She heard Polly, *sotto voce:* "Hey, Daddy, she's coming."

James looked up from his work, his eyes not there behind the sunshades that swamped his Louis Pasteur metal-rimmed glasses. She always had the feeling that he was either blind and didn't want her to know it, or that he came with two sets of eyeballs quite naturally. If he squinted, maybe he saw her in triplicate, twice over, like a government form, or the dragons on the draperies at Pembroke Avenue.

He addressed her. "Sleep well?"

"I don't know. It was full of crazy dreams."

He asked no further questions but rather looked away. She was cut off. Were her dreams any more boring than his?

"Hey, Ma, what's all that junk on the floor upstairs?" Polly spoke from behind the sun. Alma looked down at the young body, slithery with suntan oil and sweat.

"Not much," Alma said. "Old letters, some of them sad."

"Can I see them?"

"They're your mother's, Polly." Alma realized that in some way James spoke in defense of her. It felt good.

"There's nothing secret in them anymore," she said expansively, "at least not from us. You can read them if you want, Polly."

"Okay. I don't want to, I just wanted to know if I could."

Alma sat down hard on the picnic bench next to James. Zapped by her young. Why am I so vulnerable today? "Oh, God, Polly, why are you always testing me? It's like some loyalty quiz."

"I was amusing myself, Ma." Polly rolled over and purposefully stretched her legs to reach her toes as far as she could, in a lazy, self-confident gesture of victory. She jabbed her father's boot at the instep.

"Hello, down there," he said to the young woman laid out on the lawn. He smiled broadly at Polly, a radiant tribute of admiration and love.

"Okay, you two," was all Alma said. She got up, still carrying her coffee mug, and began to inspect the roses as if she needed a magnifying glass to understand them. "It all makes me uneasy, uncomfortable, unwanted," she said to Pascali, the white tea rose, bursting with delicate blooms, and she moved on past the grandiflora, Betty Prior, pausing briefly to smell the floribunda, Queen Elizabeth, her sharp nose buried in pale pink petals. Across the oval from the father-daughter tableau, she addressed the dramatic apricot blowsiness of the two Medallions. "What is she telling me? That she has a sex, too, my sex? That she can wrap her father around her toe, her father, my man? It's bitchy of her, and it's normal, I suppose. She's flexing her muscles at me and I fall for it. I feel challenged. Come on, Alma. You're her mother, you should be able to ignore her." But she couldn't. The pit of her stomach felt as if the long arm of a giant crane had reached in to pluck out the center, and her body was blocked up back to her throat. Nausea. "For God's sake," she said to all the assembled blossoms, "what is the matter, Alma? It's okay. You were a man's daughter once. Still are, remember? It's all right." She asked her stomach to travel back down her intestinal tract.

Slowly she moved about the small garden, away from the others. She needed the privacy, but she strove to look busy. The tomatoes had tiny yellow flowers drooping over from the fibrous vines. The expectation of fruit. Time to be staked, she thought. The marigolds along the border needed to be thinned. She picked up the trowel with the metal tip once painted orange, half hidden in the grass, and stooped to carefully loosen the soil around the green peppers.

Gradually her innards settled back into place, and she began to relax the control she had placed over her arms and legs. Crouched on the balls of her feet, she felt her left leg begin to vibrate like a plucked string. Quickly she clamped her heels down on the ground and wrapped her arms around her knees. Oh, Dr. Freud, she intoned to herself, what are you cooking up for me now when I least need it?

She poured her tepid coffee onto the lawn and hoisted herself up out of her squatting position. She concentrated on organizing her head—grocery store, cleaners, fertilizer—and felt all of a piece enough to approach James, nestled in tin cans, papers and dirty dishes. She resisted tidying up.

"I guess I'll go shopping. Anything you need?"

"Pick me up some more beer, will you? Tomorrow's Sunday."

"I don't want to, but I will. Don't forget the expensive bourbon and the twenty-five fine wines at dinner tonight. One for each simple little course. And then there's the ancient brandy that you don't like but won't be able to resist because there it is."

He paid no attention to her, never even raising his head from his book. He was out of her reach at any level, and she wanted to be nurtured like a kid, loved in spite of herself. She turned away from him, defeated, unsure, a whole wealth of little insecurities popping out on her forehead, beads of sweat.

"It's hot," she said.

"Right," he agreed.

She returned to the kitchen and the comfort of her son.

"Say, Ma," belly-deep from one who was once a soprano. It always startled Alma.

"Hmm." She picked up her shopping list from the counter.

"I want to jam with Mark later today. Gotta get my amplifier and stuff over to his house."

Here we go, Alma thought. He can read my mind.

"I was just going shopping."

"Yeah, but I need the car, Ma."

"Whose car?"

"Okay, okay. Can I borrow the car?"

"I need it, Ned."

"Well, I'll drive you down to the store, see, Ma, and then I can pick you up anytime. You just name it." Ned's tone was remarkably friendly.

"Right on the dot," Alma said sarcastically, "just like always. Let's get going." I'm being conned, of course, she thought. It's the only token of attention I get today.

Ned piled his dirty dishes in the sink with an air of someone doing her a favor.

"I give up on you," she announced. "What'll you do next fall at college without your sister or your mother?"

"Find someone else."

She tut-tutted at him. "You really mean it," she said, and she knew that she would miss him.

"Come on, Ma, get off my back."

Shafted from all sides, she thought. I must be asking for it.

Ned backed the car into the curved drive that knit together the colony of two-family houses comprising Prichett Circle. Alma watched him as he thrust the gear into first, his back unnaturally straight, his shoulders pinned back. Driving gave him a sense of stature, she saw. And she remembered how much power she used to feel when she had first learned to drive, the power to move too fast, even the power to destroy.

She would drive anywhere to no place, just to speed along the highways and . . .

"Hey, Ma. Fasten your seat belt."

"You're quite right, Ned." Her return was gradual. "Safety is the most important thing about driving."

Alma struggled into the strap pulled across her shoulder and breast, and settled back against the vinyl seat cushion. She felt like a child snapped into one of those car carriers, snug and protected by parental concern. She realized her son drove with accuracy, care, complete competency. More than she could say for herself, her mind always miles away from the clutch or the blinking yellow light.

"You really drive very well."

"Thanks," Ned said. She enjoyed his acceptance. After a while he expanded on his favorite theme. "It's really nothing. You just have to learn to keep your eyes on the road. You wouldn't be such a bad driver if you didn't get so uptight about speed."

"I used to drive too fast when I was your age," she said defensively, "but somehow it was safer."

"You gotta understand, Ma. Back when you were young, there weren't many cars on the road, life was a lot easier. Now you keep moving or you get hit on the highway." He stopped with majestic skill for a red light.

Alma pushed her brake foot hard into the floorboard.

"See what I mean, Ma? I was right in time with the other cars."

"Okay, dear," Alma said, "maybe I'm so old I'm in my second childhood. Just deliver me to nursery school and wait for the nice policeman to help me across the street."

"You're a funny old lady, Ma. How long you want to be in the grocery store?"

"Not more than an hour. You'd better just leave your things off at Mark's house and come right back for me. You can help. I may be so decrepit I can't make it around the store on my own. Maybe I need a nanny like my father's Bess."

"You're not that bad, Ma. Dad can manage you."

"Oh, is that so."

Ned pulled up along the avenue at the crosswalk.

"Not later than two," she said.

"Sure, Ma."

Alma stepped onto the pavement and the traffic policeman held up his white-gloved hand. She waved to Ned through the windshield as she stepped from the curb to pass before him.

Adult again, the protector of the old lady/little girl speeding down the street someplace out of recall, the reality of the marketing scene seemed especially poignant to Alma today. The fruits looked bruised, the vegetables limp. The cucumbers felt like an old man's muscles, overgrown and spongy; the peas labeled "fresh" were pocked with the brown spots of age. Alma fingered the broccoli, cabbages, chose a bag of garishly orange carrots, a lettuce, the ripest of the red-yellow tomatoes. She drove her cart against the flood of traffic, collecting the irritated looks from her once fellow dreamers and colleagues for going against the rules, being out of line, the deviant. Pausing at the meat racks, nothing appealed. No fantasies, no friendly exchanges about the high costs, fat content, roasting temperatures. The beef reminded her of blood, the chickens looked withered and pale. When Alma reached the delicatessen section at the back of the store, the outlook brightened. She selected a large piece of sharp cheddar cheese, a perfectly ripe Brie that would pass in a few days. Her stomach rumbled and she realized she hadn't eaten breakfast. But when she squeezed the rounds of Italian bread, her thumb sank deep into the soft surface. Why was it impossible to bake hard-crusted bread in this country? It hadn't always been so, and she remembered from early childhood through the years until she left her primal home, the sweet smell of the bread store, the many-shaped loaves along the shelves in the storefront room, the white flour on the floor, the huge ovens and the long-handled paddles to reach the dough in and out of the heat. When she was young it was her father who made the daily trip to the bakery, always in the early evening; she held his left hand while he counted out the small change with his right. But even at sixteen and more, when she drove up the streetcar tracks to the cluster of shops, one of the pocket ghettos that dotted the city, she was afraid of the bulbous-headed baker, rolled in flour, who grunted and signaled his message through his dumbness. She learned early that between twice-a-day baking he slept on the huge table where he kneaded and formed the loaves, a huge, snoring animal, ungainly but menacing like a sleeping drunk. Grown, she could reach to hold silent the bell at the top of the shop door, and tiptoe in to leave the money, pick up the bread, without disturbing the old man at his rest. The memory of her father's hand was gone. In its place it was his grotesque figure that lay on a wooden table, his body floured as if for frying or braising.

Alma dropped the bag of bread where she stood and quickly pushed down the nearest aisle. Her throat, filled with fear, would not clear with the slow deep breaths. She abandoned the shopping basket and moved with alarm to the door marked "Women." As she inserted her dime into the slot she swallowed repeatedly. At the toilet's edge she vomited, hitting the seat, a mouthful of creamy liquid and then the trickle of bitter-tasting bile that accompanied the dry heaves. She stood bending over the porcelain bowl, simply breathing. After a while the rest of her returned and she decided with herself that she felt better. At the sink Alma mopped and wiped, rinsed and spat. The other women in the ladies' room stared at her, disgust and sympathy battling in twisted mouths and scrunched-up brows. She felt like the loser in the long-distance run, half a lap behind and still trying. As she regained her grocery cart, the crowds failed to cheer. One man stood close to her and smiled wanly, exactly mirroring her own lack of life. She moved away from him and in a flurry of no thought, filled up the basket with cans and boxes, the fast foods that the children liked and James didn't. Never mind, she told herself, he would be fed like royalty tonight. Alice Marshall would make him happy, and she could try again Monday evening after work. Right now the point was to get out of there.

She began to search the paper towels, the cereals, looking for Ned. Plenty of skinny jeans, heavy boots, dirty T-shirts, but none that she could claim. The lines at the checkout counters were long and the clock already read two-ten. Motherly irritation began to overtake the street-gutter-waif feelings. As the groceries moved along the belt to crowd against each other, she noted all the things on her list she had overlooked. She fostered a comfortable feeling of martyrdom seeping back to help reestablish normalcy, and began to bag her own groceries. She pushed the full cart past the hot dog stand, the flower shop, the liquor store, her mind completely absorbed now with the business of growing angry. In the parking lot, with flamboyant militancy, she encamped near the entrance, the better to catch her prey. A ten-minute wait and Alma moved her wares so that she could lean up against a telephone pole at the edge of the hardtop. She watched the cars move in and out of the painted white lines. Each car had a place in the scheme, each group of shoppers emerged from the supermarket with a load of bags—the family together, the couple, the single on the make—to load up and drive off to a sporting Saturday in the sun. She removed the melting ice cream from her other trophies and bent to set it down on the ground. Despite the plastic bag, the green of pistachio dripped down the front of her pants. Here I am, she muttered to no one, a middle-aged orphan. My father has gone to live with his thin-blooded pink people on his television. My daughter is claiming my husband, her father, right this minute, and he calls it plain old-fashioned affection. He laps that stuff up. And my devoted and obedient son has run off with an electric guitar, and in my car. I wonder if they'll remember me when they open the refrigerator door to see what's for supper tonight. She recollected a green enameled ashtray somewhere in her life. Chipped. In the middle was one of those sexless, sad loners of William Steig, limbs all twisted in on itself, eyes bulging with longing. Underneath this soulmate it said in script: "Mother loved me but she died."

Alma sat down in a clump of wild blue aster ruthlessly alive in the dirt of the verge bounding the parking lot. Her shopping cart rolled into the telephone pole. Big William Steig tears rolled down her sunburned face. If I don't stop crying, she thought, my skin will corrode and my face will be like the tissue of an unhealed wound. But like eating peanuts or chewing gum, it hurt when she stopped. She drew lines in the dirt with a stick and examined the designs made by the thongs of her sandals pressing along the sides of her feet. She welcomed the wonderful warming teardrops on her toes.

"Hi, Ma. Sorry I'm late."

When Alma and Ned reached Prichett Circle, James came out to the car. He saw that one face was normal flesh color shadowed by a slight beard and that the other was a patchy red and streaked with dirt like a little kid's.

"I thought you two were lost," he said cheerfully, rolling down the back window of the station wagon.

Ned began hauling bags from the rear of the car. "Ma went up in smoke just because I was a little bit late."

James put his arm around Alma's shoulders as if to lift her from the front seat. "You've no business behaving like that, Ned. It's not your car, dammit. She's doing you a favor when she lets you use it. You'd better learn respect for other people or try taking the bus."

Ned passed his parents. "Right, Dad." He strolled toward the house balancing two bags of groceries in his arms, feather light.

Alma and James watched him go in silence. Then she folded herself in his arms against his chest. "Oh, God, James. I forgot your frigging beer."

Chapter 9

WHEN ALMA OPENED her eyes, she shut them again immediately. Her sleep hung heavy across her face, her legs ached, her skin was pocked with the bumpy pattern of the bedspread. She could sense his presence in the room before she heard the pull of a bureau drawer. She waited to hear it shut. As usual, James left the room leaving the drawer open. It was some sort of cliff-hanger incompleteness in her life, akin to the way he felt about a tie caught in a closed door. She rolled over and squinted at the clock. Oh, my God. Six-thirty. She rolled back. She had just gone to lie down for a few minutes before setting aside the children's supper, cordoning off the untouchable commodities which if plundered would never go to make one complete meal, let alone several. That had been somewhere around four-thirty, five o'clock. Now it was time for partying up. James had just finished shaving. She could hear the agonizing gasps like death throes as he applied after-shave lotion to his cheeks. It was a delicately painful ritual, just another one of his noises that she had learned to ignore and that left her with a wolf-wolf feeling about his physical agonies, real or imagined. If he smelled expensive it was the Roger & Gallet, and it would be on this occasion. For just your ordinary old teaching days he wore a modest number by Yardley called Ship Ahoy or Wagons Away, something like that. Such were the conceits of man, and she had a half-evaporated bottle of Christian Dior which she habitually forgot about until some other woman, smelling sweet and delicious, floated by her at the whatever gathering they were attending. For the office she chose the youthful freshness of Ivory soap.

She threw her legs over the side of the bed, miles to the floor, thus catapulting the rest of her body upright. She shuffled into the bathroom and turned on the shower. The pressure was low, a trickle of nonpleasure, indicating water running in the garden, the kitchen sink. In the other life, the one where she would have everything she wanted, there would be a private, unlimited water supply, hot and cold, coursing through her own indestructible copper pipes as if cascading down from the highest mountain top. She distributed the splash of water here and there about the surface of her skin to bring it back to life. She remembered and laughed. She used to watch her mother beating, slapping at her cheeks to bring out the girlish bloom. Margaret Hughes was far too vain to wear the accepted rouge like everyone else, and too good-looking to allow the hint of lackluster.

James appeared in the bottom half of his white silk suit, French blue shirt with onyx cufflinks set in gold. Clearly he intended to have a good time tonight. He held up two ties: a matching white Indian silk or a blue and coral pattern. She pointed to the white one, preferring the simple, elegant Chicago gangland style for this evening.

At her closet, she scanned the array of corduroy jeans and wraparound skirts. There was the soft brushed-nylon nightgown, empire with plunging neckline, that she could never wear because James said he couldn't ravish her in something that looked like a ball gown. She inspected her few outfits. The simple gray dress labeled Bonwit's, svelte; the black two-piece drape model from Saks, vamp; the hot-pink pants suit, Lord and Taylor's, a trifle *sportif,* perhaps, but gay. Still, she liked it this evening and wished it were *de rigueur* to paste the label across her heart to show in a subtle way that it was in the right place and she was just like everyone else. As she carefully manipulated the tiny screw pin on her earring, she thought how chic it was of her not to have pierced her ears a couple of years back when everyone was doing it, with an upholstery needle, an ice pick; some even went to a doctor. Suddenly she felt very pleased with herself and smiled charmingly into the mirror. A face full of intelligence, wit, warmth. Juicy, tender lips. "You are all that I could desire." A mouthful of crowned teeth and silver fillings, a neck turning the slightest bit scrawny, a mop of matted blond hair. She began to brush it into place, addressing herself. "You would have made a splendid actress. Lillian Hellman or Edward Albee."

By the time James and Alma were ready to launch themselves into the evening, she thought they looked good, the beautiful people, and spirits were high. They cheerfully abandoned their children, heavily engaged in a brand-new flick, *The Big Sleep,* starring Humphrey Bogart—discovery. The dears were hunched over the television set at the kitchen table which was smeared with catsup and low-cal dressing to resemble a Jackson Pollock. With a "Leave a note about your plans" and "Don't do anything I would do"—"Jesus, Dad"—they stepped into their 1965 Dodge Dart as if it were a Porsche or one of those little old MGs. On the way into the city Alma speculated on the guest list.

"I wonder who'll be there."

"I don't know, maybe the Albrights. They live next door to Alice, after all."

"Ugh."

"That's what you always say, but I notice you gravitate to him every time."

Gordon Albright was a literary critic on the best newspaper in town. He also had several books to boast of and once taught literary history, eighteenth- and nineteenth-century England. Alma had known him since college, where he was clever and offensive, a snob and a name-dropper. What else was there? Oh, yes, he ran with the arty crowd and lusted after hot-potato-accented boarding school girls while denying he liked money.

James had escaped him at this time, being in vigorous training for his lifetime assignment in scholarship. Success suited Gordon, and providence and a thousand years of psychotherapy had rewarded him well. He had a nice wife and two attractive children. Normal, even. If his shagginess was stagy, it appeared to be an occupational necessity, like wearing a uniform in the army, and considered objectively, he looked no better or worse than the dozens of writers, critics, editors that Alma saw each day, and liked.

"I guess you're right, James."

"Who, me? Such an admission. Another sign of your flagging mental health."

"Okay. I get you," she said. "But honestly, James, I never thought about it. I always remember Gordon as someone who had no time for me because my cashmere sweaters were basement quality and I didn't wear a gold pendant between my breasts invitingly. I wasn't rich enough to join the Communist party and I didn't want to write, direct and star in a twelve-act play at the Workshop Theatre. But I'm always glad to see him now. He's like the memory of my father drunk. Familiar."

James swung his right knee toward Alma, his foot still on the accelerator. "The memory of your father drunk. Listen, your old man trying to lay you when he was drunk is too familiar to remind you of Gordon Albright. Get this straight, I like your breasts fine, so none of your little daydreams, see."

"Oh, come on, James. Gordon Albright. You must be kidding. Besides, I like his wife." Alma was titillated by both James's claim on her and the new idea of sleeping with Gordon Albright. After all these years, she thought. What a blast. I have only just come to appreciate your body, delectable Alma Thomas, née Hughes. I was blind to your beauty, but I have matured. Your eyes are like sapphires; your breasts as shapely and coveted as Elizabeth Taylor's diamond, double booty; your twat is ruby red. If you're going to stick your finger in it, Gordon, better cut your nails.

In the city now, they maneuvered the one-way streets, up and down the hill where the established lived, passing city-size cobblestoned courtyards, tiny gardens elaborately planted, some of them walled off with flowering vines hanging over to the brick sidewalks. The Georgian town houses of the rich or the well-born, an occasional balcony with wrought-iron balustrade, polished knockers, a lion's head, the curve of a duck's neck, each mounted on a handsome paneled door. They passed the Marshalls' house twice, searching for a place to park. James looked at his watch.

"You'd better go in, this may take a while."

"I'm in no hurry, I'll go with you."

"We're late, Alma," James shouted. "I'll let you out."

"We should have taken a cab," she said. Both tempers frayed.

"Take a cab and listen to you give me that old frugal New England crap all the way?"

"Hey, James, what are you so keyed up about?"

"I don't like to be late, Alma, that's all."

"Depends on where you're going," she said. "You fly into the masked ball and sweep everyone off their feet. I'll park the car."

"You will not. I can be as much of an inverse MCP as any other male behind the wheel of a car."

"I thought driving made men come all over ruthless power before the little woman."

"No, it's just that men drive better than women."

"I challenge you on that."

"Don't, you'll lose. Now get out."

Alice Marshall opened the door herself, endearing in a filmy long thing with luxuriously full sleeves and comfortable brown street shoes. A woman after my own heart, Alma thought, and liked Alice more than ever. Alice greeted Alma shyly, inquired after James, and led the way through the foyer, as big as the rotunda of the Capitol but warmly papered in figured gold with white painted trim, a graciously curved staircase, opulent Oriental runner, the whole open space festooned with *objets* from the Far East. Extremely handsome, Alma rediscovered, and mentally began counting her own: one Bavarian glass vase, parts of a silver tea service, six Canton plates. By the entry door to the drawing room she was up to the Picasso lithograph and a silkscreen done by Ned in the eighth grade.

The inner rooms were grandly decorated, sparsely furnished, comfortable. From a glimpse beyond the first living room into the dining room, Alma could see they were going to be ten for dinner. The Marshalls, Tony standing mid–Chinese rug in his stocking feet. Mute in his greeting, small, thin, uncomfortable in his own home, with his eccentricity and the mystery about how he earned his money—consulting, but about what?—he was intriguing to Alma but she always drew away from him. He carried the simplicity and closed-mindedness of a recluse with him to all the common or exotic parts of the world he traveled, and he cared for only one person, Alice, who was chirping her way through hostessly introductions. His eyes followed her. Amidst all this money spent in which Alma stood, she had the feeling Tony would just as soon eat off a paper plate, or better still, not eat at all.

Alma turned away from Tony Marshall to greet his guests. The Albrights, Elizabeth and Gordon, who was bent attentively over a small, perfectly shaped, younger blond woman. Alma didn't know her. She wore a pink pants suit, the lapeled jacket tailored at the shoulders and waist, the pants tight at her thighs. A small gold chain traveled down her suntanned throat to disappear in the plunge of the neckline. Pure, rich spite oozed up in Alma's diamond breasts like the flow of mud in the first spring thaw. Gordon twinkled at Alma like a tired old pixie and flapped a hand at her.

The lovely American woman in pink was the wife of the lovely man in the pale gray suit, a prince from Thailand or some such place. Alice had found them on one of her trips. Alma never knew how to feel about these collector's items. Like the Englishmen of the fifties, the war protesters, fearful they would not be brought to trial, of the sixties, in the seventies it was right to have exotic, obscure royalty at the mantelpiece. The lovely prince, a Yale law school graduate and a practicing civil rights attorney, had recently come to study public administration, sure that in the classroom situation he could still learn about good government.

And then, of all people, there was Bernie Miller, standing at the elbow of a dark-haired woman who was talking to the prince. What happened to his wife? Bernie rushed over to greet Alma.

"I guess you two know each other." Alice giggled. "Bernie has just come to live on the Hill, but maybe you know all that, Alma."

Bernie kissed Alma on the lips. "You look just the same, Alma."

"You, too, Bernie." He didn't. He had less hair and more belly, and Alma wondered how much she had changed.

There was an awkward silence, then Alma remembered to ask for a drink. She followed Bernie to the bar, greeting Elizabeth Albright, the prince and the dark-haired woman, named Joanna, on the way. People began to sit down. When James was led into the room, Alice holding his hand and announcing his presence, Alma noticed how relaxed and friendly he looked. Temper abated by gentle, loving attention. Wait until he sees Bernie, she thought. But spotting her, he smiled encouragingly at the two of them seated at the far corner of the group. Perhaps they looked like strays into the barnyard rather than conspirators.

"Where's your wife?" She had to ask it.

And then she heard the story of Bernie's recent past. Move to the suburbs, happy children, wife elected to school committee, meals thrown together, shirts never ironed, local politics in his living room too many evenings. Ennui. Bernie upstairs before the television, Bernie in bed early with a good book. The conversation across the room sounded interesting. Individual rights and libel loss. Just up Bernie's alley, but he paid no attention. Alma noticed that Tony was actually talking. James and Elizabeth Albright had joined Gordon and the pretty blonde. Everybody was laughing.

"And to leave the garden, the house, the children, too. That was the hardest, Alma. I was just getting into family living."

The children, for Christ's sweet sake, she thought. A bit late. "Yeah, but what happened to Public Issues, Inc.?"

"Oh, that's dissolved. I find the environment the most abused area. I'm forming a group to abolish all pesticides."

"Oh, Bernie, there must be dozens of those around here. You really had a good group of well-known people speaking up, a couple of Nobel Prize winners. People read what they say."

"I kind of let it go, I guess. But what I can't stand, Alma, is the not touching. She wouldn't touch me. When I left she didn't ask me to stay or cry or even call me up."

"I'm sorry, Bernie," was all Alma said. It serves him right, she knew, and in the end his good works, his turned-on charm, his solicitous interest in her new burgeoning freedom, the smooching in the supply closet—it was all like a brief high, like Sodium Pentathol. Three cheers for Bernie's wife. But seconds later, Alma realized what an ass she had made of herself; James was right all the time. Bernie was a phony. My confidence in your judgment is shaken, whispered Alma to Alma. Well, I was on my own after all those years of playing the little Dutch housewife to the protective, we'll-do-it-my-way male. Everyone makes mistakes. Alma depressed Alma. She looked at Bernie, balding and with bushy eyebrows. He reminded her of a moment in her childhood. She was about ten; it was after her father became president of the bank. At the reception at the house on Pembroke Avenue, some big man bent over her as she sought to escape him. He backed her into the grandfather clock, menacing her, his red mouth wide open. She was afraid of his wild-looking eyebrows. She wiggled free of him and fled past her smiling mother emerging through the drawing room doors. She remembered the awful man spoke to her mother and laughed, and she thought her mother joined him.

On the pretext of getting another drink, Alma slipped from the room and into the pantry, where, in a deluge of kitchen chaos, Alice was assembling. Empty copper pots and cast-iron pans lay about, sticky-looking with spent soup and meat drippings. A huge mixing bowl of half-whipped cream rested on the drainboard. It was a marvel to Alma and against the best French Chef tradition that this creature of disarray and childlike ingenuousness was an excellent cook and could read cuneiform.

Alice willingly let Alma whip up the cream and return it to the refrigerator, whose interior was like a city sacked by the Saracens.

Seated at the table, sparkling with silver and crystal and made more decorative by a huge silver basin of pink peonies just beginning to open, Alma drew Bernie again on her right and Tony Marshall to her left at the head of the table. This was definitely not her day. During cold melon soup the gathering groped for common topics of interest. Bernie's move to the Hill, how nice that Joanna lived in the same building, the difficulties the prince and his wife were having in a city where profitable investment in real estate was hard to come by. With the crabmeat mold garnished with watercress and served with a rich creamy sauce, the wine began to flow and Alma watched the little tête-à-têtes forming. Bernie held her knee and told her it was good to see her. Alice and James were so much in agreement that she should go easy on her thesis to do a thorough job —allowing somehow to perpetuate the project for another eternity—that when Alice rose to clear the fish course, James leaped to his feet to help. They cast the dishes into the pantry as if disposing of the remains of a picnic in the park, a walk to the nearest trash can. On his way past Alma, James scooped up her half-empty wineglass and drained it. Oh, swell, thought Alma. What's mine is yours, but the hangover tomorrow is something we cannot share, dahling. James carved the leg of lamb at the sideboard while Alice fed him red wine. He carefully layered the slices across the beautiful Sèvres dinner plates, spooned on the pink juices, placed the baked tomato half and the sprig of basil to one side. Each serving was a work of art which took easily days, so that expectation and salivation level was almost unbearable. Everyone watched the performance with awe, except Tony, who opened up at this moment to Alma with the most unusual and detailed account of the day the Internal Revenue men came to audit his 1972 income tax return. My God, she thought, for most people it's fear and trembling down to the district office with as many old bills and canceled checks as can be mustered up. For Tony Marshall they come to his house, full apologies, no doubt. Alice probably serves them spinach pie and Turkish coffee and they don't catch the delicacy of the problem.

"I wouldn't show them everything, of course, but the only item they made me back down on was Alice's tuition," Tony said. "Not a professional expense."

"Can you imagine, James," Alice squeaked.

"Wait'll your thesis is published. All those royalties," he joshed her good-naturedly and she rocked toward him with laughter, spilling wine on the rug.

"Oh." Alice rushed for water.

"Alice."

She froze at the pantry door.

"Forget it," Tony ordered.

"Put salt on it," James said majestically. Alice dumped the salt from one of the blue-glass-lined dishes to form a little anthill heap on top of the spot.

"There," she said, grinding it in with the sturdy heel of her walking shoe. She returned to the serving, incident complete. No, one last touch. "Oh, James, you're wonderful."

The whole show was so extraordinary for Alma to watch, she hardly knew what she felt. She began mixing. A cup of amusement, a fistful of sour grapes, two cloves of possessiveness, a pinch of admiration. She must remember to remind James of his reversal in roles sometime when he could dish up the spaghetti sauce with the same grandeur at his own table.

The conversation took on a one-upmanship quality. Travel. It was like an elimination game at dancing school when Alma had been a kid. Elizabeth Albright and Alma were tagged out soon. Each had been to France, England, and so forth. One had even lived in Rome, but it would be classier these days to admit to a weekend in Montreal. The two of them smiled at each other. Gordon hung in through Scandinavia. Joanna was born in Germany, which gave her an upper hand. Bernie had gone to India to deliver peace some years ago and found filth and poverty. The wine flowed again. James had all his behind-the-iron-curtain to share with the truly international. How to say thirty-three in Polish, marinated cucumbers, strange figures lurking, smooth vodka, Pasternak's grave bugged. But even James had to drink in silence with all of Asia to be covered. To do it right, it seemed, all it took was time and money.

The swimming in Istanbul, the herbs in Yerevan. "Never will I fly into Ashkhabad again," the inevitable Katmandu, Angkor Wat. As old-hat as Kipling, or even Marco Polo. Alma was naïve enough to believe you could not go to most of these places now, but then she believed everything she read.

Maybe only she could remember. From the time when she was very young, her father was a regular airplane-hopper, too impatient with the tired and true trains, which arrived when scheduled. A flight from Boston to Washington as often as not ended in Philadelphia or Richmond—a storm, a broken wing, an engine fire, nothing—making him angry and only a half a day late to his appointments. The telephone calls from unknown landing points were frequent, and the anxiety was high at Pembroke Avenue when he traveled. Alma had a repeated dream. Nightmare. A plane crash in Afghanistan, a word acquired in world geography; romantic, faraway, unknown. Her father was always face down in the shattered plane. She knew him by his suit, his shoes, his tiny hands, just like hers.

She watched James nod his head in total agreement to everything anyone said. His face was, by now, cherubic, his eyes reduced to slits of color in his grin. Whatever trip he was on, he was clearly without her. Maybe he was sailing with the Greeks to Troy, or with Alice to the British Museum to search out clay tablets. The beginning of the end—Alma recognized it—and she drained her wineglass to supply fortitude, or to dim the reality of the evening's future. I can feel you getting crabby, she said to herself. Hang on, she called back.

In her reverie, Alma had lost the story line. She missed the salad. The circle had been made and it must be strawberry time in Kent. A crystal bowl full of luscious berries, the whipped cream and champagne.

"I'm impressed," she said to Alice.

"Oh, thank you, Alma; it's all for James. Tony and I just wanted him to know how much we love him." The table rose with her and toasted "the most adorable professor in the world." Hmm. Giggles, smiles, glowing words. You don't sleep with him when he's drunk, hey, everybody. Pause. At least I don't think so. Conversational pause. Now we have the Chinese, and Alma raised her glass high and smiled at him like a gargoyle in hopes he would receive the message. He looked at her and reflected. No speech. Oh, bless you. And then he began to kiss Alice, sloshing champagne down her back. He slithered around the table, mostly upright, shaking hands and kissing lips and cheeks and necks. More champagne. When he reached Alma he pinched her earlobe and whispered, "Right, dear." He returned with an afterthought. "Remember, I love you." Oh, yes, she had forgotten.

Alma excused herself. In the bathroom she talked fretfully into the wash basin while she rearranged the expression on her face. "Now I have to mix caring with anger, goddamn him. I have to remember he came through with the right sentiment. I can't just plain hate him like any healthy woman. The horrible burden of love is just another form of self-destruction."

She emerged, tossing out her tender feelings like a boomerang, determined to extricate and claim the body before the brandy was served.

Chapter 10

————··⋘∞⋙··————

"For the last time, James, where is the car?" Alma propelled her cargo—at once as cumbersome as a sack of good-sized field stones and as hard to hang on to as a helium balloon in a high wind—through the picturesque streets of prosperity and high birth, where the bricks of the pavement conspired to heave up unexpectedly, thus stubbing her toes for her, and the romantic vines and even the handrails that guarded commodious, welcoming doorsteps tended to snatch out at them.

"I told you."

"Where?"

"You know the street, the short one, the one that doesn't go all the way to the top."

"We're there and it's not."

Alma sat down before number 56, unburdening herself of her baggage. It threw itself down somewhere close beside her. The time was late, the light was dark, the air was thick and it was after James had had two snifters practically full of brandy and a prolonged farewell with each individual in the cell and then collectively. She found him tiresome and inconsiderate. Was she kidding herself? She found him sexually repulsive and loathsome.

"It's after one o'clock and I want to go home."

"What's the matter? Turn into a pumpkin?"

"It's after one, asshole, and you're drunk."

"Your abuse touches me not." James began to sing. " 'It's one o'clock in the morning, we've danced the whole night through.' Remember your mother singing that? Some song from her childhood in the Dark Ages. Good old Margaret Hughes. Not a bad girl, for a certified witch. 'I've been to the most marvelous party.' Hey, remember her old Beatrice Lillie act? She thought she was hot shit."

Alma glowered at him. "Even drunk you're no match for my mother."

"Bet she was a lousy screw."

"You lay off her. I mean it." Alma flushed in anger. "When you hoist yourself into that damn bed you think is so great, it won't be much of a love nest tonight."

"Want to bet?"

"You're a shit, James. Everybody knows drunks can't get it up."

"Alma, you're one sweetheart of a foul-mouthed kid. All fun. Mrs. Hughes's little girl."

"I hate you, James Thomas. I hate you more than anything in the world when you're drunk."

Some word hit James. He made sense. "Why is it that when I'm drunk it's my fault, and when you're drunk it's my fault. That's sharing, Alma Thomas style. Your mother was right."

"Right about what?"

"Before we got married she took me aside and told me you were awful in the morning."

"Why didn't you tell me? What a nasty woman."

"Remember, sweetie, nothing against the sainted mother."

"Shut up."

"Besides," James said, "she was wrong."

"You just said she was right."

"No she wasn't. You're really awful at night."

"I hate you. Come on, I hurt from these stone steps." She dragged him to his feet and they started up the hill again.

He soliloquized as they stumbled along. "You hate me because I'm successful. You hate me because I can have a good time, and you're an old prune-faced hag. You hate me because other people like me, and your prune face shows. You hate . . ."

"I hate you because you're piss-assed drunk."

He turned to face her abruptly. She drew back. "Oh, the perfect prune-faced princess, never touched a drink in her dried-up life." His words became indistinct again and he slumped against her. She was no longer afraid of him and her anger flooded back. She squeezed his arm as hard as she could, digging her nails in to hurt him.

"You kid yourself into thinking you're having a good time out of a bottle. At least I know when I'm miserable."

He didn't hear her; he barely brushed away her fingers from his arm.

Jesus, she thought, he's gone again. They walked to the end of the street once more, turned left, and left again, and down to the bottom of the hill, right and up again. Alma imagined she was a Salem witch scanning the sea from a widow's walk, despite the juxtaposition of a couple of centuries. After she found the car she would work on a good curse for the drunken bastard at the end of her tether. Halfway up the third street, in a private alley, she spotted the car. There was a white traffic ticket tucked cozily under the windshield wiper. "All that fun and it only cost fifteen dollars and another marriage down the drain," but her words were wasted. James slumped against the side door, comfortably resting his head into the glass. Alma accosted his backside in her search for the keys. If anybody sees me, I'll get picked up for rape or assault with intent to kill. She removed James and propped him up on the hood. "Stupid ass," she yelled into his ear, and drew away in haste. He was still close enough to slug her, but he didn't move. She was safe.

Alma drove home carefully, sedately, as if she were chauffeuring the King to the opening of Parliament or a presentation at the Guild Hall. Her king catnapped at her side, resting up for the strain of the ceremonies to come. His complete absence from life, and from her life, when he passed out like this left her with a consuming sense of abandonment that often brought on physical discomfort, even intense pain. Now her head ached, her loneliness squeezed at her temples like a sweatband. Sometimes it punched her in the gut, leaving in its wake circles of throbs reaching out across her abdomen, or sent shooting stabs up her calves, or temporarily paralyzed her left arm. Usually they fought about it afterward. He called it sleep, and why the hell shouldn't he sleep once in a while? She called it irresponsibility in as snooty and decisive a tone as she could put on, in hopes that he wouldn't stumble upon the hurt, the sense of loss. He didn't bother to argue with her; he didn't care. The only guilt he felt was the truth, and she feared the truth to be escape. His abandonment of her was real. At moments like this, at times like this one in her life, all his conviviality out of a can or a bottle was really a raceway to independence from her, even if it brought only blessed, sweet nothingness. If she challenged him to a rematch to make him take it back, he only screamed at her angrily, "I love you, now shut up," and left her feeling abandoned once again. It was something she could not drive away or murder and bury in a secret grave, and she just barely realized that it was a very odd feeling, going way back to before she first knew James, but understanding certainly was not half the battle, as the soothsayers declared. If she understood nothing when he left her stranded with his message of retreat, she would at least enjoy her anger, instead of carrying this lifetime sentence to ambivalence, a solitary confinement behind bars, a latticework of love and hate, when she longed to be allowed the freedom of indifference.

When she was young, Polly's age, her father's drunken embraces, the haughty hurt in her mother's aloofness, sent Alma out on long drives where she played with speed. Then she was still young enough to understand nothing, to feel her rage and know who it was against. Then she didn't care what happened to her. She was free of them and of herself, too, or so she thought. Hers was considered a difficult adolescence. With the notion of the quest for security, the novel idea of sharing, came caring and the commitment to want to live. It was called growth, maturity. Sometimes Alma thought there were more diminishing returns to counting up the years in a life than just the tired old journey to the grave, unless she lived to be as ancient as her dirty old man, made pure by his extreme years. So far removed from his own past and therefore no longer responsible for it, it was too late for him to have a future. He was the only person Alma knew who was entirely satisfied to live in the present, dreaming about a past that was all rosy and romantic. "What a price to pay," she said out loud to the nothingness within the car, and looked away from it sleeping next to her and outside herself for relief.

The night lights of the city blanketed the ugliness that humanity cast upon it by day. She began to notice things. The buildings became friendly, the almost empty streets were avenues of space. The leaves on the urban oaks whirred like the ocean, their branches swaying gracefully in the gentle dead-of-night breeze, to reach out to greet her. As she left the city to cross the bridge over the river, the moon provided darts of light across the waffled water, giving the illusion of whitecaps waving at her. By the time she drew into Prichett Circle, a thin layer of good will covered her baser thoughts like melted paraffin poured into the jam jars and left to harden to seal out the slow rot.

Alma reached out her hand to shake James by the shoulder, but he eluded her. His eyes were still shut against the glare of the moonlight, but the car having stopped, some instinct had obviously told him the conveying was over. He stepped from the car of stiff pins and pointed toward the front door like a mechanical man. Inside the house, the falling barometric pressure in the front room must have brought him comfort, for Alma noticed his eyes come into focus with each other. The atmosphere was thick with cigarette smoke and the sweet smell of dope. The beer cans along the coffee table looked like the course markers for the grand slalom. The stereo played rock as accompaniment to the background music denoting the passage of a supersub along the bottom of the sea which wasn't quite all there on the television screen. Ned and Polly were entertaining a few friends well known to Alma and James as Liza and George and Perry and Melanie and Amanda; stars in their own right, they had shed their surnames. And then there was little Donny Southland, with a beard and one broken tooth, sitting in Polly's lap. He looks as though he'd like to taste Polly, and she seems happy enough to touch him, Alma thought. Her sixth sense told her to try to ignore the whole scene or run the risk of turning instantly into a parent.

The clump on the sofa moved uneasily as Alma and James entered the room. I'll give them that for manners, she thought, the discomfort of recognition.

"Hi," said Ned, without seeming to take his eyes off a spot in the center of the room at about average hip height. His eyes were a delicious raspberry color.

"Hiya," returned James, sharing the same object of sight with him. His eyes were about the same color.

"Hello, Mrs. Thomas. Hi, Mr. Thomas," around the room.

"What's up, Ma? You look funny. Anything wrong?" Polly moved out from underneath Don.

"You look as though you'd had a good time, Dad."

"You bet I did, Ned. I know how."

Ned and James continued to commune with each other somewhere in outer space.

"Have a beer, Dad."

"Thanks, old man, I will." James slipped away into another party and Alma went to the kitchen, huffing her shoulders as hard as possible until she could feel the cartilage tearing in the bone sockets where they met her arms. She sighed significantly.

She turned on the flame under the coffeepot. One for the road. Where the hell are *you* going? she asked herself. I don't know. She reached for a cup. The black liquid looked sluggish, brewed and rebrewed. She searched for a pattern, a direction in the faint stain on the surface like drops of oil, but there was no future to be told. Squeezing into the place beside the sink, she stretched one arm across the old porcelain basin. Polly came into the kitchen, tucking her shirt into her jeans. She paused to display her dirty bare foot to her mother by placing it on an empty chair seat beside Alma. James was right behind Polly, beer can in hand. He stooped clownishly and pinched Polly's bottom through the stretched denim. Polly stamped her foot down and slapped her father's hand.

"Fuck off, Dad, that hurts."

The familiar pain from the rebuff revived James. "Did you hear that, Alma? She said fuck off to me, your kid."

Alma stood in her fury. She pushed him back against the stove. He blinked at her, startled. Her voice came from the pit of her stomach. "Listen to me, you sot of a father. Keep your hands off your daughter." She was near screaming now. "I mean it. It was too much for me, and too much for my mother, and I hate my father for it to this day."

"It's okay, Ma."

"It's not okay, Polly." Alma took Polly's hand.

James tried to drift from the kitchen, but the two women pushed passed him. "Hey, wait. I didn't mean anything." No one answered his call for help.

Alma lay rigid on her side along the edge of the great ocean liner of a bed, waiting for the ballast to shift, the storm to hit and rock the boat. James rolled over onto the other side. In his deep sleep his flung-out arm scraped across the side of Alma's face as his body repositioned itself. She coiled up and struck. She shot her legs up, knees almost to her chin, and placed her two feet against the small of his back, and then she pushed with all her force, her hands grasping the bedpost above her head to give her what leverage she could find. She felt him slip over the side, heard him fall hard, his legs against the metal of the radiator.

She waited.

He rose up intent to kill, like a wild stallion, his arms raised over his head, palms flat as if to stomp her to death with his front hooves.

She cried out in her terror. "Don't you hit me."

He beat back her arms, her hands, and slapped her across the face. The thwack sounded in some echo chamber of her head, and as the sting spread along the surface of her skin, she tasted the blood that dripped down the back of her throat.

She screamed.

He stood over her.

"I never want to sleep with another drunken man again in my life."

Part
Four

—◦◦∞◦◦—

1949

Chapter 11

THOMAS HUGHES STOOD at the hotel window, his shirt sleeves rolled up to the elbow, the neck open. He knew that the collar was limp, crumpled, and he probably would have to change into a fresh shirt for the afternoon session. The ice had melted in his Scotch, leaving it stale and tasteless. Down below, ten stories down, he could see the heat rise like the surf breaking from the New York pavement, he could feel it like a colonic cramp despite the spacious air-cooled corner room where they stayed most of the time between the official meetings of the conference. He moved to the table to make himself another drink and returned to his perch at the window. The streets were hot and stuffy, the hotel airless. The bars in town were too dark, the restaurants crowded. And he had to be careful where they went, whom they met. The people of New York depressed Thomas. They so readily accepted dirt, rapid transit, cheap fashion, frozen vegetables, the new mindless television, adopting a kind of neighborhood provincialism in the name of progress, the avant-garde of the country at the center of the largest city, each one without individual ambition or achievement. Only a few knew New York's wealth, and these bought their way to decent living outside the city as much as possible, the move to the suburbs, the getaway house in the country.

Tomorrow was Saturday and he would go home. He could go home tonight, for that matter, but for Miss Carmody and the loneliness of the evenings there. But he welcomed the freedom the weekend days brought at Pembroke Avenue. To drink on the back porch, maybe listen to a ball game. The first crop of peas ought to be ready, and Margaret's roses would be in full bloom. June was certainly rose month. He liked to watch Margaret as she plucked and nurtured, her long hands protected in cotton gardening gloves, the line of her lithe body almost the same as when they were first married over thirty years ago, nearer thirty-five. She wore her hair short now; it was a golden gray. She never knew he watched her. It was his secret. And he thought of her for a moment with a sweet sadness, a sense of loss he had carried off and on all these years, before he let his anger in to comfort him. He had given her all he could—money, property, even her children, which she had quickly persuaded herself were all of her own doing. She wasn't one to enjoy the facts of life. She had never wanted his touching her and she had never freely given him her body. After the miscarriage, it was years before she'd go to bed with him, and then it was like the travails of the martyrs, as if she had to cast off her very skin to allow him near her. Even her kisses seemed a sacrifice; he'd long ago given up offering her his. He was almost forty before Mary was born, forty-six when Alma came along. People commented on Margaret's frailty. Frail, my God, he thought. Frail like the slender blade of her sewing scissors; she was a bastion of tasteful grace and sexual frigidity. His penis, which Margaret had never seen or touched, had drawn screams of vanquished pride should he penetrate her between her tight-closed shapely legs.

He almost dropped the glass to the ledge made by the radiator cover beneath the window and raised his empty hands to his temples. The ache was there and he began the deep breathing to keep back the wheeze gathering in his chest.

Sometimes I hate her for her perfection. Never soil herself. I've always been something dirty to her. My needs are something that will always threaten to consume her, to be extinguished like the Japanese beetles that she plucks from the perfectly formed petals of her handsome roses and thrusts into kerosene, to lie in layers like the formation of the earth itself until she has a whole jarful of decomposition. Does she get the same sense of accomplishment by burying me, a little bit at a time?

The rasp was in his throat now. He reached into his pocket for the atomizer and went to sit down in the armchair beside the bed. He inhaled deeply as he squeezed the black rubber bulb at the end of the tube.

Miss Carmody stretched across the bed to rest her hand on his arm.

"I'll be all right," he said savagely. He hated Miss Carmody to see him this way.

She withdrew her hand and returned her eyes to the notes in her lap. "The speech will go very well," she said timidly. "There's really no need to worry, Thomas."

The speech, yes, he'd forgotten for a time. His breathing was almost normal; he had escaped a real bout. Now he looked up at Miss Carmody, whom he had forgotten so easily, dark and purposefully brittle, her face exposed too sharply by her hairdo, a bird's nest of little curls atop her head. She was not stylish, her whole sense of being a little bit behind the times; her smile too girlish, her skirt too short. She wore a worsted suit much like his own. But she was a proficient secretary, useful, quick, and when she let her hair fall loose she was quite pretty. He always thought of her as Miss Carmody. She was his sidekick. He must remember to give her something.

"I've no business talking on foreign exchange." He spoke as if to himself. "I'm a banker, not an economist."

"But it's a tribute to you to be asked, to your superior knowledge of both foreign moneys and banking procedures." Her voice was warm. She knows her stuff, he thought.

And then he told her what he didn't want her to know. "I feel like a phony," he said.

She looked at him, startled. "No one would know it," she said ingenuously.

"You do," he answered. I hate you for it—silently, furious with himself. He began to unbutton his shirt. "Take off your suit and do something about your hair."

The clock read three. "The time, Thomas."

"This won't take long. There's still more than an hour before my little performance."

She carefully placed her blouse and skirt across the seat of a straight chair, hung her jacket from the back. He watched her, poised like a diver, first one foot on the chair seat, then the other, as she unfastened the garters, shyly lifting the hem of her white slip at the four corners of her upper legs. She went into the bathroom.

"Forget it," he called after her. He was naked now beneath the covers of the bed. His clothes lay in clumps about the rug.

Her voice came from behind the bathroom door, modestly set slightly ajar. "We agreed I have to use the jelly each time even if I can't take it out yet."

The slimy stuff was uninviting. He never knew if the wet was hers or from a tube. He waited impatiently and when she came toward the bed, he made note again that even at thirty-five her breasts hung too low, her hips were mottled with an unwanted layer of fat. Margaret would appear to have the figure of a young girl, he thought, just like Alma's.

Thomas reached out to grab Miss Carmody by her breasts and she fell forward onto him. Her weight felt good on him and he struggled to pull aside the bedclothes between them. He bit her lips, he pinched her nipples, he thrust his fingers into the wedge between her legs. She called out unexpectedly in pain, but he worked on rubbing his fingers through the labyrinth of soft tissues. Outside it was dry to his touch. I hurt her, he thought, but I don't care. He stopped to roll over on top of her, placing her hand upon his penis. She held on to it like the handle of a safety ladder, gripping it tight. Still it sprang to her touch and he quickly freed it and thrust it into her a stroke before ejaculation. He had to act while he had it; an erection didn't last very long now. And then he lay on her, exhausted, his anger spent, and he felt the guilt move in; guilt toward her, toward Margaret, even guilt toward himself, what might have been. It was so familiar it had become just another among the steps from desire —or the will to desire, more likely now—to the washing up afterward. He was too old for this kind of thing, he thought; almost sixty-two. Next Wednesday. He let the idea fester awhile. Not the end of the road, not by a long shot. He could still do it.

Miss Carmody rolled from beneath him and he let her go. He saw that he had made her cry again. It was as familiar as his guilt. It didn't bother him; he'd given up wishing he could do better by her long ago, and it was not for her, he realized, that he cared. He cared only for himself now, sentenced to the age-old self-doubts. He drew a deep breath and felt the rasp in his throat again.

"Be careful about your breathing, Thomas," she said.

"No more asthma," he snapped at her.

In the bathroom he inspected himself before the full-length mirror on the back of the door. His hair was gone, mostly, and what was left was gray and fringed his head, his skin sticking to the contours of his skull. His eye sockets were recessed, his teeth uneven in his jaw like a handful of squash seeds broadcast in his mouth. The flesh across his shoulders seemed slacker now, somehow diminishing their breadth, their strength. Patches of gray hair across his chest, his pubes. Too much stomach, too little muscle, a sprouting of moles, the trunk of his body set on ever slender legs, a mushroom cap of a penis, a fungus of a pin to hold him together, his testicles hanging long and limp. He looked at his hands, veined, lined, but still perfectly shaped, flat open palms, small fingers fanned out to form a crescent. Hands and legs, the extremities remain stable, some sort of frame to carry the sagging seat of the body.

And for a moment he could imagine his own skeleton. The idea was so bizarre it made him laugh. He looked at his smile. A friendly fellow, and he waved, mocking himself. It's funny, he thought. The dignity of age: we hear about it all through youth; in middle age it begins to appeal as an idea, and then we learn it is all a subtle deception. Underneath the balding head labors a brain burdened down with painful experiences, addled with knowledge, spun loose by change. He felt no more the dignity of age than he had at sixteen, thirty. He had just added up more losses. His beauty was only skin deep. He laughed again; it seemed a good joke. His skeleton was there beneath the growth of him so visible in the mirror.

He turned to run the hot water in the shower. He added the cold slowly until it seemed right to the touch. Then he stood watching it pour down from the spray head to the bottom of the bathtub. Water spilled plentifully on the tiled floor, soaking the terry-cloth bath mat. Wasting water was one of the things you paid for in a hotel room. And he remembered to congratulate himself on having the forethought to install showers in three of the five bathrooms in the house on Pembroke Avenue when he built it. Two of them were closet showers, separate behind a curtain. That was fifteen years ago, before the shower was much of a vogue at all. He stepped under the water boldly and immediately the physical pleasure of the warm water on his skin brought the most moderate temper to bear. He began making happy resolutions, aware that he was like a child splashing in the bath. He would be more open with Margaret while showing kindness, his warmth to Miss Carmody. He would listen to Alma, because she mattered to him. He must let her know it. She would be sixteen in October. And he would write to Mary, gone from him now in her marriage. He would drink less to please them all. Better for him. Perhaps he would treat himself to another reseeding of the lawn—he'd had difficulty with the grass this spring—but he would have to wait for cooler nights. He'd buy Margaret one of those television sets.

He paused in his daydreaming to soap himself lavishly. He made curls of foam across his belly. He pondered his successes. He had come a long way to bank president. Educated, country-boy edges gone, grand house, wife, mistress, children who were expensive to bring up, but he gave them everything. He had respect, independence, energy, ambition. Did anyone love him? Sometimes he missed the warmth he grew up with. He often thought of himself as a simple man, with simple needs. He knew it was not so. Elizabeth Roberts and the ministry—even now he had a sort of contempt for the notion, and if he had missed out on an easy kind of loving, he knew it was an affection, a dependence that he would have trampled right through in a few years, like an army combat unit across the face of a village. He stood still to let the water do the final rinsing.

Bank president, member of the governing board of the Council for Foreign Investment, consultant to the federal government. He wondered what time it was. He imagined the audience seated in the great ballroom, the press table, the speaker's podium. Treasury officials, academic economists, investment counselors, fellow bankers, newspaper reporters, statisticians, foreign-exchange experts. Mrs. MacNeil should see him now. It still gave him pleasure to know she had admired him in proportion to his income, his possessions, his prestige. And old maid Aunt Polly. He'd won Margaret away from them, but they never knew it was too late. Had they won in the end after all? But then there was Miss Carmody. They'd turn over in their graves, the pair of them.

There was a rap on the bathroom door. "It's going on three-thirty."

Miss Carmody. His speech. Margaret. "It's all right," he said, irritably, "I'll just make it. I've got half an hour." He stepped swiftly from the shower and began to shave. "Put in a call to Mrs. Hughes," he called out. "You go down. I'll meet you in the lobby." He heard her soft voice speaking to the hotel operator. By the time he emerged from the bathroom she had left. He dressed in a hurry, plunging the tails of his clean shirt in his already belted trousers like a man reaching into a grain sack. As he flicked one end of his tie around the other and pulled it through the loop to form the knot, the phone rang. He stepped to the mirror above the dresser, straightened the tie, smoothed down the pointed tips of the starched collar. He looked good, he knew, despite his years. He carried himself with dignity. He was an important man in his profession, an innovator. Others looked to him for leadership.

He picked up the phone receiver.

"Yes, this is Mr. Hughes. . . . Hello, Margaret? It's Thomas. . . . No, not yet; in a few minutes. I just wanted to talk to you before my little performance. . . . Oh, I'm sorry to interrupt you, Margaret. . . . Yes, I bet you're good." Her tone of voice hurt him. He had interrupted her ladies' reading group; they were doing *The Tempest*. A romance. Ironic. And for a moment he was jealous of her many friends. He had never felt close to many people; too often it hurt. "Yes. Ariel." Of course she was reading Ariel. A magic, invisible sprite, a youth, often played by a young woman. The thought of her, beautiful, delicate, unpossessible, pierced him. He wanted her. "I thought I'd come home tonight, if that suits you?" Why did her aloofness undo him so? He should never ask her permission. "You say your group will be gone. . . . Good. Then I'll try to make the six-o'clock plane. . . . Yes, I must go. Wish me luck." He had heard the click, but still he waited to receive her encouragement. As he put the telephone down, his lungs began to fill up with the familiar tightness. He took a deep breath, reached the pages of his speech off the desk and left the room.

In the elevator he inhaled on the atomizer just to be sure. By the time he reached the lobby, he felt he had it under control. Miss Carmody rose to meet him.

"Good afternoon, Mr. Hughes." She glanced at her watch. "You are expected in three minutes. Are there any messages before you speak?"

He looked at her, and then he remembered there would be people who mattered watching them. "See if you can get me a seat on the six-o'clock plane. I think I'll go home tonight."

"Will that be all, sir?" She sounded hurt.

"Yes, thank you, Miss Carmody."

He walked past her toward the ballroom.

"Good luck," she whispered.

He turned for a brief moment. "Thanks," he said, and an almost paralyzing sadness filled him as he set the expression on his distinguished face and entered the crowded room.

The huge assembly hall was almost filled. After salutations to the dignitaries to the left and right, Thomas Hughes stepped to the platform and took his seat on the right of the aisle, the place of importance. He grinned expansively across at the council's president, a stockbroker on the Exchange, a stuffy fellow with passé trading ideas who was afraid of Thomas Hughes. The thought pleased Thomas and he mused warmly on the flattering presidential introduction he would receive in a few minutes from this man. All self-doubts forgotten now, as if they had never been, Thomas settled into the pure joy of his supreme self-confidence. He was at his best and he knew it.

From his seat beside the podium he studied the audience, lifting his small hand in greeting to those who passed before him in search of their seats. His friends and acquaintances. The powerful men of the nation. The dean of the country's most prominent law school. A tribute to Thomas Hughes. Several members of the Council of Economic Advisers. An aide to the President's appointments secretary, just another hick from country-town America, like the President himself. The Jew-boy from Russia who would challenge the Hughes Theory on International Recovery with his newfangled statistical economics. Thomas looked forward to victory in the foray.

At the press table, the representatives from publications all over the world were turning the pages of the press-release copies of his speech, quickly, quietly. The national newspapers. The *New York Times* financial expert. Thomas saw that the man from *Fortune* magazine was making notes in the margins. There was the *Wall Street Journal,* several of Washington's news sheets. The *London Times* in the front row, as was correct. He welcomed them all. The attention of these men was the highest mark of interest. They knew Thomas Hughes had given them good copy.

To his far left, next to his bank's investment vice-president, sat Miss Carmody, stenographer's pad open on her lap, her almost childlike face beamed in on his, the elusive vessel on her radar screen. At times he knew he needed her, aware that she was the wrong woman, but in the moments of his full power, she was a loyal employee, the king's scribe rather than his mistress. The irony was that Margaret and Miss Carmody each suspected him of total dependency on the other, and neither of them was entirely wrong.

The meeting called to order, he listened distractedly to his own curriculum vitae, to the list of adjectives describing his achievements and talents.

". . . and now I will delay no further the pleasure of hearing our fellow member of the governing board of this council, Mr. Thomas Hughes, who has always given us the daring to do more as individuals and as a nation in the arena of world finance."

Thomas felt the applause was at once respectful and anticipatory. He had been justly introduced, and he took his time reaching the lectern, arranging his notes. He settled his heavy horned-rimmed glasses on his Roman nose and prepared to address the forum, Caesar come before them. He enjoyed the theatrics, he relaxed into the full knowledge that he would bring the whole room to standing ovation. Years of such appearances had brought him perfect control. From the first word his voice was as sonorous as a gospel preacher's.

"Mr. President, fellow members of the governing board, gentlemen of the press, ladies and gentlemen. It is a great honor to be asked to address this, the twenty-sixth annual meeting of the Council for Foreign Investment. We have heard some very distinguished speakers in these past few days—the president of the World Bank, the Undersecretary of the Treasury, a representative from the Federal Reserve. Billed very grandly as an expert in foreign investment, I come before you something of a fraud, a humble banker, although I hasten to say I once taught economic theory, but that was a good many years ago. Now, while you experts may feel that we in the banking world are too often concerned with the immediate needs of the individual and local businesses, we never lose sight of the nation's investments, both domestic and foreign, by the federal government, by industry, privately owned corporations, and by private American citizens. And it is to the international scene I wish to turn for a few minutes today with some little ideas I've had in the past months."

Thomas Hughes took his first reading of his audience. Attentive. Expectant.

"The lessons of two postwar periods have taught us that the world had come to see the United States no longer as the borrower of the pre–World War I period, but as the international loaner. While European reconstruction came late after World War I, the twenties was a period of substantial private investment throughout the world. I ask you to turn your attention for a few minutes to pages six through ten of the text."

While Thomas elaborated informally on the investment charts covering the post–World War I period, his thoughts were elsewhere. I have always been ahead of the times. I made my first packet in something as simple as the safety razor, five or ten years before the rest of you saw the light. A modest return it was, but a beginning.

"It is already clear from the information presented in these tables that the world had begun to look to us to perpetuate stability at home as well as abroad. The Great Depression of the thirties . . ." And now I stand before you city slickers, once a poor country boy, foreign-born, you called it. But I had the brains and energy to beat you at your own games. It was a piece of cake. ". . . and so I say that the greatest contribution . . . establish on a long-term basis a stable . . ." I could do this in my sleep. On and on. Not too fast now, a brisk clip, just enough to leave the duffers behind. ". . . maintaining a liberal and constructive trade and investment policy overseas. I have projected a . . . which you will find in briefest outline on pages twelve through fourteen. Let me explain."

There was the rustle of pages while his audience struggled to understand. With an exaggerated leisure, like the patriarch of a large and well-to-do family, Thomas Hughes took out his pocket watch and snapped open the gold lid. Half after four. Right on schedule. Time for a tough tone.

"I must speak specifically now about the straits of our individual allies. . . ." He ran swiftly through a detailed account of the present economic growth of the continental Western European countries. At the top of page twenty he paused. I want them all to hear this, he thought. He took off his glasses and looked over his audience. A few strays returned to the fold during this well-timed silence. From here on in it was to be a personal triumph. The world would know that it was a Welshman, Thomas Hughes himself, who was both brilliant and bold enough to save the bloody English from themselves. He adopted a paternalistic tone.

"It seems clear that the situation in Britain is serious enough, due to both overly optimistic and unrealistic planning internally and overwhelming external pressures and obligations, to require that Britain not only have a freer hand in industrial trade and on the currency exchange, but she must foster an entirely new attitude toward a way of life by the whole country, and by a country not yet out of wartime restrictions, although a victor in that war. The base facts appear in Table Three. Let me go over them with you."

As Thomas Hughes read from his script he also read the faces before him. Interest. Acceptance. Alarm. Challenge. Controversy and control. This combination elated him and he pushed on to the end, explaining the balance necessary in the policy of the United States toward Britain, moral and financial support to the point of producing incentives, parent to child.

". . . Faced with the need to reduce British costs and prices, a new economic policy within Britain and for the world at large must be adopted."

He paused again. Here it comes; I know my dramatics just as well as Margaret does. He raised his lyric voice to sound across the huge room like breakers pounding upon the people seated there.

"I ask Britain . . ." Pause. "I ask Britain, with the support of the nations of the Free World, to consider devaluing the pound." Pause. The silence through the room was complete. He could move on. "In this mounting atmosphere of speculation and anxiety over the pound, and to avoid the disaster of further deflation within Britain, I believe this action, contrary to repeated denials by British and American government officials, must and will be taken. While it seems a shocking concept to most of you—I can observe that—I believe members of the sterling block will adjust quickly to realistic reevaluation of their own currencies to bring prices into touch with the world market. Such reevaluation will restore confidence in money, restore freedom to individuals, industry, business, banks, travelers; it will give individuals and business alike the mobility to convert from one currency to another, perhaps give life to the vision of multilateral trade. In short, such a bold move—I repeat, so frequently denied of late—while seemingly drastic, is the only wise step to bring economic stability to this changing world.

"I thank you, ladies and gentlemen."

Thomas Hughes stepped back to sit down. The applause began to rush across the rows of men and women until it grew massive and uncontrolled enough to bring the audience to its feet, first a few, then a whole row, the roomful of people standing. He noted with satisfaction that even those hardened reporters at the press table paused briefly before making for the telephones. He'd done it, of course. It was almost a letdown now, it was so predictable. The jousting would come later, in person, in print. He returned to the podium, carefully filled the water glass and sipped, then raised a hand in acknowledgment and strode purposefully, triumphant, from the speaker's platform, down the main aisle to the exit, accepting handshakes along the way.

Plenty of time to catch the six-o'clock plane.

Chapter 12

———————··❮❮∞❯❯··———————

"LET'S TRY the entrance again, Dorothy. You are Shakespeare's Prospero, the rightful Duke of Milan. You worship your lovely daughter, Miranda, yes, but you address her with innate majesty." Margaret Hughes spoke decisively.

Prospero, the woman Dorothy, stood awkwardly rooted to the Afghan throw at the marble hearth. Behind her, gold nymphs, a series of three to the pair, held up the candles in their outstretched palms at either end of the mantelpiece. Sparkling crystals revolved slightly on delicate pins. "It's difficult for me, Margaret. I feel self-conscious, so silly going through all these motions at my age. You can really become the part you play."

Margaret Hughes approached her friend with open arms, her still lovely face filled with a warm smile, her eyes admiring the delicacy of her candelabra. She paused a moment, noticing just briefly the good taste of her expensive possessions, then gently led the middle-aged Dorothy to stand before the bay window at the west end of the drawing room of the Hughes house on Pembroke Avenue. She drew back the draperies, closed each day against the growing summer heat, the red-eyed dragons woven across the mustard linen background collapsing into the folds of the material like the pleated bellows of an old accordion she remembered in her childhood. Who played it? Certainly not the celebrated Aunt Polly.

"Stand right here, Dorothy. You'll feel more at ease. Perhaps the sunlight will cast a spell on you and get you out of yourself." Margaret laughed melodically. "You'll make a strong Prospero to Eleanor's adoring Miranda."

And the other women in the play-reading group took their lead from Margaret Hughes, their president and most accomplished actress.

"Stand up straight, Dorothy, and speak out."

"Just hold your handsome head up, my dear; that's all you need to do."

"And remember, you have supernatural powers and an airy spirit to work your romance. It's really a wonderful part, Dorothy."

Margaret grabbed a heavy silk-and-wool shawl, her mother's, from the arm of the black velvet sofa and draped it about Prospero's shoulders.

"There, that helps," she said.

Dorothy settled into her stance, her sensible brown-and-white laced shoes, for better comfort, in ludicrous contrast to the fabric-and-texture elegance of the drawing room furnishings, or indeed to the very notion of an isolated island, a wizard's cave, the heritage of a dukedom. "I feel like an ungainly girl," she said, "playing at games in all those frightful bloomers and middy blouses."

The women laughed with her good-naturedly. "Give it a try." "Those bloomers really were a sketch." "This is only in fun, Dorothy."

Dorothy smiled back, encouraged, and let her large body slump, her beige fly-front dress, Egyptian cotton, hanging from the shoulder seams now. The women chatted with one another like schoolgirls at break time.

Impossible, Margaret Hughes thought. Dorothy Scott was a big, homely woman, almost sixty, she guessed, and perennially stuck in the gracelessness of an adolescent, like Margaret's sister

Mary, but certainly not like her well-brought-up daughters, one of them still young enough to be, as yet, not fully formed. Surely Alma would soften as she grew older. She must remember that Alma was only fifteen. And what's worse, Dorothy Scott hadn't a morsel of the commanding presence of even a bad actress. And Eleanor Black, an overgrown ingenue at fifty-two, artless, without guile, petite, and shrunken still more with aging. Perhaps we are all fools, Margaret thought, and yet these amateurish attempts at parlor theatrics by the Friday Afternoon Mothers Club were the only chance she, Margaret, had to recapture some feeling of triumph over the gaps and holes of her own world, her private self. These were the moments when she felt free of her inadequacies, and when they ended, the group dispersed until the next meeting, she all too often faced for an instant the truth, that the peak of her life was played out some thirty years back now, in a railroad station in Providence, Rhode Island; from that time on she had been on the road, living out a purgatory of yearning and regret.

Margaret knew that she appeared to her volumes of friends everything she chose to project—at ease with her life, like the rest of them, each an extension, some an adornment, to an established man. She and her friends and neighbors were all comfortably stationed and housed—many of them born to it. Each one of them a helpmeet, mother. The more practically competent were community minded, the highly educated— humanists, some innovators—absorbed in independent studies, secure in the shared knowledge that delving lifelong into literature, botany, languages, whatever, was truly more laudable in the equation of purity versus success, while their professional husbands—lawyers, doctors, bankers, educators, politicians, investors—navigated a worldliness necessary but somehow less noble. The women who had earlier chosen a man's world were admired, sometimes beyond their achievements, for their courage, but they were not often picked to reign over a man's house, nor indeed his bed. The majority of married women in town felt the spinsters had chosen irrevocably and poorly.

But few saw inside Margaret Hughes; it was her choice that it be so. And even those close to her would wonder at the real fear, timidity, she felt and concealed before the worldly-wise and successful men who were married to these women, her friends. At dinner parties at the Scotts' house, for instance, colossal at the edge of the reservoir woods, so perfectly tended by the servants, so gloomily squired by Dorothy and William, whose money, continually reinvested, brought no further glamor to his New England frugality. Sometimes Margaret would envy the little wanting that the Scotts seemed to have. They lacked for nothing, they longed for nothing. It must be a kind of peace, she thought, and while she knew that she was the woman who made William Scott a wee bit giddy there seated at his right, his wineglass in his hand, she was always one of the two people in the room who knew that all her seeming woman-liness vanished upstairs in her own handsome house, in her marriage bed. And suddenly right now, watching her friends at ease in her house, at play with her and each other, the awful terror of the memory of Thomas touching her between her legs was there again, as repugnant now as it was the first time it had happened so long ago, and with the repugnancy she felt the sadness, the failure, the embarrassment, as if she alone could not have the love other women received because she was afraid of it. A paradox. And she knew it. She shielded her eyes with her hands; her face must show her pain. Let the others talk a moment, she needed the time to enter herself and then rejoin them.

She must keep the memory and the doubts out. Why were they seeping in now, when she had most of what made her happy? She dwelled on herself. She struggled to remember her vigor, her intelligence, and her still prevailing beauty. It was the greatest pleasure to her. She was even a match for burgeon-ing Alma, Thomas's favorite. Margaret bathed herself in her own good looks for a moment, like stepping into scented water. Slim, her blond hair silvered now, and short, framing her face, a picture, her bone structure everlastingly good. The happy thought was enough to bring her back to her grand drawing room and the society of well-to-do women, her friends and admirers.

She took charge again. "We'll push this end table aside, that's right, over there beneath the window. Thank you, Eleanor. Let's give this Prospero some space in his tempest, and we'll let the light shine into his cave."

"You direct us a little, Margaret. Dorothy and I will find our parts, if you just get us started."

"Yes, you get us going, Margaret."

Margaret stood poised a moment. She listened to the heavy tread, a bouncing stride down the stairs into the hall. The front door slammed shut. Exit Alma, she thought, noisy and intrusive, but no one else seemed to notice.

In a busy manner Margaret Hughes set the stage. The curtains already drawn back, the furniture removed, she placed her characters to this side or that of her proscenium, tucked them behind the back of the Queen Anne chair at the left of the fireplace, Marion Middleton ready at the right of the bay window, a dazzling young Ferdinand to come. Straight and bony, with the aristocratic carriage of to family born, Marion, Margaret thought quickly, might once have made an engaging Renaissance page boy. And she, Margaret MacNeil, the stepping stone up for her own family, here in the substantial house that Thomas had built for her, she would slip into her part as Ariel with all the perfect ease that Shakespeare intended for his magical sprite. Margaret Hughes knew the pleasure of playacting.

She listened to Prospero's story told to his adoring daughter.

". . . rememb'rest aught ere thou cam'st here . . ."

"But that I do not."

"Twelve year since, Miranda . . . Thy father . . . A prince of power."

And in that center of her mind that would go back, always back, she fought to maintain her distance from the series of pictures, the tableaux: Thomas, middle-aged, still handsome, seated in the green armchair, the one pushed against the wall now to give space to this other fantasy. And Alma at five, astride his knee, bending forward to reach the coffee table where the silver tray presented the bottles and glasses, even the slivers of lemon rind, the potions that would take husband away from wife and into himself. Alma was permitted to stir the mixture, which she did vigorously, bruising the gin. Yet Alma went unchided.

"Alack, what trouble was I then to you!"

"Oh, a cherubin thou wast that did preserve me. . . ."

Or Alma, about twelve, cross-legged on the floor before her father, still in the dirty green pinny she wore to play at field hockey despite the approaching dinner hour. He holding out his glass as if an offering. She trying to explain the rules of the game, the victory of the afternoon. She thumping her fist on the rug to startle away the benign smile he showered on her, pounding her round red thigh to jostle the machinery of his brain to comprehend her, like the irritable tappings on the crystal of a watch temporarily slowed or stopped.

And where was she, Margaret? She was always the observer.

"Come away, servant, come; I am ready now. Approach, my Ariel. Come."

And Margaret Hughes reentered her real world, leaping gracefully across the imaginary line that separated drawing room from stage, her arms extended, elbows bent, her fingers splayed out to exaggerate the make-believe quality of the character she would become so perfectly, a tight fit like a pair of good kid gloves.

"All hail, great master. . . . I come to answer thy best pleasure, be it to fly, to swim, to dive into the fire, to ride on the curl'd clouds. To thy strong bidding task Ariel and all his quality."

Prospero swung the shawl as if it were a cape, across the breast to the shoulder.

"Ariel, thy charge exactly is performed; but there's much work. . . ."

"Is there more toil? Since thou dost give me pains, let me remember thee what thou hast promised. . . ."

"How now? Moody? What is't thou canst demand?"

"My liberty. . . ."

"Dost thou forget from what a torment I did free thee?"

"No," spake Ariel. The choice made so long ago was indeed a torment, Margaret recalled. Did Thomas free me?

And Ariel went on, obedient to the scolding master Prospero. And finally, "Pardon, master; I will be correspondent to command and do my spriting gently."

"Do so; and after two days I will discharge thee."

"That's my noble master. . . ."

To be discharged, thought Margaret. Discharged to what? Within the world of Thomas she lived out her success and her failure. Was there another world?

Ariel crossed from center stage, anticipating an exit right.

Commanded, "Go, hence with diligence!" by the master Prospero, Ariel moved almost weightlessly toward the wings— the side window and the inlaid card table, the creamy-colored Ming vase blossoming with tea roses. The slightest breeze, moving the glass curtains, filtering through the open screened window, briefly scented Margaret's quickened breathing. She leaned against the window sill, silent beside Marion Middleton, who squeezed Margaret's shoulders and whispered, "Marvelous!" into her ear. Now Margaret's pensiveness was heightened by her almost hysterical feeling of affinity with the character Ariel. She was particularly good this day, she knew, and yet her thoughts were shadowy, jumbled like some people's shoe racks and bureau drawers. She was longing. For warmth, and on such a summer's day? For protection, here amidst the details of acquisition that meant security? Some terrible foreboding, the unknown storm approaching, a tempest, perhaps. But no sense that there would ever be peace in it for her. The will to fly away, to escape all feelings. To die. And with the sort of clarity she had felt when anesthesia—induced sleep—had in the past sharpened her hearing so that, remote, she heard the doctors clearly discussing her as if she were not there, she knew that she had two lives within her, both her own. One dead in marriage almost thirty-five years now. One dying.

She was almost as frightened for her exterior command as by the painful fluttering in her breast, like a great black-backed gull murderously trapped inside her, struggling to be set loose, vast feathered wings beating against her very body from within, battering her, plundering her, killing her. The nausea was high in her throat. She grabbed Marion's extended hand.

Face flushed, the invisible Ariel, singing and dancing, led handsome young Ferdinand onto the stage to do idyllic romance with Prospero's daughter, Miranda.

The afternoon progressed; the other players, freed from themselves, joined Margaret Hughes in her world. Ariel performed magic as if there would be no other day. Margaret's performance ignited the others to bring the playacting especially alive, so that when at first not on stage, Margaret dared to close her eyes to listen to the art and song of the meter, but the words meant too much today.

She opened her eyes.

A moment's further collecting of herself, and Margaret resumed early on her role as director with outward diligence, and she was versatile enough to act out smaller parts in the drama as well as her own spritely Ariel. She must be in control, she told herself, she must. But now it was across the romance of the young, Miranda and Ferdinand, that she kept tripping gracelessly in her mind, as if, on a journey through a familiar meadow filled with daisies and black-eyed Susans, the grasses feathery and gentle against her legs, she kept stumbling forward, stubbing her toe in newly formed fox holes or against unexpectedly dislodged field stones.

Such an unbelievable couple who courted each other with such elaborate games and verbal embraces. It was stored way back in her memory. While as director, of course, she knew she manipulated nonpeople, it was actually the unreality of the romance that unsettled her. Was she afraid for herself? Surely not now. For Alma? Apprehension, maybe, but not for Alma. For herself. Why was she not enough? Her warming hands, her welcoming kiss, her comforting embrace through the bouts of asthma, when his breathing came slow and scratching, sometimes not at all. And she knew hers was a dream of romance, too young for her years ago. She was not a peasant in his bed, just a lady in her house. Her upper lip began to quiver. She clamped her teeth shut with unaccustomed violence.

"Control." She said the word out loud. The actors paid further careful consideration to the business of the play.

Margaret quickly consoled herself in knowing that although the most artful actress among them, she really could not have played the role of Miranda well. It was insipid, vapid. Eleanor Black was naturally cast. She turned again her full acting attentions to the joyful Ariel. And when finally the playwright ties up all the minor tragedies with comic smartness and Ariel sings in anticipation of freedom: "Where the bee sucks, there suck I. In a cowslip's bell I lie," Margaret twirled the imaginary rapier as Ariel attires Prospero. "There I couch when owls do cry. On the bat's back I do fly. After summer merrily." She stretched up before Dorothy to place the duke's crown on Prospero's head. "Merrily, merrily shall I live now, Under the blossom that hangs on the bough."

Margaret Hughes, light-footed, seemingly so light-hearted, brought the production temporarily to a halt. Her admiring friends clapped and clumsy Dorothy Scott embraced her as her aunts and her father, when she was very little, would hold her tight when she had done something especially well. The comfort of clasping arms made her hear the words of the song she had sung so happily, and she cried openly, thus bringing her friends closer to her. It was this genuineness they loved in Margaret, her openness, her ability to feel things more deeply than others; only she knew of what they were unaware, that these were not the tears of joy, as they appeared, but the terrible sorrowing in the knowing that no mortal could be free. Therefore, not she. And free for what?

And so when the maid entered the drawing room to announce that Mr. Hughes was on the long-distance telephone in the library, Margaret was truly loath to take the call. She started to tell Bridie to refuse the call: "Bridie, please tell Mr. Hughes I will return his call later, after . . ." but her friends urged her to speak to Thomas. "Oh, nonsense, no one minds the interruption, Margaret." "Don't be silly, speak to Thomas." To protest too much would be to have to explain.

Margaret followed the maid from the room, adjusting the open collar of her lavender-colored linen dress. She wished to appear quite cool to him in her agitation. How foolish, she thought; he can't see me. She noticed as she parted from Bridie in the hall the slight, attractive tightness beneath the waist of the girl's gray afternoon uniform and the fact that she did not wear her cap. The backs of her knees reminded Margaret of Miss Carmody's too short skirts. She would be there beside him on the hotel bed, a copy of his speech in her lap. His speech . . . he's calling to tell me about his triumphs. She grabbed up the telephone receiver at the corner of the huge leather-topped desk in Thomas's walnut-walled study.

"Yes." She spoke harshly into the instrument.

His tone was solicitous, even eager to please. Was he so sure of himself that he would think Margaret did not know that *she* was there beside him? Margaret determined to ask about his speech, and in the same breath she let him know she was busy herself. Art before politicking. He was coming home tonight. She fairly dropped the receiver into place. How peculiar to change his plans. And there was something in his manner that made her think that he made the decision right then and there, even while speaking to her. What could she suppose? Only a change in Miss Carmody's schedule. Young, intelligent, a single woman in business—what a wonderful freedom she must feel, the right-hand man to such a brilliant success as Thomas Hughes. "Dr. Hughes," Miss Carmody called him. Margaret pursed her lips so that the smooth pink tissue pinched and curled like the skin on a dried plum, wandering as she did through the library doorway into the great hall, where she stood musing, inspecting all the while the medallion patterns woven into the Chinese Oriental rug that swept the full width of the house. Martinis, she thought. And Alma. Sometimes she wished neither of them would come home.

Through the porch doors, open now, she saw that Bridie was

grouping the teacups and glasses to the side of the hutch table, its round top one solid maple board rubbed smooth with age and dull-finished by the oils administered to all Margaret's antique woods for proper care and preservation. At an informal occasion such as this one, and served out of doors, it would be a pity to cover a surface so handsome with a damask cloth. She felt steadied by the thoughts she recognized, and the voices of the members of the Friday Afternoon Mothers Club reassured her further. Stepping to the screen doors, she called to the maid on the piazza. "There will be three for dinner, Bridie. Mr. Hughes will be home."

"Late, then, Mrs. Hughes."

"Yes, I suppose so, Bridie."

She returned to the drawing room, to the conclusion of the drama, the business of the afternoon. In the garden the playing began, the comments on man's world, the gossip, the laughter that men never seemed to share, the exchange among women. Margaret served tea—hot in paper-thin Canton-blue china cups, or iced with sprigs of mint fresh from the garden. The flat silver simple, rather modern. The tea service Georgian, newly polished. The tea napkins a delicate lime color. Cucumber and watercress sandwiches straight out of Oscar Wilde. The expanse of lawn, the maples and elms, the herbaceous borders to the flower beds, the dogwood at the garden's edge just past flowering now. And the wild array of roses, teas, climbers, lowbush, and the lavishness of the old-fashioned beach-house roses, as full-bloomed as peonies. The red brick of the façade, the English ivy slowly traveling up and spraying across the expanse of stone to the white trim. It was all the new film color extreme. Technicolor, Alma called it. And it was handsome, the creation of Margaret Hughes. For a moment it seemed her life's work.

The afternoon ended and Mrs. Hughes's guests departed. The white gloves donned, fingers drawn in and fitted, first one hand, then the other; the effusive praise and thanks delivered; the next meeting anticipated. Margaret Hughes was alone. While Bridie cleared the tea things and moved indoors to lay the dinner table, Margaret waited for the return of her family, the magazine section of last Sunday's newspaper resting in her lap. She sat quite purposefully upright in a wicker garden chair rather than abandon herself, self-satisfied, on the chaise. The heat of the day long gone, she would seek the tranquillity of the early evening light.

It had been one of the best performances of the group she could remember, and yet it was an awful afternoon to look back on for her, the star. She felt diminished by her travails; too much doubt pushing out of her, spent without purpose, like an overflowing bucket, the hose thrust into it and forgotten, to run unattended. She would try to think in dramatic concepts. The unreal and the real. Yes. Appearances and the secrets of every man's life. Literary tensions. Love and obligation. More like it. The comic in everyday tragedies. Past, present, future. She was haunted this day: pleasure, fantasy, expectation. Thomas and Alma. At home tonight. And the fluttering little bird of hope slumped back in her breast. Haunted, by anxiety, not knowing, the unknown.

She turned the pages of cheap news sheet. Picture ads of women with spaghetti legs and protruding pelvises modeling summer shirt fronts. The economy. The cold war. "A Doctor looks at Marital Infidelity." Something about thinking clearly about this major hazard to modern marriage. A marriage, the institution of legal union, should be prepared to defend itself against the shattering impact of infidelity with facts. She read completely absorbed, as if at last a set of rules and she would be free from the hurt and humiliation. "Number one," she read. "Infidelity is no answer to disappointing sexual experience. Even in a penthouse-and-champagne atmosphere, the guilt, the secrets, the hurried exchange of intimacies that accompany an illegitimate sexual relation, will automatically defeat its objective."

Exactly, she thought. Then why does he do it? She would just show him this article, show him what a fool he makes of himself. And of her.

"Number two. It is useless, however, to meet the unfaithful mate with a moralistic sermon. In extreme cases, his behavior . . ." Yes, his, she thought, but that young woman should know better. What would her mother think of her running around with the boss? ". . . his behavior may be vile, but he is to be regarded as ill. He is suffering from a severe personality disturbance that in one form or another will plague him whether he remains married or is divorced. It affects not only the sex life, but the ability to work ably on the job, function as a responsible parent, or achieve any kind of real self-respect or personal contentment. He is in need of psychiatric help."

"It's his fault. It's all his fault. It says so right here.

"Number three. Only the marriage relationship offers the possibility for the development of a fully ripened, sophisticated sex life. The capacity for sexual pleasure does not depend on a vast knowledge of different techniques. It grows and flourishes with living together, raising children, building a home, with mutual trust and confidence and with the sharing of happiness and sorrows.

"It is under the normal, accepted and conventional conditions of married life that the sexual relationship is most satisfying to both partners."

But we have a normal, accepted, conventional . . .

Margaret Hughes heard the front door slam shut.

Alma.

Chapter 13

ALMA LEANED her back against the heavy paneled front door, her hands behind her still grasping the knob Bridie was always polishing up to make the outside look good—the Hughes false front, Alma called it. It was a kind of dirty joke among her friends, who thought her clever to know so much about inside people and what showed. The knocker had sounded its abrasive tap as she pulled too hard, too quickly on the way out, in a hurry to keep contained the terrible dissatisfactions she felt within the house at Pembroke Avenue, like slamming the lid on her Pandora's box. She felt she'd succeeded, none of the ugly puffy moths of her mother's self-pity or piercing mosquitoes of shame leaking out at the seams of the great brick container. The silly frowzy ladies and their pretensions, her mother the worst of them with her dancing steps, projecting her high squeaky voice as if she were some sort of magical spirit. Alma threw up her arms to the heavens and made her face sag hideously the way she had seen her mother do once when her bunch of biddies did *King Lear.* She closed her eyes. "How sharper than a serpent's tooth it is to have a thankless child." She mimicked her mother to the bushes on either side of her. If she did that in Miss Eliot's English class everyone would laugh out loud at something so really corny. And there was her mother making a fool of herself, and of Alma, too, in that awful lavender dress, the one with all the buttons down the side, which said "no" in embroidered white thread on the linen, only Ma refused to see that that's what the design spelled. She was above all that. All she could bring herself to hug was her silverware. Never Alma. Maybe Mary. She extended a cheek toward Daddy sometimes. Margaret Hughes with her faded skin and proper thises and thats. Alma had given up trying to please her. She didn't long anymore to be hugged the way she used to. Leave the loving to Mary, her mama's goody-goody.

And the house itself. It always smelled of her father; musty bookshelves, stale sweat. Drink.

Alma had to admit sometimes she missed Mary. Her wedding had been fun and she was actually living with a man now. Alma knew that when they wanted to they slept together naked. Ever since Mary had gone away there was no one Alma was supposed to talk to. Bridie was all right, in her way. She called Daddy "his nibs" and got away with it. But as she thought about this day, Alma guessed mostly she was just plain glad to escape the house without getting called in to perform, the handholds and pecks on the cheek, the how-was-school-this-year-what-are-your-summer . . .

And she began to do just that, to plan. She had a whole afternoon of freedom ahead of her. She could do anything she wanted to and no one would know the better. She leaped down the broad steps to the gravel path, pulling tight the loops at the waist of her light cotton skirt to accentuate her small waist and to emphasize the fact that she did have breasts. Small. Too small, but round, not hanging thin like fat bananas. Her nipples stood up whether she pinched them or not. Her movement forward brought the feel of air fresh against her skin at her neck, drying the dollops of moisture there; she created her own breeze. Her sneakers allowed her an extra spring or two. And then she set out for the bottom of the hill, for Martin's house down by the car tracks.

Martin was someone Alma Hughes had grown up with. He was like an old pair of sweat pants, too hot and sticky against cold flesh, something she just snatched off when it was her chance to plunge into the game. Alma made a point of it to never wash her sweat pants. While Martin was still welcome at her house on Pembroke Avenue along with the rest of the neighborhood children who were also Alma's classmates at school, after the bicycle race five years ago Alma's mother expressed a kind of nervousness about him—and some of the other boys, too. Nothing spoken, just oversolicitous. And her father openly encouraged her to show more respect to those sons and daughters who lived at the top of the Hill and in the High Street area, the children of what he called "solid" families, "professional" people. Money, that's what he meant. He was a snob, and that was against Alma's own personal principles. Though Martin's mother was a teacher at the high school, that wasn't good enough for Mr. and Mrs. Make-it Hughes, a couple of schoolteachers themselves. No; Mrs. O'Shea only taught music, and nobody knew what Mr. O'Shea did. Welfare work, delinquent children, something like that. Mr. O'Shea kept pretty much to himself and Alma didn't blame him, the way people never mentioned him. Alma had a special affinity for Mr. and Mrs. O'Shea. After she had tried so hard and had beaten Martin in the race and on a boy's bike with handbrakes—back when they were ten or eleven, sixth grade—and Alma couldn't stop the bike or avoid the telephone pole, Mr. O'Shea had held her in his arms until the throbbing in her head had subsided. He put his own clean handkerchief into the blood on her forehead and on her lip, and he had looked inside her mouth to inspect her teeth. That really had impressed Alma. Mrs. O'Shea had mopped her face gently right at the kitchen sink, the blood on the drainboard, and Mr. O'Shea had told her she was a good sport—tears didn't matter—and she was a winner. Martin was pretty nice about being beat, too, because even if she couldn't stop, she'd won, after all.

Alma's mother had thanked Mr. and Mrs. O'Shea and then driven Alma to the hospital to get the stitches in her lip. On the way home, Alma remembered, she made note in an observant, detached way just how long it took for her face to swell. Her mother talked about growing up and perhaps not being so busy playing with a gang of rough boys; it was time to be quiet and clean, pay more attention to piano lessons and English grammar, soft stuff like that. And all the time Alma's face was swelling up like a water balloon. Oh, yes, and she should try to be a credit. The Benedict girls never got into any scrapes and look how pleasant they were. Alma thought the Benedict girls were just nobodies, all three of them. By the time Ma had maneuvered the too big Buick into that garage built a million years ago for some ancient little car, Alma recalled that her face had flamed with pain, which swept across like a brush fire kindled to burn strong. The shot they had punched into her in the accident ward hadn't numbed her for long. She left her mother fumbling through her pocketbook, bent over the front seat, and right in midsentence, something about not throwing herself at boys. What did Ma know about boys? Slam on the little garage door. Mr. O'Shea had known that Alma had tried. And besides, she hurt.

In the bathroom mirror Alma had recognized her eyes and nose like lily pads in a swamp of patches of gravelly skin where her cheeks should have been, crisscross lines like a little kid's skinned knees. Her forehead was askew, a big egg lump to throw it off balance, and her upper lip protruded. But the most awful memory of all was when she sat down to go to the john. The blotch of red stain soaking into her white cotton underpants. It was a long time before she knew what had happened. It wasn't the curse, as she had suspected; it didn't keep coming, and mostly she was afraid to touch herself down there. Alma had to figure these things out for herself. The curse was supposed to flow. When she finally told her mother, Ma had clutched her hands between her breasts, like that hefty woman in *Aïda* trying to grab a breath, and asked Alma if it hurt. When Alma told Ma she hadn't even known the blood was there until she saw it, her mother stopped throwing her arms around long enough to look surprised. Then she led Alma up the curved staircase and laid her out on her great high bed as if she were a corpse. She looked between Alma's legs. Nothing had ever hurt so much inside; she had felt ripped open, exposed. Even now the snapshot of the scene made the flesh of her inner thighs burn hot with a kind of blush of embarrassment. Ma told Alma that probably her hymen had been broken and Alma had better be careful. It wouldn't be long now. Even girls on High Street got into trouble. Of course, Alma knew right away it had to do with sex, but she had had to do some more thinking and poking through the dictionary to take it all in. Looking back, it seemed the silliest thing in the world, except for the deep humiliation of such an inspection, which she could never forgive. Some people never heard of privacy. But the hole was open and she wouldn't have to go to the doctor for that the way Penelope Peters's sister had had to before she got married. Even Mary hadn't had to do that.

And Alma knew she'd go all the way someday. That was more than Mary could get up her nerve to do before it was legal. Alma had always liked to kiss and have boys feel her breasts. Once she and Tassie Funkhauser had taken their shirts off up in Alan Powell's attic and fastened their barrettes on their nipples, but that was way back when they didn't really have much to show. Now when Martin put his hand up her skirt and down into her underpants, she loved the journey across her stomach, but she held her legs tight. She didn't like it when he got over the bone. But when they had been dancing close at the boat club party after school let out, she could feel his thing hard against her crotch, and it frightened her. While she was laughing at him about where it would land if he were very tall, say, or better still a midget, he said he couldn't stand her any longer and rushed her outside onto the launching platform. He unbuttoned his fly and thrust her hand through the mess of shirttails. She had stopped her giggling fast. The lump was hard and growing right there in her hand. She took her hand away but remained in his arms to think. It was something she had always wondered about. What would a penis feel like, just to touch, she meant, and she knew she wanted to see one, at least.

Suddenly Alma remembered where she was headed and stopped walking to lean against the Powells' fence, bending back into the shade of the tall lilac bushes, the leaves spotted white with rain water, the aromatic blossoms long gone by. She studied the clusters of seed pods, tiny brown dried-up sacs. Brittle. Why did science teachers always talk about plants and animals as if there were something human about the reproductive process and therefore difficult to explain?

Sure she'd go all the way someday, but it would be with someone she didn't know yet. He would hold her across his arms when he started kissing her, the way they did in the movies, and he'd be tough, he'd be a somebody. But very gentle. And she would know what to do. She hoped.

Alma crossed the avenue, climbed the embankment and peered through the great iron fence poles into the cemetery that ran parallel to the road. When she was a little girl she used to be able to squeeze sideways through the bars at any point along the fence, the black paint rusted and peeling green even then. Now she had to skinny under where the dogs had dug, way down by the greenhouses near the dump, on the other side of the hill. Either that or go around to the front gate, but that seemed wrong to Alma somehow. The cemetery was for illegal entry. When she was younger it had seemed spooky. She laughed at herself now. She had stood, stubby legs, Dutch haircut, staring at the stones that marked where dead people would just lie there feeling nothing and wasting away. She really hadn't much liked to go in there when she was a little girl; she only did it because Emily Wheeler wasn't afraid and Alma always wanted to be like Emily. Emily seemed to be good at everything, especially at being a girl, although she looked like a colt with her slender long legs and mane of brown hair. And Emily's grandfathers and great-cousins and all that had lived in the same houses for hundreds of years. For a moment Alma missed Emily, off to boarding school most of the time and now at the family summer place by the sea. She was more like a stranger now, and Alma wondered if Emily had done it yet, and wondered again that she didn't know. A kind of loneliness set in; she recognized it—a sag in her gait. She realized she was clinging to something way back. She turned from the cemetery

view and began to wander down the path, left arm outstretched, slapping the palm hard against the posts as she went.
She felt like making it hurt, just so she could feel something,
anything real, right here and now. Pretty soon she took to
stubbing the toes of her sneakers, at the rubber tip, on the
ancient heaved-up roots of the maples that knit the embankment solid. She traveled on, still headed down the hill, and she
dwelt on herself with fascination: the weird notion that she was
really two Almas, the one that was trapped inside her family—
angry, mostly, and lonely—and the one in her own world, shyer
than she wanted people to know. Both Almas were confused,
she couldn't see either one of them clearly, and she didn't like
herself for that. It sometimes made her be boisterous, a circus
clown. That's what her mother meant when she talked about
acting like a young lady now that she was fifteen. Alma could
cover up things she didn't even know how she felt about by just
letting some smart remark slip out. Wisecracks, her parents
called the things she said. She tried to keep her mouth shut, but
no one believed her. And if she knew how she felt about things,
maybe she would act better and please them. Like how she felt
about how Daddy was with her, gooey and hugging when he'd
had too much to drink and smelled like the toilet in a filling
station. And her body. Mostly she guessed she was lumpy and
ugly, and might as well give up. But sometimes she thought she
was more beautiful than her mother, and everyone said, "Mrs.
Hughes—what a striking-looking lady for her age." Alma saw
her mother like a mirage between the retina of her eye and the
light of reality. She scrunched up her nose and made a snout
like a pig's.

"I don't know," said Alma to the traffic piled up at the stop-
lights at the foot of the hill. "I just can't figure everything out
all at once. I'm smart in ways that don't show up on French
tests, but I can't find all the answers." Across the avenue she
spotted Martin O'Shea's bare feet sticking out onto the city
sidewalk. She shoved all her thoughts in a pig pile under the rug
at the back of her head and crossed the street.

The rest of him was there, too, under the chassis of his Model

A Ford, a little red coupe with a rumble seat and a black top, the body of it all shiny from his polishing, as if such an old thing could look new. It was fun to ride in and even better to drive. When it worked, that is. But Alma couldn't see how anyone could spend a whole lifetime beneath there trying to do something to get it to run once in a while.

She called out to him and when he didn't come out from under or even answer, she stretched out on the gravel alongside the car, which Martin had pulled into the laundry yard behind the O'Shea house. He lay on his back, shirtless, the scant dark hair on his chest trickling out to form a line that led her eye down the middle of his rib cage, across the divide of his waist, where she could see the top of his abdomen at his navel, sunken like a smooth riverbed between his pelvic bones at the belt of his jeans. She knew the trail of hair traveled on down his stomach, and she knew he never wore any underpants.

"Hey, you," she said, offensive so as to be heard.

She watched him swing his eyes in her direction. Then he turned his head gently toward her and hoisted his body to lie half propped up on his side. One shoulder reached up to rest wedged against a greasy pipe. The other nestled miserably in bluestone chips. It hurt him to move, and the sight of his stuck flesh reminded her of the little jabs at her elbow and along her hip. The physical discomfort, the pain, excited her. It was something she could feel and identify.

"Your hands are covered with black." As if on demand, Martin stretched them out to look them over before offering them to Alma.

"That's a stupid thing to say," he said.

"You're stupid to spend all your time under a stupid car. Come on out," she demanded.

She watched him consider, and then his eyes began the inspection, starting with her face and hesitating a moment at the wedge of skin that showed at the neck of her blouse. According to plan, she thought. She knew he always looked her over, and she remembered to suck in her stomach so that her breasts would stick out.

"I've gotta finish this," finally, and he began the tortuous motions to lie again on his bare back.

"You're all dirty anyways." She didn't want to sound disappointed. Not knowing what was to come made her feel bad with herself. He's stupid, she thought self-importantly. Common, like her parents never said but always let her know. But still Alma hung around, dangling her hands loosely along the laundry lines that stretched overhead, limp like the strings on a discarded ukulele. At one point she shinnied up one of the green laundry poles that stood at attention all in a row outside the O'Sheas' kitchen window, and balanced her seat on the small flat top, her hands between her legs, clutching the beveled edge. When she raised up her head Mrs. O'Shea waved the dish mop at her through the window. Alma tried to look as if she meant what she was doing, but even she knew Mrs. O'Shea could see her embarrassment at being caught just doing nothing because Martin wouldn't pay attention to her. She pushed herself off the pole, leapfrog style, and hit the gravel eight feet down hard. The impact traveled fast up her body like a high fever up a thermometer, and the force collected in her temples for a moment. She shook her head to make it go away. Why did people call her mother stunning if this is what it felt like to look at her?

When Martin maneuvered cautiously out into the open, Alma was ready for him. She was crouched over him like a sprinter stopped to tie her shoelaces before racing on.

First he drove her up the hill and all the way down to the dump site. She sat in the rumble seat, her head thrown back to let the wind mat her hair flat on her head. When he stopped to turn around, she stuck her thumbs up at her ears and wiggled her fingers at him and thrust out her tongue like a good-natured gargoyle. Back at Martin's house, she put on his sister's bathing suit under her clothes, and they went out to the reservoir to swim. Martin parked the Model A bold as brass right in the municipal parking lot, but as they approached the sign saying "No Trespassing. No swimming. $100 fine," Alma began to wonder.

"Maybe we shouldn't."

"Why not? Anyone is allowed to walk along the path. If we go over in the woods by the Scotts' place, there's a big gap where the fence is gone. I know."

"But it says not to swim."

"The water comes right in close at this spot I know. If you don't splash and squall about how cold it is, just get in fast, no one will notice way around on the other side where the buildings are."

That did it. "I don't squall," announced Alma, and she led the way down the path.

The water was cold, an initial attack against her body, but she plunged right in and kept her mouth shut. When she surfaced, Martin disappeared from view, with a good deal of visibility, she thought, his head and rump appearing here and there as he made his way toward her. She had an uneasy feeling of impending trouble that kept her almost motionless, just her feet paddling to keep her afloat. Across the wide expanse of hues of blue, water and sky, behind the encompassing fence, the webbed metal a blur of glistening silver in the midafternoon sun, she knew authority lurked at every bush, hurrying to her now, to catch her in the act. She pivoted to swim back in to shore. A solid mass passed between her opened legs and hands grabbed at her. Martin's head broke through the surface of the water like an impatient baby's burst into the world. Alma screamed just as Martin drew in a desperate long breath of air.

"Shut up," he hissed at her, and covered her mouth with his. The wonderful sliminess of his tongue and the water slipping in between their bodies to tickle her skin where he pressed against her alerted her, and she broke free to swim swiftly to the edge of the reservoir. She scrabbled quickly over the rocks that lay exposed between water and woods, cutting into her fingers and the pads of her feet. She turned to watch Martin swim away from her out into the reservoir, long strong strokes, feet splashing rhythmically. She saw that he moved fearlessly, as if he knew where he was going. Hovered down on the needles beneath sheltering trees, the sun screened out, the damp bathing suit blotching wet through her clothes, she envied Martin his freedom, and she made herself promise to shed her indecision when the next chance came along.

Her mind made up, her nerves collected at the front of her head, pressing painfully against her forehead, she watched Martin continue to play irresponsibly on his own, way out there where anyone could have him. The waiting for him made Alma sick at her stomach like cramps, gathering up to split her gut wide open and then passing away as if nothing had happened, only to form and peak again. By the time Martin joined Alma in the shade of the woods, shaking his head like a dog come in out of the rain, she had already trotted the whole course from envy around rejection and finishing at hate. It was one of the fastest heats she'd ever run. He didn't even have the courtesy to feel worn out from all that fun he'd had with himself.

"That was good," he said, jumping up and down on one foot, pounding his ear as if he had just emerged from some difficult passage across the Atlantic Ocean and had a right to behave as though he'd accomplished something, instead of just splashing around in that bathtub of a reservoir that any four-year-old would consider nothing more than another night's scrub. When Martin put his arm around Alma, she told him she had to go home, but he said, "You do not," and took his time squeezing out the pant legs of his sopping blue jeans.

Alma was afraid to go back to the parking lot, her hair plastered down on her head. Anyone could tell they'd been swimming. She went through the woods and up the rise to the highway and perched on the low rail fence to wait for Martin, the meanwhile flapping the hem of her skirt to dry it light blue again. But when she stood up, the damp showed a broad dark band around her hips and thighs. She'd be found out for sure.

Alma was in no hurry to get home now. A confrontation with her mother would mean having to admit what she'd been up to. Breaking the stupid law always brought the old disappointed sigh from Ma, the not-a-credit, all that stuff, and a load of warning and the responsibility of law-abiding—a week later sometimes—from her father, the bad news saved up for his eventual return. The waiting for his angry slaps, the tongue-lashing like a licking, was miserable for her, her anger blooming under the white blotch where his hand smacked her jaw, and in some strange way she understood that he liked it. Alma never knew what to think about these ritualistic beatings, but at least they were attention. Ma had once told Mary in secret that anger was better than nothing, and anger was mostly what Alma got from her father, that and those queer embraces. So when Martin turned left down Fairmont Boulevard, which came to an end right in front of the gates to the cemetery, she welcomed the respite that a return to the familiar paths might bring. At this time of year the growth would be particularly lush and full, and the terrain so varied that from the top of Tower Hill in the old part of the cemetery down the steep ravine, Alma almost forgot the grave lots that nested on tiers among the ancient elms, the oaks and expansive weeping willows, the exotic raspberry rouge of the Japanese cherries still hanging on in clusters, the sticky limbs of the ginkgoes from China, the tropical yucca from the Southwest, huge blossoms bell-like receptacles upon the tough fibrous stalks, the slender locust, delicate branches extending bent, the fern leaves drooping like the forearms and palms of a ballet dancer. She had come to feel that these trees, established together in a communial parish of international harmony, shaded the hillside to invite the secret games of childhood, the privacy of discovery. She liked the trees. Nobody she knew could give her such a feeling of comfort.

Martin left the Model A down by the crematorium, which always looked to Alma like a smokehouse. It was supposed to be disguised as a toolshed or something, surrounded with honeysuckle bushes and seedbeds. It was the place where no one went. They agreed the car would be pretty safe there even if the whole world knew who it belonged to. Alma was excited about all this secrecy because it made a trip into nothing, the usual prowl around with old Martin O'Shea, seem like a new adventure. They walked along the drive not looking at anything, because, of course, they'd seen it all a million times before. But down by the pond where the crypts were—Wheelers'

Alley, Emily called it, some of her family were there—Alma just couldn't help feeling squirmy about the tidiness of those people packed away in drawers in stone houses like her mother's wardrobe, the handkerchiefs in rows like a shelf of hymnals, the second drawer full of stockings, the third vests for summer, on and on. They hung around, squinting through the bars in the doors trying to read names. Hazard, Paine, Wheeler, Coolidge, Zilanski. Who was that? Not all of the drawers were taken. "More to come," said Martin, as if he were filling up the parking garage down by the town hall. "Don't be so ghoulish," Alma came back at him. She liked to think of all this death around them as being over. Up the grade to the entrance of the tower, Martin held her hand, as much to get her up there as anything else, she knew. The stone steps were narrow and smelled of mold; it was like being trapped in the study with Daddy, no room to move around in and the awful musty odor. She passed Martin and began to take them two at a time. At the top they made a promenade of the balcony and came to rest leaning over the parapet. Martin made a fool of himself, leaning way out so that Alma would be afraid. She looked the other way to make him quit it, and when he grabbed her for a kiss she had the feeling that all the dizziness that engulfed them was holding them up in thin air. She opened her eyes to see the view that extended over the roofs of Pembroke Avenue, down across the river to the swamps, the giant high pampas grasses little tufted-haired children swaying in obeisance. "I feel like a princess." "Hmm," and he pursued her lips with his. "Come on," she called, and this time she did the leading, all the way down the interminable curve of the staircase to ground level. They stood in the doorway of the castle and Alma curtsied to the crowds to her left and right, and then they both began to run down the steep ravine, Alma hanging on to the trunks of the trees to hold herself upright, swaying as she went as if in a country-dance swing, the air blowing up her skirt to touch her thighs, her hair spun out like a cap of moss. Halfway down the slope she stopped to catch her breath. Martin was already at the bottom in the tiny valley, hands spread out on his kneecaps, shoulders hunched forward. Down there among the headstones, he looked as if he were in effigy.

The idea appealed to Alma—she was always startling herself. Martin suddenly frozen in midactivity, his legs sticking out from under his car, in bronze, maybe; his elbows and the side of his head as he turned to take in a breath while swimming; running naked, his penis erect like the figures on a Greek vase that Alma once saw on one of those boring school trips to the museum. The caption had read: "Youths at Play." She laughed out loud and stepped over the calf-high wrought-iron ornamental railing into the family plot of the Somebodies. There were two slabs marking the graves, dirty pink marble elevated on stubby Doric columns like a miniature Parthenon, the floor the spongy grasses that barely saw light in this protective forest of death. Here were stored the Balfour family, Alma read, safely housed within the black picket fence. Charles Henry lay alongside Elizabeth Atkinson; even under the earth they slept in twin beds, like Ma and Daddy. Alma perched hesitantly at the foot of Mr. Balfour's stone, right over Martha Balfour Weston—his daughter, it was clear by the dates. She lay at the foot of her father's bed, trapped forever between his dirty sheets.

Alma watched Martin mount the hill coming toward her, pulling himself up in exaggerated struggle by the trunks of the trees. When he reached the Balfour site she lay back cozily on the stone, her bare legs dangling awkwardly over the edge, her head pillowed on her hands cupped at the base of her skull. At the edge of the enclosure he carefully slipped off his jeans and stepped over the fence in a slow-motion calm that alarmed Alma. She kind of wanted him to be all thumbs, to show his usual old clumsiness, and it suddenly struck her that she was not his first. In her bewilderment she let him strip off her skirt, and the bottom of the bathing suit, and when he got around to unbuttoning her blouse she obliged him by sitting up on top of Martha. Neither one of them said anything, business being at hand, but then when he reached behind her to unhook the bra of the swimsuit she crossed her arms over her chest. "No," she said. "Why not?" he questioned, irritated by the interruption in the natural progression of things. "Martin O'Shea," she said, "you forget who I am. I have some pride, after all." "Listen, Alma Hughes, the flat-boob untouchable, you're no different from any of the rest of them. You've been asking for it all afternoon." And with that he pushed her down hard on the marble slab just as she was mustering up her hauteur to give it to him right between the eyes, and before she could shove him from her he stuck his thing in her, stiff like the leg of a chair, right in her crotch where there was no place for it to go. Just when it seemed like it was going to fit and she began to remember that something very important was happening to her, he was gone, and she felt the warm air cold where he had been.

"Hurry up," he urged her, frantic. "Someone might see us."

"I can't," she said, frantic herself now. "All this ick between my legs, and it smells so strong, like nothing I ever knew before."

"Well, now you do," he said, and scooped up a handful of leaves. "Here. Wipe yourself off."

On the way back to the car, Alma began to worry about what she had done. Martin didn't say much except "Come on" and "Gimme your hand," but she could tell he was nervous, too. And when he asked, "What about the curse?" all she could say was, "I don't know if it's okay," and she thought of all those girls on High Street that Ma was always tut-tutting about. Oh, God, would she get it, and she began to be afraid. Afraid to tell, of course, and afraid to ask Martin any questions, for in some way she didn't even know what had happened to her, and when Alma felt stupid she knew the best thing to do was to keep quiet and suffer. Oh, Lord, how she suffered.

Martin drove back down to the dump; neither one of them wanted to go home. They sat in the two-seater and watched the fires spread across the brush and the old paper bags and flare up before settling down to a good steady burn. The heat reached them even way back from the fire. The smell was so pungent it was almost a comfort to Alma in the midst of her unspoken misery. After a while Martin patted her knee the way you pat the rump of a dog when you're telling him to beat it.

Finally she asked because before much longer she just had to know.

"Was that the way it's supposed to be?"

"Sure."

"But it wasn't anything at all."

"It was okay by me."

"But there wasn't anything to it except you shoving it in. I thought it was supposed to be special, something about feeling all together with the person you do it with."

"Who told you that?" He looked at her for the first time since they had stopped to stare at the fires.

"Everybody knows that," she said defensively. Maybe she had it all wrong.

"You got that from being on the top of the Hill, all that romance and the right person. Serves you snooty people right. The real people in the world know better."

She'd get him for that. "What makes you think you're such a big guy at it? I know lots of boys . . ."

"Alma, you don't know anything."

Her ears pricked up. He was on edge now; maybe he wasn't such hot stuff, like he'd like her to think. "That was just a big show, Martin O'Shea. You hadn't ever done it before either."

"Oh, yes I have, but I always get scared about the baby and get out fast."

"Oh, God, Martin. I gotta get home and wash."

Chapter 14

———————⧈———————

ALMA KNEW she had slammed the door too hard in her exaggerated care to be quiet. Across the long foyer, through the screen door, she noticed that her mother was seated in a wicker garden chair on the piazza. They both raised a hand in greeting, but oddly enough, Ma did not call out to Alma. Jesus, she thought, does she know already? In that see-into-everything way of hers, were her eyes up there in the branches of one of those ancient trees? Panic overtook planning, two steps at a time up the circular staircase. She rested a moment on the blanket chest at the head of the landing. The latch clicked shut, and she remembered that the key was missing. I forgot, she thought disinterestedly; don't sit on the blanket chest. Right now it hardly mattered.

While the bath was running, fast and deep, she scrubbed the shorts of Martin's sister's bathing suit too hard, the fibers of the cotton knit tearing to form a small hole. She balled the wet cloth in her hand, squeezing the water out, and flung it into the wastepaper basket; on second thought retrieved the evidence, and unlocking the door on Mary's side of the bathroom, she stole naked down the shallow steps into her sister's empty room and to the closet, where the chute led directly to the incinerator two floors below in the basement. With some urgency, she returned to the seclusion of the bathroom and stepped into the tub, water so hot her ankles and calves were instantly red, as if the heat would kill any living thing. Alma lowered her bottom slowly into sitting position, the heat numbing her skin like the ocean in March; she washed lavishly with 99 and 44/100 percent pure Ivory soap. Doing something put her in charge again. Oh, God, make me pure, she intoned through tears of relief and anxiety, and I promise I will never do it again. Really, I promise. At least, not that way. Not until it's safe. Please, God.

Purged, cleansed, Alma dressed in a ruffled smocked pinafore thing, tiresome because it forced her to sit feet on the floor, knees together, rather than cross-legged in the chair, but unquestionably the right choice, since she knew it gave her mother the illusion that her daughter was demure and pure— oh, no, not now. She prepared to descend the serpentine staircase majestically—that meant slowly, one step at a time, posture A-plus, thank you very much, Miss Hughes, and all that— in hopes that Ma would see her first and greet her normally, not knowing what Alma knew, because Ma really couldn't know if Alma kept her wits about her. But at the foot of the stairs, Alma glanced right and saw the summer moths clustered about the overhead porch light, which gave no illumination in the evening daylight. Ma was somewhere out there, and Alma could bet she was harboring her old hopes and mistakes in judgment in that all-pervasive silence of hers that sometimes hung over Alma like a poncho, smothering her while she wore it for protection. The secrets between them this evening would be noisier than ever, but of course, Alma knew all Ma's secrets. Miss Carmody and sin and what a great boring English teacher Ma really was. For once Alma would miss the protection of her mother's disapproval of Daddy's "big-city ways," as she called it. She meant his drinking. There would be nothing to shield Alma, to help her keep inside what was bursting to get out. In fact, the longer she paused here in the hall, the more her thoughts stuck like a wad of chewing gum concealed under the edge of that marble slab. For a moment she saw the name and dates branded into the flesh of her back. Charles Henry Balfour,

1852–1917. The whole thing had come out wrong; nowhere could she remember any pleasure. Wasn't it supposed to be fun or special, something all warm to dream about? Could awful Martin O'Shea be right? Oh, the thought of Martin O'Shea, of all people. Now he'd never get out of her head.

She snorted out her perplexity. On another night, she might have chosen to make a grumpy remark and be allowed to eat in silence, but tonight Alma bore a new guilt, far more uncomfortable than that of being a disappointment to her mother. She resolved to be as pleasant as her principles made possible, depending on the topics up for conversation. Okay about Aunt Charlotte and her damn dying pain. And what was wrong with the tea sandwiches. But no talk about how Alma should be friendly with Betsy Benedict—Betsy never would do it, not even when she was all grown up—about summer plans, and for God's sake no talk about what did you do this afternoon.

Alma crossed before the doors to the dining room. The table was set for three. Immediately she glanced into the living room. Sherry or gin? Silver tray, ice bucket, mixing glass, gin bottle. Whiskey for daytime needs, martinis for after five. Daddy was expected. Knowing this, Alma didn't want to see him after all, particularly now, and she wondered if she could possibly still smell after all that washing. With his old peasant nose, he could fish out just about anything if he got mean enough. Between the two of them, I'm in for it tonight, she thought, and contemplated feigning illness, but that would only bring questions and the threat of examination. No, she would just have to brazen it out.

Out on the piazza, Alma watched her mother at a distance across the lawn—Ma was pinching off the hips on the lowbush roses—and she had a sudden glimpse into her father's face. She'd seen him studying Ma secretly and seen the unacceptable sadness on his judgmental face. The memory confused her and anger bloomed like a hardy perennial to fill in the pothole in her mind. Ma was graceful, Alma would give her that much, and she weighs less than I do, she thought. She regretted her choice of outfit for its appropriateness and slipped off her huaraches to appear barefooted, at least. But I'm taller, she went on, and younger, and someday later that will count.

Margaret Hughes turned and posed briefly, then glided diagonally over the grass toward Alma, holding the hard centers of the spent roses in her gloved palm. She inspected Alma's feet.

"You look very nice," she said pleasantly, dropping the fertility pods into a discard basket at the edge of the ivy bed.

Alma's tongue just froze at the back of her upper teeth, right in midformation. She never had had any small talk with her mother, only business, and she found it impossible to say thank you to anyone.

Without noticing Alma's silence, her mother passed her by and entered the house. For once she doesn't care about me, Alma realized with alarm. She went right in as if I weren't here. She's way off somewhere, hoping I'm not there. And Alma followed her mother quickly into the hallway.

"Daddy's coming. How come?"

"It's his home, Alma. He called to say he'd be home tonight for dinner." Margaret Hughes pulled off her gardening gloves and readjusted the lion's head ring she always wore on the little finger of her right hand.

"He'll be late," Alma announced, dropping her shoes on the rug.

"He'll be here any minute and we will sit down to table after cocktails." Margaret stored the gloves carefully in the bottom drawer of the highboy.

"Bridie will love that." Ma ignored the remark.

"Oh, dammit, Ma." Alma was getting back into shape. "Supposing I want to go out."

"You haven't discussed any plans with me, Alma. Now watch your language and put on your shoes before your father comes through the door."

They both heard the car door slam. The taxi had arrived; he was only thirty feet from them now.

"His nibs it is," said Alma, allying herself with Bridie, who moved quietly but attentively about the table in the next room, laying out the serving pieces. Alma looked in upon her. Bridie giggled.

"Shush, Alma. Bridie will hear you." Margaret was conspiratorial; mother and daughter shared a moment of levity. Could be worse, thought Alma.

"His nibs," she went on. "Sir Thomas Hamer Hughes, home from the wars, hail conquering hero, savior of mankind, friend of the dollar, royal statesman and lover. . . ."

Her mother hardened into a figurine of hurt like plaster setting fast in a mold.

Oh, God, I wish I were nice like Mary. When I do say something it's always wrong. I wish my tongue would drop out, and she bit it hard.

"I'm sorry, Ma," was all she could say, and she moved to extend her hand to her mother's shoulder with all the tentativeness of a young woman holding her baby for the first time.

The latch rattled; the door stuck in the summer. Her mother still motionless, Alma stepped forward awkwardly to open it. On the other side, a shadow of odd lines and angles in the diminished light, Thomas Hughes bent over where the door handle had been tugged unexpectedly from his hand. In the other he held a suitcase; his briefcase was pressed between his knees. He looked like a little boy who needed badly to go to the bathroom. Alma turned back to her mother while her father composed himself.

Thomas progressed the foyer, Margaret at midpoint like Hecuba awaiting Priam's greetings, only it wasn't. Baggage still in hand, he lifted his arms to embrace his wife; she turned to offer him a slippery soft cheek and moved from his reach. The suitcase dropped; he placed his hat on a side chair, his briefcase beside it. The defeat of both parties in the struggle lay upon the hallway, enveloping them all like the heavy smoke from a yet green log. In this moment of impotency, Alma wanted to hold both her parents, but she could not free herself from their sadness and her own monstrous ineptitude even to hug her father the way she should. When she was a child, small, when

Daddy came home then, the game had been to rush him and jump into his lap, only he was standing, she hanging from his neck. For his part, he would swallow her up, his arms squeezed tight about her waist, tortuous nibblings at her neck and ears. Ma had always stood behind her; Alma could feel her moving in, the way fog came off the water. Mary, too, waiting to kiss his cheeks. At the time Alma knew she took for granted that she came first. If Mary's face up there alongside Ma's looked pinched like a monkey's, it had seemed to Alma then that she deserved it for acting so superior because she was born good. Ma used to admonish Alma: "Your face will freeze that way," when she put on a pout or let the tears stream down her cheeks just for the sheer joy of being watched, but Alma never paid much attention to Ma since she knew she wasn't going even to be like Mary, much less look like her. After a while, as she grew older, Alma began to wonder. She noticed that when the bear-hugging was over and all the little pecks delivered, the business began; her parents got serious, the way adults do. Everything past and future—like how Alma threw a rock through the garage door or dug mouse holes in the wall with her new penknife; the expense of the dress Mary would need for the party, the recital, to receive the achievement award at school; the furnace on the blink, the automobile on the bust. Or the high interest rate to be placed on some kind of loan; balance of trade, problems at the bank. The present was simply swept away in the progression from hallway to drawing room, and with it Alma, and Mary, too. It was as if Alma had been sent as emissary to cross the no man's land between the two factions, the flag of truce that brought opponents together to get on with their warring. With time, she was even to become the spokesman for a cause. "Ask your father to consider a new stove." "Tell your mother we seem to be out of cognac." And now, Alma all grown, all thumbs when it came to loving, as they were, but at least mistress of her own secrets, she felt like a hired mercenary moved from one camp to the other according to supportive need.

Husband and wife proceeded to set places for the next scene, she on the end of the sofa, lost in the opulence of pillows, he in the club chair leaning over the cocktail tray. As Alma drifted stealthily out of view toward the stairs and her respite, she heard the opening round, rung in by the sound of the silver spoon with which he stirred the gin and vermouth, moving in and out among the cubes of ice, tapping the side of the mixing glass. The triumph of his council address countered by the success of her literary affair; soon to move on to the comments about this man or that—"a perfect fool"—and but-for-you-I-would-have been an exceptional teacher, a sensitive actress, sung together in parts, a cappella now, no captive children in support. It was a smooth performance, perfected over the years of partnership. By suppertime they would have reached the crescendo of silence: he searching out the food on his plate, his fork and knife as unsteady as his tongue wandering about his mouth as if a stranger to words; she in perfect complement, every movement controlled, every monosyllable a public speech. "Thank you, Bridie." "Would you care for more butter, Thomas?" They belonged to each other, they were bonded together, and Alma never knew where she came into it.

This evening will be longer and more unbearable than ever, Alma thought. And she stole up to her room, her dejection complete. She remembered the old joke she used to make with her friends about how her parents had only been to bed together twice—and oh, yes, there was the miscarriage. She used to say it in defiance of her parents' norm about suitable subjects for conversation, and it always brought on the giggles and the admiration of the assembly for daring to link sex and her own mother and father. She closed the door and flung herself across the double bed. What a baby I was then, another dumb kid. It was never a joke. I only stumbled on what was true. She called it out. And what with Martin and the graveyard today, and the not much that happened that flooded her head every time it emptied out, she guessed she was wrong all the time. She just didn't understand anything at all about sex.

Alma was called to dinner. The network of ties that enmeshed her parents was strung so tight this evening that Alma was squeezed out, unexpectedly allowed her own thoughts. She watched them, unnoticed, and realized that their silence was reflective, each one in his or her own discomfort. Her father's face was flaccid, the lids of his eyes drooped; she recognized the sagging as if the alcohol dried up the muscles of his cheeks like a worn-out old rubber band. How many times had she watched that come on? A sadness hung from him like the pouches of skin. And across from him her mother bowed her head. In supplication? In shame. It hit Alma and the food rose up in her throat. She swallowed hard. No, that's my secret. The fear traveled back down, her stomach settled. No, she said again to herself, they're with each other, only on opposite sides of the river and suddenly there's no bridge. Me? They don't even care about what happened to me today. If I told them right this minute, they're so far removed from me I couldn't even mechanize them into action. And she vowed to hate them again; it was better than this doubt.

But Daddy didn't give her a chance; he didn't wait until the end of the meal. When the salad was placed before him, little lettuce leaves from his own garden, he lifted a petal toward his mouth as he rose, trapped in a half crouch by the arms of the dining room chair. The oily dressing landed on his tie. Alma watched the spot saturate the silk dark to reach its perimeter. And she heard him begin his slow mount up the stairs, her mother watching from the foot of the table, so placed that she could see into the hall. It could hardly be much after eight o'clock.

Bridie came in to clear, and when her mother rose and went to settle into her seat on the sofa, ready to receive the coffee tray, one demitasse and the sugar lumps, Alma headed for the kitchen to sit on the stool amid the comforting debris of garbage on the dishes and the sink heaped with pots and pans. But then Bridie seemed desultory tonight. Late dinner meant her boyfriend would not come, since he had to be gone by ten. And Alma knew her mother had her reservations about the wisdom of having him stay to such an hour.

She moved to the back door and placed her hands above her

head on the highest of the wooden crossbars that formed the panels of the screened frame. She laid her forehead on the fine wire netting and it gave way slightly, forming a pocket to cradle her. In her listlessness she was able to recognize the smell as summer night air, and then she could remember to let the gentleness of the evening brush past her, caressing her. She cried softly into the brittle screen mask, which hugged her whole face now as she pushed against it; such gentle tears were a tenderness she rarely allowed herself. She knew she could ring up a friend, or pedal her bike around the block, making broad swoops on the empty street, testing her balance, and wondering what was going on in the lighted rooms as she passed the neighborhood houses. She could even visit Martin's family —Martin himself didn't enter into her sadness now. But only the truth interested her, about herself, so stark and lonely that there was nothing to be done about it. She must prepare herself for it, and pushed open the door. In the heavenly blue light she went to lie on the cool earth beneath the dogwood tree, her head placed at the base where the roots went underground, out of sight, reaching into the darkness to provide the nutriments that grew the tree up there for the sun to kiss, the world to see and praise. A tree was a lucky thing, Alma conjectured, and felt a little bit smart in ways she knew mattered only to her. A tree was given a new chance every year, the dead limbs pruned away, the new growth encouraged to produce. But it was too late for her, almost sixteen and hopeless. And she stretched out straight, on her back, her ankles crossed, her hands one on top of the other over her breast. She lay down to die. She might as well.

The only thing she wanted was to be cared about—just for herself, sometimes in spite of herself—but somehow she wasn't worth that. Her parents couldn't find a moment outside themselves to fill her up, and she worked so hard to be noticed that they never saw that all she wanted was them. If she could just shrivel up and die for lack of nourishment, then they'd know what they were missing. But sometimes she wondered about that, too. Maybe they wouldn't care any more than the relief they felt when she wore the right dress or did something okay in school.

"Alma, you're out there."

She didn't answer and Bridie slammed the door, mad. The lights went out in the kitchen.

Alma rolled over and clutched her stomach, her knees pulled up, her pinafore bunched, exposing her bottom to the yew bushes. She rolled back and forth to dirty herself. "And the worst of it is"—she spit out a sour fallen petal—"I don't even know what love is."

Chapter 15

———————— ·❦· ————————

SHE REALLY HAD no intention of falling asleep; hanging on to life seemed more important now than death. If she really began to think about it, the idea of death disturbed Alma more than all this worry about loving, and right now she had this scary feeling that if she shut her eyes something so terrible would happen that she shouldn't even waste time trying to imagine it. She lay on her side, almost motionless in her bed, the thin percale sheet pulled up to cover her naked body. While she had brushed the dirt from her arms and washed her hands, it gave her some pleasure to feel the soil between her toes, and she knew that the scaly tissue of her heels looked like the heaves of parched earth. She began to feel comfortable here in her own bed where only she belonged.

She rolled over onto her back, her hands beneath her head, her elbows jutting out so that her arms formed a triangle, the wide-angle point where her cleavage would have been if she weren't just about completely flat-chested, particularly in this position. By pulling in her stomach she formed a cavity between her pelvic bones, her ribs sticking out; she ran the toes of her right foot up the shinbone of her left leg. And she thought of the pleasure she took in her own body when she was alone like this, no one around to make her feel lumpy and ugly, awkward and unknowing.

She remembered very clearly, and she was still puzzled and hurt. She saw the little Alma, four years old perhaps, standing near the lowboy in the dining room, where Ma kept her pocketbook in the racks amongst the silver trays and platters. The little girl was holding one hand out to receive the nickel from her mother that would buy her a Good Humor stick when the man pedaled his ice cream wagon along Pembroke Avenue to settle in at the corner by the Wheelers' house. Her mother searched out her change purse and turned around to face her. Alma stuck out her finger and touched her mother's summer dress at the joining of her legs.

"That's where you weewee."

Her mother struck Alma's hand with such force that it turned white before the blood rushed back in under the skin, and she wore her stubby child's finger in a splint for two or three weeks. Nothing had even been said; Mary and Daddy were told she'd broken it playing. And the unspoken wrong, a secret between Ma and Alma, was forever a reminder that bodies were not to be shared.

And now she thought with shame on the events of the afternoon. How Ma would be disappointed in her if she knew, for being fast and cheap—"A boy will take advantage of you, Alma. It is your responsibility to be in charge; boys just get carried away. But if you let one do so he will never respect you again" —and even worse, it was despicable Martin. Somebody named Martin O'Shea had something against her. That would upset both her parents. The badness of being Alma Hughes just seemed to come naturally to her, more and more now. Growing up made it secret and that made it worse.

The sound of her father's wheezing in the corridor outside her door startled her, as if he had heard her thinking. It must be almost midnight. Ma's sleeping and Daddy's up again. Did nothing ever pass between them? The latch on her door came loose the way it always did to the slightest motion, and she stared up at the wedge of white ceiling illuminated from the light in the hall, door ajar. She held her breath, then relaxed: the measured shuffle of his slippered feet on the runner to the head of the stairs, the slow pace down, one step at a time, across the foyer, through the dining room to the pantry, where the brandy lived under the flower sink with the cutting scissors and the picnic basket, a family closet. Alma didn't have to be along with him to know where he was going.

Oh, dear God, she thought, I hope he doesn't want to lie beside me tonight, to stroke my hair and tell me what a nice little girl I am, and all the time him smelling so of brandy and cigars—"his little pleasures," he called them as if they, too, were his children. She wouldn't be able to breathe, especially this night when she was already choking on her sins against him. Alma's mother always said she had no proper morals, no ethics, and on account of him. He had refused to let Mary and Alma receive proper religious education at the Episcopal Sunday school alongside the other children on Pembroke Avenue. He had told Ma to go to the devil, there was nothing in this church hogwash. But often Ma hung her head and told Alma she'd have been better off knowing the Bible, right from wrong.

And suddenly Alma recited the Lord's Prayer, learned for desperate occasions, about trespass and forgiveness and evil. Loud and clear she spoke it and hoped it would hold back whatever it was in her that made her be just exactly what they didn't want.

Her atonement complete, Alma felt more comfortable within herself again, and she may have dozed; in fact, she did. When she awoke, the summer's night was darker, and Daddy was there, slipped between the sheets this time, lying at her side. His closeness terrified her, no covering to divide them. She abruptly turned her back on him, feigning sleep, and inched away. He followed her, his hand stroking down her bare arm, his frowzy voice mumbling things she could not understand; she only knew he was in pain like some injured animal and she had let him down again, for she could not bring herself to answer him. There, beneath his pajama bottoms, she imagined where it would lie between his legs, and she feared for herself and the thought of it. But she knew he would never touch her where he should not; he was only asking for her affection in some way she did not know about. It would be all right: he was her father; she had not wanted this. She reassured herself as she continued to move imperceptibly on the sea of her bed, floating out of his reach to safety and the floor.

Too late. Between her buttocks she felt the soft mass of protruding flesh, squishy, formless, squeezed against her skin. Her thigh muscles rippled instinctively like the shank of a horse dusting off a fly. His knee touched the back of hers. She lurched forward to the edge of the mattress, clinging to the horizon. He moaned at her the way she imagined the dying left a message to those still allowed to live, and listening, she hesitated a moment. He clasped her in his arms, his hand brushing her breast, his soft stomach nestled into the small of her back.

She stiffened.

The slit of light on the ceiling ten feet away slowly broadened to form an ill-defined rectangle.

The scene froze; no one moved. This present would be with them forever.

Alma dared to look down and saw a shapely gray silhouette. It could only be her. Her mother was standing in the doorway.

"Thomas," Margaret whispered. "Thomas." The familiar voice gained the strength to move in front of the epilogue curtain. "Thomas," she said, and there was silence.

"Thomas. Think of the child."

Part
Five

Chapter 16

———————···⟨∞⟩···———————

ALMA THOMAS could not sleep. After the brief respite from her turmoil, swaddled in her anger at James, for some minutes she enjoyed the welcome relief that follows violence, a sense of a job well done, good riddance, and she dozed in a cozy after-noon-nap way. But gradually the enormity of her act dawned, the preposterousness of her feelings toward him, and then the stunning realization that she was struggling with something buried in the pit of her brain like a tumor as big as a water-melon, pressing against her skull, the vine weaving in and out the crevices, the yellow flowers as big as her fist ready to form more fruit. And with terror she knew her head was going to burst, splinter, brains, bones, pieces of skin blown all over the walls of the bedroom. She left her bed in escape, and standing in the hall, noticed that the door to James's study was pressed tight into the frame. The unnaturalness of this barrier into the room excluded her. Carefully she pressured the swollen door from its frame and looked in. The sight of him filled her with an unexpected tenderness and the sudden thought that she might have driven him too far away this time; he might not make the return journey to her. She studied him. He lay on the old day bed under the Indian throw, curled up like a fetus around the untied springs, and she remembered with pleasure the stab in the back she used to get when they made love on this their marriage couch. That's twenty years, give or take, she thought.

And she saw her isolation from him for the first time in her life. This time he would have to choose her. She could not cajole, request, demand acceptance. Good girl or bad must go. She was who she was; maybe he'd like her, maybe not. The back and forth of their relationship exhausted her. Somewhere locked up in her overstuffed head was the clue to their peace, but she felt no assurance that she would ever find it.

She drifted down the stairs like a sleepwalker, unawares, passed other rooms that housed the pieces of her life, the doors shut against intrusion, and she thought how lighter than air she would feel when she had finished with their growing and could get back to her own. In the kitchen, she turned on the gas flame under the teakettle, a kind of automatic gesture, a filler, a what to do before the plumber comes, the doctor, the undertaker. She stood at the back door and looked out into the darkness, noticing how light the night sky was at this time of year, the shadows of the railing on the porch, the zinnia heads just forming, the branches of the maple tree, even the neighbors' lawn furniture across the boxwood hedge that separated one garden from the next, each receding band in the watercolor a thinner wash so that in the far distance the chain-link fence seemed like a mass of silver light beyond the darkened obstacles in the foreground. The faint moon wore two masks, pockmarked both tragic and comic.

She listened for the escaping steam, then turned and saw the base of the aluminum kettle glowing red over the edges of the flame. Hastily she extinguished the heat and moved the empty kettle to cool on the enameled surface of the stove. So much for administering to the needy. I can't even make myself a cup of tea in the midst of my mourning, and she wondered at the intensity of her undefined calm, as if she had not the capacity to even identify what she had lost.

Back upstairs, Alma glanced at the mess that was her childhood still strewn about the room and lay down again on the bed to study the ceiling, dirty white, fingerprints where she had steadied herself changing the light bulb, water stains over in the corner. The roof leaked, a punctured lid just like her own self-deceptions, which had conveniently provided protection all these years from the other half of the truths that combine to make up the whole game, like one of those smarts tests: Draw a line indicating which word listed on the left matches up with one in the right-hand column:

mis	laid
hand	made
maiden	head
double	bed
de	cease
make	peace

She felt the numbness branch across her right shoulder, fear just stretching in an expansive way after a restorative rest. She closed her eyes; that's enough, she said to herself, and as if to roll over on her own thoughts and bury them alive, she curled up on her side, struggling to bring the summer coverlet, a crumpled rag at the foot of the bed, along with her. She opened her eyes briefly to locate the sheet as well.

In the murkiness cast by the drawn shades before the sun bursts through ethereal night's retreat to promise burgeoning life anew each day, Alma purloined the sheet from where it hid and tried to hang on to limbo. Before her tight-shut eyes the pictures spun into bright colors which became shadows. She gave up and looked at the clock. The Roman numerals glared back at her. Almost five-thirty, five twenty-five more like it, the stubby arrow just out of the V, the leaner, swifter hand just moving in. The face looked out at her, tired-eyed and pleading, a fringe of graying hair, large nose, sensuous lips. Her father's middle-aged specter faded. She sat up abruptly, prepared to escape the bed again. Her mother stood in the doorway, van-ished, reappeared, then vanished again.

Alma bolted, past the closed-off rooms that sheltered every-one who made up her new life, the pads of her bare feet touching the fuzzy weave of the stair runner, hitting the smooth boards of the hall, cushioned by the carpeting again, hard across the kitchen linoleum. On the soft grass she stopped and approached the rose bed rather gingerly, holding out her hand to the side as she had done when she and her father had snuck up on the opened coffin twelve years ago, only this time she was alone. She heard her father's voice, uncharacteristically small and wobbly, and she heard the speech he had delivered over the body of his dead wife, her every hair in place, hands manicured, her face young-beautiful in the subtle rejuvenation death had brought like a birthday gift. "Well, Margaret," he had said, "I never thought I'd see you like this. I always planned to go first."

When Alma touched the dew-damp white tea rose in front of her, the tough thorn lodged in her forefinger, and as she drew her hand away the movement caused her nightgown to brush the stalk. The rosebush clung to her in a forever embrace. Alma began the careful disentanglement, gently lifting the tricot nylon off the tiny spears, the pulled threads forming a jagged path like stepping stones leading from her breast down to her thigh.

"I didn't know anything about that sort of thing, Ma," as she worked the material, one hand bunching up the nightgown so as to create no tension, the other plucking at the bush tentatively, aware that each prick meant another spot of blood to stain. "And my guess is that Daddy didn't know much either. Honest, Ma, I know you thought he was a sex fiend, what with Miss Carmody and all the others, but I bet you he wasn't." Ouch. She paused to suck her thumb. "He had no business doing that to either of us, but he was so boozed out of it he couldn't even know the awfulness of what he was doing. He probably never even remembered the next morning." She drew back, finally freed. "Christ, Ma. Drunk like that, how could he even get it up?"

Poor bastard, she thought, and started back to the house, the wet grass sticking up between her toes, providing a sort of soothing, porous sponge to her heels. The confusion was flowing down her trunk to collect in her roots like warmed-up untapped sap.

She went directly up to James, shoving impatiently, her shoulder to the doorjamb. In passing through she noted her junk in his room and made a mental note that this was the day she would move her childhood out of the way, out of his territory, store it all in the basement, the subterranean beginnings of her part of Ned and Polly's lives. She and James were the foundation; the structure was up to them. She paused in the middle of the room to consider what would happen then to her, what superstructure could she build. The way cleared, maybe he'd invite her into his seclusion. There'd be more room now, and after all, she was just one neat and tidy package, really. Sometimes she needed a new box, a fresh gay ribbon around her, but James liked receiving gifts. Maybe this time when he opened her up he'd know what to do with her. Not in the filing cabinet; she'd had that, handy reference. Nor on the bookshelves. No. Perhaps this time the centerpiece of his worktable, mixed in with his manuscripts and books, and those crummy paperbacks that were his secret delight, his craving like a dieter's spoon plunged into the peanut butter.

She pulled off her nightgown and hunched in under the smelly cover, curled around his body, pressed against him to realize him. He heaved and halted the natural extending of his left leg. The pain almost woke him and he groaned. Oh, God, she thought, always the initiator, good and bad. And then she remembered her promise to herself: not anymore. For the first time in several days, or was it months, she felt sleep climb into her limbs, lie down on her eyelids to celebrate some peace attained. She savored every moment of falling into it.

The telephone rang, one, two, three. Let someone else answer it. And then it came to James that he was not in his own bed, Alma's famous monument to marital discord, sleeping next to the bedside table where the telephone was placed so that either of his children could call at one in the morning, let's say, highway accidents, drug arrests galvanizing him into alertness, to tell him that Tom and Liz had just come into town and needed a place to stay. Now he found himself lying on his right side, crowded against the wall of his study, body stiff, the back of his head pushed painfully forward against his temples, his nose touching the white plaster. The slab that lay pressed against his backside moved in and out of the curves of his shoulders, small of his back, bend in his knees. Breasts as smooth as marble squeezed into the flesh of his shoulder blades; exhaled breath tickled his neck. He was wedged in between Scylla and Charybdis, the mountain of blank wall that sometimes mirrored his own inadequacies to match the rock that presently threatened to suffocate him, and like Odysseus, he thought he had better get out fast or be crushed between his fear of Alma's rejection of him and the awful anger he sometimes felt just plain having to put up with her. And so, godlike, as wily as his Greek counterpart, he prepared to move swiftly to escape extinction.

The pain pierced up his left leg to lodge in his groin, the poisoned arrowhead, the memory of her unforgivable act of violation the night before too deeply embedded in his aching brain to be easily extracted. Hostility shoved hangover aside. He hit her inert form with his left fist, catching her at the hipbone, where he knew she would carry a hideous patch of bruise, purple to black to yellow, for several days. She shrieked and jumped from the couch to stand foolishly draped in the bedspread. Exposed to her, he slowly rolled over onto his back so she could fully see the quiescence of his manhood, the thing he would never get up for her again.

"You're mad."

"You're surprised?"

She was; he could see her face searching in the costume box for the right expression. She couldn't find it.

"I'm not going to play games with you, James. I promised myself I wouldn't. Not this time."

"Well, quit it right now, then."

"You can take me as I am, like it or not. I've got to be me, James."

"Oh, tell me at last you've found yourself." He rolled over. "Again and again, play it again."

"This time I mean it, James."

"Shove it, Alma."

"Don't speak to me like that, James. You're worse than either of the children."

"Alma," and he raised his unmanageable body to sitting position.

Alma backed off. She could already feel the clout at her side. Once she had drunk a whole bottle of Fleurie to accompany the steak and mushrooms she had fancied up for herself to rejoice that he was going off on a not-quite-all-expenses-paid lecture trip to Oxford, Bonn and Warsaw. When he came in that evening she had called him nothing much bad for leaving her with the hard part of life, the damn domestic scene. Well, he'd been out for the beer-with-the-boys bit, some inner-circle talk, and was feeling pretty good about getting rid of her for a month, she could tell that, and he got scary angry and gave her a black eye. All he did when she said, cool and to the point, "James, you're nothing but a jellyfish," was walk up to her where she sat at the dining room table in her solitary splendor and say, "Alma." Then he punched her. No one believed the walked-into-the-door line, and she wore dark glasses for two weeks, all through the pre-Christmas shopping season. That was some years ago now, maybe five. He moved in slow burn cycles, but she could feel this one coming on. He started to try to get off the day bed, but she made it through the door before he could figure out how to move his injured leg. Later, she said to herself. He'll understand all about everything, her daddy and Ma and everything, later. And he'll know who I am then. He'll be glad, won't he?

Alma dressed in work outfit—bare feet, cut-off jeans and a sleeveless cotton shirt shrunk up and stretched out in the hot cycle of the dryer to fit over a barrel of pickles—proper seasonal discard clothes, because she already knew that the easiest way to make order out of chaos was via the trash baskets. She hoped she would be able to make this second trip through her uncomfortable gains, her family possessions, a quick one. It didn't matter that the face of the old man read twelve o'clock, the Sunday morning gone, or hang too heavy on her that at this moment James was not a sure win, her bet placed. Somehow she felt it had not been one of those lost weekends from which the routine of her job on Monday morning sometimes came as a relief from misunderstood conflicts unresolved.

She began again, with a fresh cup of coffee. She could tell in the kitchen that the children had been playing grown-up house —the garlic press on the stove, the slightest of juices dripping over the edge of the burner, the very place to mix a salad. But she went again to the garden, always the place of her preliminary codging. She halted abruptly on the porch to take in the scene.

"Hi, Ma." Polly lifted a damask napkin in greeting. To Alma's astonishment, she was dusting off place mats, the ones from Polynesia or Haiti or some rattan sort of place. On the picnic table the wineglasses glistened in the sun, the silver ready to be set. The salt dish would be filled with Malden's sea salt, the pepper mill with something to grind. Ned hovered over the hibachi, stirring the red-hot coals with a pair of long-handled tongs to send up little satellites of sparks into the heat of the midday, something James was fond of playing at, a man's chance to relive the illicit lighting of matches, the secret of his childhood. The steak was on the ironstone platter, ready for the cooking.

"Hello there, Ma." Next he will be doing that calypso motion with the martini shaker like the handsome young executive in the poolside advertisement.

Alma spotted the salad bowl on the bench, carefully pushed under the table, and along with it the butter plate, the wine jug, the covered bread basket, a thoughtful plan to keep off the sun. And most unlikely of all, the realization filling her up like a water tank, a pint of worry, a quart of disbelief, a magnum of pleasure, Alma noted that Polly wore an attractive blue patchwork sundress, her shoulders bare and smooth, her toes nestled into a pair of thonged sandals. Ned had on the embroidered shirt his grandmother had brought him from her last trip—was it Greece?—open neck exposing the depression between the clavicle and the tufts of hair on his chest. Until now he had refused to wear it on the grounds it made him too good-looking.

Alma looked down at her dirty feet and ragged pants. She felt a perfect fool, little Miss Hughes revisited, and she had nothing to say until spoken to.

"Hand me the clippers, would you, Ma. I think some of your roses would look nice on the table." This from Polly. Imagine.

Alma formed the question in her head, but the words failed to come out, Obedient and unusually subdued, she returned to the kitchen to collect the cutting shears. Polly followed her to fetch a pottery vase, the acme of Alma's years at the wheel when the children were middle-aged and the family kept at-home-after-school hours, Alma on duty. In those days she had filled her mornings with crafts and good works. She handed the shears to Polly and was allowed to hold the vase in return. She filled it with water while Polly clipped, stem just long enough for arranging but expertly leaving the cluster of leaves to branch into new growth and further bloom. Alma watched in awe.

"It all looks so nice," she said, addressing the host and hostess as they moved about their preparations knowingly, casual, so-cial sophisticates. "What's the occasion?"

"Well, Ma, maybe we weren't quite fair on you and Dad last night. After all, it *is* your house."

His understanding mate took up where he left off. "And re-ally, I shouldn't be vulgar to Daddy; I know he doesn't like me to use that kind of language, and he really means well. He loves me. Sometimes he just doesn't realize he's getting old and needs to be a little more careful. He doesn't want to be one of those disgusting old men who talk about breasts and how 'comely' girls look. You know, like Judge Nutter."

I couldn't agree with you more, Polly, Alma thought. Judge Nutter, now about eighty-something, had always been a lech as long as Alma could remember, about as inviting-looking as the underbelly of a fish. But the stunning idea of anyone thinking of James as old made her giggle. The innocence of his little girl's patronizing was ironic. In his present state of capacity to love, it's just as well he missed that one.

Alma stepped from the porch onto the lawn. "Come on, Ma," Ned said, and gently. "Stretch out on the chaise there. You're not what you used to be. We're going to take care of you."

Alma looked hard at him, her pride, her joy. Wasn't that what she was supposed to feel? She produced him, carried him around all those months on the inside, all those years on the outside, to nursery school, to hockey practice, to traffic court. Had he really delivered that speech? This scenario was right off the old man's video box. "James"—she heard the dialogue—"at last you've come. Your children have turned us willy-nilly into our dotage, they're caring for us, we need them, the end of the world is come." How long had they worked to produce this charming drama?

She laid herself out as directed, crossed her bare ankles, quickly uncrossed them. "With advancing age, water tends to collect in the tissues," she had read somewhere. "It is nothing to be overly concerned about. If there is much discomfort, see your doctor at once. Try to avoid unnecessary pressure, particularly on the legs. Put your feet up when you have a spare moment. Just relax and enjoy the good things in life." The screen door slammed. There he stood, shirtless and unshaven, the belt of his gardening pants tucked sweetly under his slightly protruding belly. From the expression on his face, the next move was to apply the paint following the war council.

"The kids are making a lovely lunch for us." She tried out her wifely voice.

"Yeah, Dad. After the falling out we all had last night, we wanted to do something for you and Ma."

"Falling out." James tested his son's words. "Better say 'kicking out.' Your mother came at me like the viper she is and I damn near got my leg busted for the privilege of sharing her snake pit." He hobbled forward.

"I heard this racket up there, after Ma let me go downstairs again," said Polly. "I guess you'd gone up to bed."

"Speak to the lady in question, Polly. There she is, Cleopatra on her barge."

"We don't want to get into any of your business, Dad." Ned being protective.

"Why not? Don't you think you ought to know she tried to kill me?"

"Oh, come on"—both children at once. They spoke with such vigor that James heeded the yellow signal.

"Well, okay, but she kicked me out of bed and I got it in the leg, right on the radiator."

Everybody turned to look at Alma.

"Okay, okay." She could hear the defensiveness twanging out of her. "I did. I'm sorry. I had my own reasons and I want to tell James about them."

"I don't want to hear them. No more trips down memory lane, Alma."

"Don't be mean, Daddy." Polly began to set the table.

Ned snapped the kitchen tongs at her. "Well, after all, she did kick him out of bed."

"Cut that out, Ned." Polly plunked down a fork.

Ned looked oh-my-God at her. "Man, you women always stick together when the awful truth is out."

"Enough, kids, that'll do." James made it to the edge of the chaise and lowered himself down beside Alma's legs. Alma was reminded of Polly's challenge, was it only yesterday? The way she had stretched out lazily and just the touch of her foot on her father's shoe was enough to cement him to his daughter. Alma would try it. Gingerly she extended her toe to brush the offended left thigh.

"I'm sorry," she said.

James was silent awhile. They waited. "Okay," he said, placing his hand on her leg, "I believe you. You never say you're sorry. Now get me a beer."

"We're having wine for lunch, Daddy."

"Righteo, Polly Peachum. Pour a couple of glasses for Mrs. Peachum and myself."

Chapter 17

---·⦅∞⦆·---

AFTER LUNCH Alma suffered a drugged feeling, her stomach full where it rested on her upper thighs, her arms and feet tingly, her head heavy, threatening to snap off at the very top of her backbone. Wine and the sun, and the lovely sense of time off for good behavior, for it had been a very nice meal. She lay down on the bench of the picnic table, setting her head on James's thigh. Without words but rather with simple body language, he told her. Pass your partner, slide to the right, swing your partner, hold on tight. He slipped along the bench, lifting her head, and released it the couple of inches onto the wooden slats. A little punishment felt good. But be careful, she thought, not too much too soon. And she tried to remind herself that it was all right to be who she was. Remember, he could take her or leave her, for better or worse, et cetera, et cetera. She looked up at the underside of the table, grass clippings and dirt clinging tenuously.

He'd better take me, she said to herself, and rolled over, dropping the foot and a half to the ground.

"Good God, Ma. You drunk?" Ned moved to stand over her.

"Your mother can hardly smell a glass of wine anymore without requiring hospitalization. She ain't what she used to be."

"Don't be so unreasonable, Dad. She's your wife."

"Say, whose side are you on? I thought you just grew to manhood about one hour ago when it came to you that in the squeeze these women stick together."

"That's not always true, Daddy." Even from the tone they all knew Polly was staging a comeback. "Sometimes I like you."

The flippancy of the delivery touched Alma where she knew it would hurt James. Better anger than that, and she knew what to do.

"I was expressing my freedom," Alma announced to her family. "I just wanted to flop down where I was and be me."

James looked down at her, she up at him. She saw it coming. It had worked. "Flop down. Six feet deep," he said.

"Ma, sometimes I don't think you'll ever be a grownup; it's embarrassing. Like you get so excited about everything and then you do dumb things like that."

"Well, Polly dear"—Alma spoke slowly—"in that case, for your own sake, I hope you never grow up either."

"What do you mean by saying something like that, Mother dear?" Polly was off center enough to try patronizing again. How comforting that I can still play with her, Alma thought, even if it means playing dirty.

Ned began his shuffle of retreat. "This is getting too heavy for me," he cast back his benediction.

"Hey, wait a minute. What about the dishes?" Polly hollered. "I got to go to work. All night over a hot grill."

"Later."

"Well, I'm not doing them," and she followed her brother into the house.

"Jesus, Alma," James said, "back to square one."

"Familiarity is more comfortable, though," and Alma rolled under the bench to raise the right pant leg and kiss the hairy back of his leg.

Together they cleared the table, Alma doing the big load, James carrying the four wineglasses by the base from between his fingers so that they hung like stalactites or was it stalagmites? Alma washed up, the terrible burden of rinsing and placing the dishes in the dishwasher. Back in the good old days of Alma's serious domesticity she hand-washed and dried at least a dozen glasses emptied of Kool-Aid, just for a seasonal starter. Sometimes Polly stood on a stool before the sink, elbow deep in soap bubbles, helping Mummy, and Alma didn't mind the rewash or the mopping up afterward. Now it was a major project to get any member of the family to unload the clean dishes, it seemed like such a commitment to housework.

When she went upstairs she carried the box of disposable green trash bags with her, visions of instant order lined up before the oak banister in the hall outside her bedroom like the gay napkins bulging with celebration surprises set beside each place at a children's party. Alma's monstrous offerings of goodies would be festively tied with plastic twistums and immense enough to deck out a party for Lemuel Gulliver's acquaintances in the land of Brobdingnag. In the room, she faced the easy part first, roughly stuffing in the period-piece clothes for throwing out to form the first lumpy ballooned sack. On second thought she called down to Polly did she want any of these things as costumes.

"No, Ma. Those days are over by about six years, remember?"

Oh, yes.

And so she emptied out the bag onto the floor again to make sure and turned to hang up the handsome evening gown she knew she wanted. Come on, Alma, it's got to be now, not sometime. I know you, she said to herself. Tomorrow? she asked back. Not this time, kid. Remember everyone is getting edgy about all this mess, inside you and out. I thought you told me you understood it all. Well, I do, she said firmly to herself. Okay, then get on with it.

She restuffed the bag, closed it with a flourish and staggered with it into the hall. "How can clothes be so heavy?" she asked James, standing at the door of his study.

He moved away from his desk. "Not just clothes, Alma; your mother's trappings." He reached for something. "Don't forget this fruity hat in here," and without so much as a pang of remorse he wadded it up in his hands and threw it to her. Alma watched with horror, her mother's skull crushed before her eyes, but she stooped to pick it up and added it to the discards without comment.

She carried the books to the basement, the trash to the street, then carefully made up a box of sample keepsakes to act as a history for Polly and Ned, who after all would someday be old enough to be both curious and humane. Alma selected; her mother had made the mistake of saving everything so that all together they had no meaning. A program from the Welsh Society, a Sunday night in 1912, Vice-President Thomas Hamer Hughes singing solo. Margaret MacNeil's college-society pin. Old copies of *Life* magazine. A clay pipe. Her father's Ph.D., framed, all crinkled under the glass. A sporting golf cap, dirty white linen. The architectural plans for the Hughes's dream house, come true, of course. The bracelet engraved "Margaret Elizabeth," worn by her own aunt, dead many years before her own birth. It felt strange to handle the dead girl's treasure and she wondered for the first time what the girl would have been like as a woman. Like her father, maybe like herself? Her choices made, she turned in the flaps of the box to hold it shut and wrote: "Polly and Ned, fun later," with a Magic Marker on the top. She retrieved her soiled wedding dress from the floor of James's study, where it had spent a bridal weekend, and put it back in with her mother's. On the way down the stairs with the unwieldy white box for storage below, she suddenly wondered what it would smell like thirty, maybe forty years from now, when it was next likely to be opened. I'm preserving more than you think, kids, and she hoped her children would realize sometime when they got around to thinking on the subject that when their parents made love they knew how to like it. And that made her think for the first time that she hoped they liked it, too, when they bedded down with some permanency.

Back upstairs she pondered, the hardest for the last. And then she resolved to put the photographs and portraits back in the drawers of the highboy now in the living room, the same one from which she had unloaded them months back when it still lived in the Pembroke Avenue house. She collected the letters from the floor where she had left them. She and James had walked all over them like the faces of the dead for two days now. In an unusual way they had been used and deserved the peace of extinction. Another trash bag. But this time she could not. She slipped them back into the shoe box, string and messages to boot, and hid the box at the back of the closet mixed in with dust-laden suede pumps and wooly winter slippers. In James's study, she tried to move the gilt-edged mirror. It was to hang in the front hall, where visitors would surreptitiously snatch a glimpse of themselves in the old darkened antique glass while pretending to admire the delicacy of the filigreed festoons of gold petals that formed the peak at the top of the frame.

She turned to face James, who sat at his desk again. "I can't move this thing alone. You want to help?"

"I've only one leg, love."

"Oh, I forgot."

"Not me. Every time I move I am reminded how much you care for me."

"I do, James."

"Well, it doesn't feel like it."

Alma went to sit on the day bed and he turned his chair slightly sideways to face her.

"Listen," she said, leaning into him, "you're right to be wrong about me. It's nasty to get busted up in the leg; you're right. But unless you let me tell you how I feel, you'll go on being wrong about me and we'll both be hurt."

James inched his chair forward with his good leg until the bad one rested outstretched beside Alma's left haunch. "I have a hard time with your Hughes logic, but nothing would please me more than to be wrong about you, Alma. I never know whether to be angry or sad. Right now I just hurt, outside and in. You must know all about that, you always say it hurts worse inside."

"My God," she said, touching his left leg. "Sorry," when he flinched. "Hey, that's the most revealing statement you've ever made; you're actually talking about feelings."

"Alma, honey." She saw his face was pinched up with a new

214

kind of pain. "You always think you have a monopoly on those things. Airing them is your hobby. The way some people whittle driftwood or collect miniature porcelains." He looked tired. "Living with you is like living inside a hi-fi set. Sometimes I'm deafened by you, but when the noise clears, yes, I have feelings, too."

Alma let out a little sigh. "I guess maybe sometimes I'm too intense for you, and I never stop long enough to feel guilty about you."

James looked beyond her head into the niche in the wall above where she sat. Here he displayed his *objets,* a hodge-podge like these famous feelings he was sounding so sure about. The precious machete of his youth; a postcard picture of an old clay tablet in an ancient language he couldn't read very well; the little pillow on which Polly had embroidered a heart, back when their love affair was two-sided; the woody mushroom reading "Ned—Dad." His favorite picture of Alma apparently had fallen on its face; at least he realized it was out of view. It was one he had taken maybe five or six years ago, all artsy shadows, Alma and the maple tree. She looked wonderfully wild, the collar of her coarse knit sweater turned up like a ruff, her hair messed up and falling across her face in ragged ends. She looked like a blond version of Anna Magnani or the young Catherine the Great.

He noticed her silence as unusual and it was just such un-predictability in her that he envied.

"I love you for all the things that drive me crazy." He ad-dressed her with frightening seriousness, as if his love for her might be diagnosed as a degenerative disease.

"Well, then you'll understand." She bounced back.

"What?"

"About Daddy."

"Oh, Alma," he said, throwing his head aside as if he wished it would go out the opened window.

"In bed," she said.

"Yeah, I know all about how the drunken lout used to lie

down beside you and tell you what a princess you were. That's why you don't like it if I just go to sleep. Maybe you miss being his pet pussycat."

"Pass out, James. It's called passing out." They both moved away from each other so that leg no longer brushed thigh.

"Okay, pass out. Who cares?"

"Passed out, you're out of it. You don't know what you do."

"Not so, Alma. You've lost track of your old theme song. Passed out means out of it, you can't do anything."

"Maybe that's okay. Maybe you're right. It's like desertion."

"Alma, why are we doing this one again?"

"Because once he climbed under the sheets and pushed his no-good, passed-out penis right into my bottom."

"Jesus Christ." He moved his leg toward her again. "That's being more than a dirty old man. That's disgusting."

"Well, I don't know. Maybe I wanted him to do it."

His eyes disappeared behind his glasses. He closed them to see into his head, or not to see her, she didn't know which. "Alma," he exclaimed, "that's incest. Alma, you're both disgusting."

"Come on," she said defensively, "haven't you ever lusted after Polly, the way you want her to be gentle with you? Maybe you're just her dirty old man."

"Yes and no, Alma; I'm normal. But I'd never touch her. It would ruin her."

"I know," said Alma, thinking of the childlike timidity that guided her when she looked at her full-grown son.

"No wonder you're so unhinged, Alma." James spoke as if sentenced to purgatory. "Your whole family is revolting to think about. The frigid old lady with a ramrod up her ass, and that dribbly old man who sneaks up on you and then you want him. Did he? Tell me right now, did that fucking bastard do it? My God, I never thought of that. I thought at least you were normal in that way." James moved his leg to the floor and pushed his chair hard against the wall. His agitation drowned out the sensation of bodily pain.

She knelt at his feet, but she knew better than to touch him

216

at first. He looked down at her as if she were a carnivorous animal, his chin pressed tight down into his neck. "No, James, he did not do such a thing, and believe me, I was terrified. He was always too boozy to do anything. I think he just felt totally unloved and when he got drunk he became unlovable. That's why I never want to share my bed with a drunken man again. I don't want to make those choices between love and hate. That's why I kicked you out of bed. I wish I'd known enough to kick him out, but I only felt responsible in some way I didn't understand. I felt guilty." As she spoke she clung to his legs, her cheekbones resting uncomfortably on his two knees. She addressed the floorboards. He didn't pull away this time.

He wondered while her shaking began to quiet. "Why do you tell me this now, after so many years?" He spoke more gently to her than he had in a long time. He knew something important was going on between them.

"I only just knew it last night, when you pinched Polly's bottom. I suddenly felt guilty for no reason, and then I knew it wasn't my guilt to live with, it was his. But I bet you he never remembered a thing the next morning, James. That's what's so unfair about passing out. He never had to take any responsibility; he just passed his guilt on to me like everything else. I bet he had no idea what he sentenced me and Ma to."

"Your mother was there, too? No wonder she was so awful."

"In the doorway."

James shouted at her, "I'll kill him, Alma."

"Never mind, James," she said, collapsing to his feet, her tired-out self lying under his desk. She nestled on the floor. "In some way he's already dead. He died a long time ago."

Chapter 18

·······◦◦∞◦◦·······

IT WAS almost six o'clock, time to return to the present, to supper and the reality that this night's sleep would bring routine Monday. What Alma referred to as the Sunday-night fadeout. But instead she thought to borrow Polly's bicycle, chicly three-speed in this day of no-pumping ten, and to set out across town to reach the banks of the river, where the murky flow of polluted city waters seemed the respite she knew she needed right this minute. To be alone with something that moved slowly, sluggishly. Maybe at the edge it would be stagnant, crusty with yellowed foam. No motion at all might just stop the machinery in her head long enough to allow the mainspring to take a rest.

She conducted by herself the familiar struggle of hoisting the wheeled contraption up the decaying wooden steps through the bulkhead doors, the front wheel buckling back on her, one handlebar pinning her wrist painfully to the frame, to find herself enveloped by metal and rubber like loving a friendly boa constrictor or exercising a pet octopus. Unraveled, the bicycle at her side ready for the mount, she called "Goodbye" up to James, and waited.

He pushed up the screen and stuck his head out the study window. "Hey, wait a minute. Where are you going?"

"I just want to move around—a little exercise so I'll be able to think straight again."

"You don't have to think so much, Alma."

"Few enough people know how. I won't be long."

"You okay?" he asked.

"Sure."

"Be careful." He disappeared.

When she got to the familiar remains, the discards of too many lives there in the green plastic trash bags, lined up by the prickle hedge for tomorrow's collection, she hesitated. She felt too much alone.

"You want to come?" she hollered.

The next-door neighbor stood up from behind the hedge where he'd been kneeling in his chrysanthemum bed.

She smiled stupidly and pedaled smartly away, out of the circle and up Dover Street, which was the thin real estate line between modesty and signs of wealth. On the downtown side of the street the houses loomed large and spacious, expensive. On the side streets the maples and lingering elms stood hundreds of years tall, touching each other, branches extended in long association to form an *allée,* as if all the streets on the right side of town were to lead up to a gigantic stately mansion or palace where Zeus housed his lovers, mortal and immortal, or Louis XIV enjoyed the discomforts of his sycophantic court. Alma had a wonderful sense of freedom, possessed as she was by the breezes that only she controlled by her speed, breezes that swept her hair back from her face and soothed cool her bare legs. Rarely had she felt so pleased with the moment at hand. Other people's gardens began to interest her. The violet iris still bloomed beneath the front windows of that brown-shingled house. Changing sun and shade; so hard to remember when the planting season first began in spring. Cascades of nasturtiums, greenhouse grown, hung from a wide porch. Lily of the valley gone wild under a cedar tree; alyssum and sweet William outlining a walk. Alma planned her next year's garden as if this year's were already gone by, but then she covered days and days with visions of flower beds pulling her through the winters. More color next year, she resolved. Daisies, geraniums. Two more roses; she could just get away with them by moving the uncontrollably healthy Betty Prior up against the bare wall by the back door. Chop down remaining ailanthus, no matter what anyone says about danger. Ugly and tacky. Maybe she would try honeysuckle bushes, yellow ones and red, a thicket of them, smelling the night air up with sugar. She rode so swiftly through her miles of garden that she hardly noticed when the bus stopped in front of her, letting out a hideous escape of air and black exhaust right in her face as she artfully pulled left and began the gradual ascent toward the center of town, standing crouched over the handlebars as the grade rose. At the end of the street she coasted around the traffic circle, dangling one foot to give her better control—a thing she used to forbid her children to do, dangerous, and besides, the toes of their sneakers were always worn flat and slit open—on down the incline by the brick apartment buildings until she reached the highway before the river. Here the Sunday traffic was heavy and she stopped. Still, the only thing that mattered was to get to the other side, and on foot, with an awkward running step, she pushed the bike across in a break between the lines of cars, another forbidden rule of the road. Having made it safely, she had a sense of accomplishment. Here she was and now at least she knew where she was headed.

She turned to ride along the dirt path that traveled the river-bank, the water at the edge indeed almost motionless from residual filth, only churned up by the gentle waves spiraling in from an occasional motor launch. In the middle of the river the sun still sparkled off the blue-green, and while beneath the surface the water looked almost black, foreboding, at the far edge Alma could see the reflection of treetops. The shadows reached out across the water unevenly, so that the line they made looked like one of those graphs from the many little electrodes glued to the scalp that measure the path of the mind to determine normal thought disruption from physiological damage. She read her mind pattern across the water. After a terrible divergent jag from an extra-large leafy maple, it was smooth sailing, the little ups and downs of relative peace, almost like sleep. She pedaled with vigor and sang quite audibly, if anyone cared, but those who shared the river with her accepted her for the passer-by she was. "You can stop me from loving you. You can stop me from hugging, too," she sang. "You can say no, no, honey, that's all right, but I'll get even with you tonight, 'cause you can't stop me from dreaming." And she braked before a weeping willow tree to laugh out loud at the memory of the two of them, Mary and herself, maybe fourteen and seven, singing this old turkey in front of Mary's bedroom mirror. It was a nice memory. I suppose Mary had thought of romance by then, Alma said to herself. But for Alma it was the extraordinary pleasure of sharing a little amnesty with the one who seemed her natural-born enemy at the time, but who was after all her sister, and then Alma missed Mary so that it ached for a moment. Never mind, she thought, Mary would be there afterward.

At the bridge she walked her bicycle with the traffic light. She did not ride up the backside of the hill but along the roadway past the street leading to Pembroke Avenue until she reached the gates. She rode fast to the cemetery lot where the stone read "Margaret MacNeil Hughes, 1893–1962" on simple New England gray granite. The space at the top was for her father's name. It was the only piece of real estate Alma owned, and at that she shared the title, but even so it was an expensive and choice piece of land as these things go. That was supposed to comfort her.

She parked the bicycle along the flagstoned path that led up to the plot, the second of three in a row, the whole expanse of graves tastefully laid out and landscaped, as if all together these monuments to the dead, the headstones grouped like croquet wickets, formed the great playing fields where Alice encountered the Red Queen, double-faced, both terrifying and enticing, unreliable like death herself. It had been some years since Alma had done more than make a cursory visit to the grave that was hers to notice. Now she wandered behind the hedge of yews that bordered the newer part of the cemetery. In the distance she saw that the wrought-iron fence, all newly painted, had been extended to the edge of the road to include what used to be the old dump, now filled and seeded to house more spent lives that no one would know anything about years from now, and it occurred to her that there in some patch of grass one of those remains would, as likely as not, be her own. The occasional glimpses into her own mortality no longer frightened her the way they used to back when the children were young and her life seemed to be inexorably intertwined with the business of just keeping them alive. But now, when she thought of the natural limit put on her life, or worse still an unnatural death, she had an overwhelming sense of haste. Whatever it was she was up to, she'd better get at it fast. She had read about this feeling in the biographies and even autobiographies of great artists, scientists, world reformers, often the life line recognizably limited by diminishing through age or incurable disease. Such people seemed to her the antiheroes in their own dramas, victims of noteworthy talents and dedication that did not free them from the common denominator of all mankind. She hoped the spindly little trees planted here and there would hurry up and grow so that at least something living would dignify her demise. She trailed back across the yet virgin ground where she and Martin O'Shea had had their last conversation made up of complete sentences, such as they were. On and mostly off, from that day on, they had exchanged greetings, each mindful of sharp memories, some of hers secret even from him, and now she heard that he was a great naval architect or something equally unbelievable.

Majestically, she began humming snippets of Beethoven's *Missa Solemnis. Miserere,* she thought. When she got to *"Dona nobis pacem,"* she sang, coming in on all four parts, and pretty soon she got carried away with the fun of running a chorus of, say, a hundred voices and full orchestra, with three French horns, five double basses and the kettledrums, inside the small container that housed her brain. The noise boomed out. She even made a pretty good bass entrance by tucking in her chin as if the double-octave drop from natural contralto lay hidden down on the bottom of her lungs, the voice range lying in many-colored stripes like desert sands in a bottle. Why was it she had forgotten just how much fun it was to sing? She hadn't missed it until today, and she remembered that singing was something she did when she was happy.

She continued her ambling on past her bike to the edge of the pond. The water was lukewarm to the touch, the surface decorated with lily pads, and she knew when the sun went down the frogs would provide the music of the night. She and the frogs had something they shared. Birds made songs from the fruit trees that encircled the enchanted pond. Alma liked birds, but she made a point of not knowing too much about them for fear she would be taken for one of those bird nuts who never see anything the way nature intended, what with their binoculars and telescopes. The cemetery was awash with them on early spring mornings, popping up from behind bushes and shrubs like some comic detective in the movies. And Alma always fancied that the birds knew just what they were up to: a tantalizing pose at the tip of a well-exposed branch, beak up, throat and breast visible until, just as the focus was right, the lens adjusted, the light meter registering, then flight into the depth of the nearest cluster of evergreens. Alma was on the side of the birds.

She strolled across the road on the far side of the pond, beginning the climb up Tower Hill. Here and there among the old family graves were new names, some of them the parents of the companions of her youth. In many respects this was a reunion celebration. At the top of the hill she looked down into the familiar valley of tropical lushness, and of course she noted the twin gravestones, side by side, and wondered if anyone else shared the bedroom now. At the fence that was the barrier between her now and then, she traveled north until she could see the façade of the house on Pembroke Avenue. She looked at her watch. Six forty-five—time enough this day to stretch out on the grass for a moment. Flat on her back, her head resting on the palms of her hands, her ankles crossed, the one gesture, rigid, that kept her from total abandon, she closed her eyes against the failing light. She saw the full-moon-shaped patch, fibers completely worn down to the web of the upholstery fabric, where his balding head had rested for almost forty years. The chair was always pushed back against the built-in radiator, right by the window there, the Venetian blinds half closed against the manic-depressive nature of the weather to establish the absolute gloom of dead calm. She saw the patch on the chair, the bookcases emptied, the desk bare, the television missing from the center of the rug. He was not there. Even in the picture book of her mind the old man was gone from the house.

Alma felt the dreadful debilitation of loss reenter her body, reminding her of the early morning hours she had stood staring into the nothing from her kitchen window. The sensation was so deadening along the surface of her skin that she let the bug climbing across her shinbone and up the side of her leg reach all the way to her kneecap before she sat up to reach down to swat it. Red ant. It bit her before she got it. She rolled over and inched along on her stomach through the shrubs at the base of the fence. From this angle she could see the whole front of the house. She had seen it before, of course, since they had emptied it out, but now she noticed that the new owners had repainted the trim and thinned out the rhododendrons. The knocker looked polished; the stones on the gravel walk had been replenished. There was an unnatural newness to her house that made even the maple by the street look bigger and greener than it ought. If they had painted the shutters purple, maybe that would have been all right, but this was no violation at all. And she realized her loss, just like that, right there appraising the real estate of her past. She had spent all weekend tidying up in her mind, and here it was all spruced up in reality. There was nothing more to fight, no indignities, no ghosts. The loss was terrifying. What would fill the void? Well, James, Alma thought, maybe at last I've arrived. If all the angers are gone, we'll have to get on with all that hard work of loving. You ought to be glad. You've always said you wished I'd calm down. Maybe I'll consider a compromise, she said to him in her head. But what was the medium between passion and peace? She said it out loud.

"I'll be damned if I know." Then she spied a finial embedded in the ground. It was just a small one. Must have fallen off the top of a fence post. It had the familiar green-rot paint on it that she remembered. She picked it up and slipped it in her pants pocket, a last protest at the diminishing childlike energies and angers of Alma Hughes. And with that she started down the cemetery drive to where she had left the bike. But maybe not gone entirely; she cheered up at the thought, patting the pur-loined fence piece where it hung heavy against her thigh. Maybe there was just enough of Mr. and Mrs. Hughes's Alma in her to provide the momentum to make life worth living. The finial was a good souvenir. She was pleased.

Alma rode down the commercial street where the trolley car tracks used to run when she was a child, then up a residential side street by the blue-and-red gingerbread bunker and fenced-off area that was the skatehouse and ice rink, now a tennis club where the serious exercisers got in a few sets before the drink-ing hour settled over the town. On the broad avenue that was historic now, the beautiful old clapboards shaded by ancient copper beach or swallowed up by century-old English ivy or wisteria vines, the lavender flowers that hung lush passing now, Alma turned right, musing on individual and familiar houses that once held families she knew. Many of them had changed hands now as children grew to move out and parents became couples again, confronted with the necessity of facing each other alone after all those years. A move to smaller quarters was one answer, thought to be prudent what with age and taxes, but perhaps really a nesting in like newlyweds again, a shot in the long arm of togetherness that often as not didn't work. At the next intersection she turned left into the traffic along the city common and into the center of shops. The marquee on the movie house read *Bananas*. Just right. She had remembered correctly. An hour with Woody Allen, the sexiest man in the world. Refreshment. She stood at the curb, her bicycle resting against her rump. Responsibility. The Sunday crowds moved leisurely before her, absorbed in conversation and ice cream cones. The problem of no money and James suddenly fettered her, her freedom to choose getting all ached up in her forehead, mixed in with ideas of Sunday-night waffles and connubial companionship. Everything curdled. She scowled, and then she watched the people watching her, as if her thought processes, her conflicts, were lit up like colored dyes running counter to one another under an X-ray machine. Suddenly self-conscious, she began to push her wheeled impediment down to the sidewalk and across through the swinging glass doors into the modern day's misconception of the local confectioner's. Big three-foot-square blowups of a strawberry sundae with marshmallow topping, grilled cheese sandwich and pickle slice the size of a Frisbee, the "Blue Burger," the melted mold cheese drooling from the bun to form a sort of antimacassar effect along the sides. All plastic-shrink-wrapped so that nothing could be considered melt-in-the-mouth. Just inside the doors Alma ignored the "No Bare Feet, No Bicycles, No Dogs" sign. At least I have sneakers on, she thought. At the ice cream counter the manager called out, "No bikes in here, lady. Oh, it's you, Mrs. Thomas." Alma had already reached the entrance to the cooking area. Polly looked up from a row of hot dogs lying close together on the grill like a log roll. She stared and turned her back on what she saw, pushing the hot dogs forward with a pair of giant pincers to sizzle on another side. She wore a filthy white shirt and pants large enough to look big on a Bulgarian wrestler. As she went from one side of the small kitchen area to the other, graceful the way a professional clown knows how to move, Alma thought she looked like Charlie Chaplin, and for a moment she was overwhelmed with tenderness toward this updated version of herself.

"Ma, no bikes, you know that. That's my bike anyways."

"You'd gone to work, dear. I couldn't ask you."

"Yeah, never borrow something without asking first."

"May I leave it here a moment, dear?"

"How long is a moment?"

"Well, just next door awhile."

"Okay, this once."

The store manager stuck his head in over the counter and set the spindle with the order slips down hard.

"Ma. My job. Not everyone has a mother like you." Polly's voice began to rasp.

"I know, dear. Can I borrow five dollars? Then I'll be gone."

Polly picked up the tail of her shirt and fetched out her wallet. "Boy, Ma, you're just like a child, outfit and all. You've even got some dumb rock or hunk of dirt in your pocket." She handed her mother a bill. "You'd better call Daddy."

"You're in charge this time, Polly. If I don't come back soon, ride the bike home. Okay?" Alma darted through the door.

Polly hissed after her, "Always put back what you borrow, dear. Don't ride your bicycle in the dark, dear. Just let me know your plans, dear."

"I will when I know, dear," and Alma was gone.

Outside again, she realized she still didn't have any change. Back up the block, she purchased a ticket to the movie. When the change came down the funnel from the cash register, she pushed a quarter back through the hole in the glass. "Could I have two dimes and a nickel, please." From the plexiglass rectangle on the sidewalk that was the telephone booth, she observed the nonflow of traffic while dialing. A red VW bug was stopped in the middle lane right in front of her. The guy at the wheel hung onto the girl, lips to lips, as she backed out of the passenger door, her sun-browned legs showing up to the thighs, where her wraparound skirt parted. The inside line of cars moved over the curb to maneuver around the young bottom. Alma tucked her toes under to keep the tires from coming right on into the phone booth.

"Hello, James, it's me. . . . Yeah, I suppose you know that. Were you worried? . . . The police, how exciting. . . . Oh, you don't care. Well, then listen, that's all right. I'll be home sort of sometime. . . . The movies? . . . Well, I had to buy a ticket to get the change to call you. Okay? . . . Hungry? Yes, make something. I'll be home soon. . . . Of course I love you. Don't worry, I'm fine."

Alma hung up and leaned against the glass wall. Why did she feel she was big and brave when all she had done was what was expected of her? Almost. For she knew she didn't want to go home to him. Not just yet. In a little while. Some hollow lump pursued her and she went rather listlessly into the theater, ignoring a string of pictures announcing features to come. She passed by the ticket-taker, the popcorn machine, and went into the auditorium in a semihallucinated detachment induced by the sound of her mate's voice, like the Soma mushroom ritual of the ancient world, served up to appease the powers that be. Me, she thought, the powers that be. Sure, why not? In her mind she struggled with some simple idea that she could see but was unable to free and examine, shut up in a babyproof bottle that only a child could open or sealed onto a piece of cardboard under a bubble top of hard plastic, removable with a pair of hedge clippers perhaps, or a small boy's stubby fingers. The sound track brought her back her hearing. Revolutionary music. She looked up to see Woody Allen, pink-eyed behind those goggles, a kid in ragweed season, unable to hold two empty coffee mugs. She felt right at home. She took one last look into the see-through package in her brain. Something about love trapped in there to be let out, if she could peel away the wrapping or learn the right combination. Whose love? Her ineptitude to reach herself, her all-thumbs thoughts, wearied her, and she slipped gently into the meaningful-life dialogue between the two lovers on the screen.

Chapter 19

"So THEN he gives this order at the local delicatessen, see. Only they're out in the jungle, remember."

Alma chewed into the side of her toasted sandwich, mayonnaise and tomato seed spurting forth, a little hill of crumbs gathering before her on the kitchen table. She flicked them away from her almost to the other side, where James sat.

"Well, he goes in and orders maybe seven hundred fifty tuna on dark, a thousand egg salad on white, say. I don't remember exactly."

James lifted his beer and drank fully. "Hmm."

"All the time the deli guy is just writing down the order. Five hundred black coffee, three fifty extra-light. Twelve hundred dill pickles. When they bring on the cole slaw in wheelbarrows" —Alma waved her arms to encompass a roomful of cabbage and carrots—"that's when I knew it was time to come home to you."

"You were hungry." James sounded despondent. He looked at her privately. He still didn't know if she was coming or going. The wanting to capture her wonderful energy and knit it together with love and tolerance, like the rows of a lap robe, to keep them warm—the wanting was wringing him wet, more so than he could ever remember. His eyes were hot and he realized his cheeks were damp. He hadn't cried since Polly refused to hold his hand crossing through the hayfield on summer visits with his parents. She was eleven, and she told him it was babyish, and that she never really had been afraid of woodchucks or gopher holes; she had only said all that because he liked it. He cried then, to see her go, but no one knew. Now he brushed his hand across his face.

The motion brought Alma to a halt. She lowered her glass of milk and looked at him for the first time since she had come home. This has got to be right, she thought, and she took her time. It's got to sound like me to him. It's okay for him to care the way he does; once in a while it shows like this. If there's more of me for him, maybe there'll be more of this for me.

"Yes, I was hungry, James." She sounded serious. "I wanted you."

"Aw, shucks, Miss Alma. You don't have to say that."

"Knock it off, James. Why can't you behave as if you believe me? You want to believe me. You're not crying because you want me to go away. You're crying because you want me. Well, what if I want you? Try it on for size and keep it on long enough to feel comfortable. I'm made of good goods. I last a lifetime."

"I don't cry much, Alma." James was with her now. "I feel silly."

"Well, I cry all the time. It's good for what ails you." Alma reached to touch him. He took her hand and pulled her from her place at the side of the sink. And when she was beside him, he buried his head in her stomach. She patted his long silky hair, twisting the ends around her fingers. He clung to her, then pushed her away to look at her. She stood still for him. Her bare legs were streaked with dirt. One pocket hung down with the weight of some hard thing he had felt when he squeezed her. Her shirt was crooked across her chest. Her face was red with her animation. He laughed at her, and himself.

"I don't know why, but you look good to me. Welcome back, Alma. This has been one of the longest journeys you've ever made. I wondered if you'd make it home."

"I'm back, James. You're right, I was hungry," and she

jumped into his lap and squeezed his torso, kneeling in his crotch.

"That hurts." He got out the muffled message.

"Glad you've got the right feelings. Now I'll tell you all about me."

James peeled her away. "Later, Alma. Let's just do something peaceful tonight."

Upstairs, James and Alma nestled into the television, he propped up on some pillows, lying along the side of the bed, she curled up like a cat at the foot. The video box rested on the memorable radiator to the left of James's legs. It was twelve-inch and colorless, a halfway measure to give Alma the feeling that television in the small was not likely to take over her heart or that of James, or the children's, for that matter. Console television in color, she knew, was for those who had no hopes left to spend. Occasionally, when she and James stayed the night in a wonderfully garish purple and orange motel, the color TV, all set up on wheels like a tea table, was the raison d'être for a luscious lapse in taste. Alma had given up trying to reconcile her un-American gentility about good old black-and-white with her obvious pleasure in cops and robbers. She viewed it as the only thing comic to look at, and worried that she was not more concerned by sociological studies about the correlation of television programming to live violence and crime. Maybe to James, she had often thought, television was like joining a conversation, a slice of life, where he didn't feel obliged to talk. He was right there with the rescue squad, stethoscope in hand, but no time to deliberate, no need to dissect an idea, just back to the hospital waiting room to join the anxious wife or caring policeman. To James television was a holiday.

Alma reached out across the abyss between bed and the set to twiddle the dials. Sound blared out from a mishmash of shadowed lines, the soft lullaby of machine gun fire. Nothing would come into view.

"We're too late for a cozy rerun of *The F.B.I. in War and*

Peace," she said, and turned to another station.

"See if you can get a picture maybe," James said facetiously.

Alma shot him a beetle-brow look and twirled frantically with an exaggerated swing of her right arm, as if she were parking a moving van in a tight spot.

"Stop at that one, Alma. Sounds like McBride or MacSomething. You know, the one with the wife."

"That one's lousy. Never any action."

The picture came into focus. "Better stop while you're ahead," James advised. "Besides, I like him. He wears a big hat. I should get one."

"Your head would disappear. Your brains might get lost. Wouldn't suit you, James. You know, I think you have an outmoded image of yourself. When Ned was six he wanted to be a cowboy, too."

They were silent for a while, alone in the dark, the only light from the screen, invited into the living room discussion about crime and motive that played out before them. Alma moved up the bed to lie pressed alongside James, who extended an arm to cradle her head.

"I didn't want to come home this evening," she said. "Not right away."

"I know." He offered no more commentary.

Silence.

"Don't you want to know why?"

"I don't know if I do. I guess I just thought you didn't want to."

"Weren't you hurt?"

"Sure." He moved away from her, teetering, reminiscently, on the edge of the bed. On the screen the police car began chase through the streets of Los Angeles. James suddenly sat up to take careful note.

"Well, I'll tell you why."

"Do I want to hear it?" Eyes glued to the screen as cars careened around corners.

"Yes, you do."

The suspect captured. He came out with his hands up.

"I went to the cemetery on Polly's bike. It all seemed quite peaceful."

"Yeah."

"And I found myself on the other side of the tracks, so to speak." She sat up, too, to move in behind him. Breasts against his back, legs running parallel to his where there was room. The left one hung off the bed. She leaned her head into his neck, looking sideways out toward her bureau, where the old-fashioned pictures of her parents, costumed and young, before she knew them, hung on either side of the mirror to frame it. The sight of them, beautiful and expectant, gave her sustenance and she went on.

"I looked through the fence at the house on Pembroke Avenue." Alma paused. James said nothing. "It looked good, all spruced up, clean white trim, painted shutters. And he wasn't there. I guess that's what I really saw."

James reached back behind him; his hand found the thin layer of softness along the right side of her rib cage. "That's the point, Alma. He's gone."

"It made me sad."

"Of course it did, honey." James struggled to turn away from his escape toward her, back into her.

"But it also scared me."

"You mean death."

"No, James, oddly enough it wasn't the idea of death."

"Plenty of it there in that cemetery." James spoke cautiously. He felt off base with her again.

"No, not death. You don't understand. I was scared because I wasn't angry anymore."

"Look upon it as a blessing, Alma."

"Well, yeah, I know, but." Now she backed away from the contorted James, partially facing her, his left leg thrown over the bedpost, sitting sideways to the television set, where some woman in a laundromat had just accepted forty dollars from the Clorox man for her dirty white jeans.

Alma leaned on her arms, stretched out behind her.

"But what, Alma?" James sounded alarmed now. From the

set he heard that one side of the torn jeans was brighter than the other. Oh, God, will she just say it and get it over with? he thought.

"But you see, James, anger is so much easier to live with than love. I mean really live with, like how awful he was when he ate, for instance, and how I hate the way you run the spoon scraping back and forth across the bottom of your bowl of coffee, back and forth, back and forth, twenty times metal against the ceramic glaze. It drives me crazy."

"For Christ's sake, Alma, how did we get to my coffee?"

"It's easier to live with than loving you."

"Now, how can you honestly say that, Alma?" He looked disgusted. "Are you always going to be out of your mind?"

"I'm not nuts, James." She knew where she was going. "You think about it. Loving someone takes tolerance, patience, all that compromise stuff. It's hard on the ego."

He moved in on her, pushing her head back onto the pillows. Chin to chin, nose to nose, he nuzzled her. "Give it a try, Alma, it's about time," and rolled off her, back into the television show.

They lay in bed, in darkness and silence, one curled around the other, until the pain moved across James's arm that was tucked under Alma's shoulder. He extricated himself and flopped down on his side of the bed. Alma listened to the snores forming in his rhythmic breathing, and then she didn't hear them anymore.

The telephone, of course. Alma looked squint-eyed at the old-man clock. Not yet seven. Who in hell—but it stopped. James had not stirred. She went back into dozing, like wallowing in the deliciousness of an illicit hot fudge sundae. Some time later, she felt sure, she first heard a tap, another, and then the knock. When the door opened and Polly stood there before her naked but for the top of her thermal long johns, which she wore at night, year round, Alma knew.

"He's dead." She sat up on the edge of the bed. "It often happens before dawn."

"Ma, it's Bess. She's all blubbery; something's up."

Alma followed Polly down the stairs, and as she reached the receiver and phone box, one in each hand, from the floor next to Polly's bed, she flipped around the long black cord like some nightclub performer adjusting to keep from tangling clumsily with the snake of a microphone. She heard the sobbing on the other end of the line, but still she waited until she was seated on the bottom step of the stairs leading up to her own sanctuary.

"Bess," she said, and she listened. It had just happened. Just like that. Bess had heard the dog scratching on the door of his room and she went in on a hunch. He looked helpless, innocent. But she knew. "What will I do?" and she sobbed uncontrollably now. Alma soothed and stroked. "Of course, you did the right thing. Remember he never suffered. . . . Yes, he always did like bacon for breakfast. Too heavy, yes, but that can't have done it. Remember that was yesterday."

"You mustn't touch him, Bess, until I . . ." No, of course, Alma should have known Bess would be afraid. It's hard. Alma remembered. "I'll be leaving now, Bess. Now listen to me. Shut the door to his room and call the police. . . . Oh, all right, I'll call them, and the doctor. . . . Sure, Bess, I know it's hard for you. . . . Yes, he usually didn't have butter on his English muffin, but I'm glad he enjoyed it once in a while. Listen to me. You take the dog and go up to the farmhouse. You stay there. You'll be better off there. Now, don't you touch him, hear me. . . . Yes, as fast as I can, a couple of hours. . . . Yes, yes, I'm coming. I'll see you at the farmhouse." Alma hung up abruptly.

She saw Polly standing in the doorway across from where she sat. She's got legs like Judy Garland, Alma thought, incongruously. Then slowly she lowered her head into her lap and cried.

"How'd it happen, Ma?"

"I don't know, dear, it just did. I suppose it had to."

"I'm sorry, Ma." Polly ran her hand awkwardly across her mother's head down to her neck, then withdrew it. Without lifting her head, Alma reached out and placed her daughter's hand back on the nape of her neck. The warmth of the touch melted the icy tears, and Alma sighed several times to make room inside her for the grief to seed itself and be allowed to grow.

She stood up to hold Polly, her head on Polly's shoulder. And gradually Polly's grasp relaxed and she returned the embrace, and Alma recalled again the uneasiness she had felt when she first held a baby. "Thanks, Polly," she said. "It's not easy to hang on to a parent, but you're pretty good at it."

"What will you do now, Ma?"

"I don't know, Polly. I guess I'll go tell Daddy."

Polly lifted her mother's face at the chin and looked at her. "Oh, you mean my daddy," and she let her mother go.

Alma turned to mount the stairs. Her body traveled upward as if the brain messages that moved her legs had rusted out. The signals were unclear, the progress slow. She helped each step with a pull at the banister. At the top she smiled down to Polly. "I'm okay, dear. I sure love you for your help."

"I'm glad I did it right for you, Ma," Polly called up, pleased.

"See, there's going to be something good out of this, right, Polly? And besides, it was time, I knew it was going to happen. I knew it just in time," and Alma passed into the bedroom.

She sat for a moment, dangling her legs off the bed like a kid off the end of a jetty. I'm nobody's kid now, she thought, and she saw the shadows in the clock and at the door. This time they did not frighten her. I've got to get going, I suppose. I want to get there before they do anything to him. She pulled James, resting on his side, to lie on his back.

"He died," she said to him.

He made no response. She nudged him awake.

"He died, James."

"Who—what?" He popped open his eyes.

"Daddy died. In his sleep. Bess just called."

"Oh, no, Alma," and he pulled her to him.

"It's okay, I think, James. I've got to go there now. I've got to call the police and go."

"I'll go with you."

"No, James. I'll do the beginning alone. I want to be alone with him."

"What about her?"

"I told Bess to go up to the farmer. She didn't want to stay with him anyway. Says she's scared."

"I'd better come along with you, Alma." He kissed her eyes. Lids warmed, the tears came again.

"No, not yet." She cried fully now. "Don't be hurt, James. I'll be in touch. You won't be left out. I'm going to bring him home, where he belongs," and spent, she lay upon him. She kissed his lips, his bristly cheeks; she reached down toward his penis.

"Make love with me, James. I want to know I'm alive."

Alma drove fast, but she knew she drove well, somehow in control, alert, as if she were a teen-age driver again. The sky was clear blue, the sun already hot. It was going to be a long scorcher, she could tell. In more ways than one. When she thought about her father she saw him kneeling on the lawn before his neo-colonial dream palace in his ragman's outfit, digging out dandelions. In a funny pair of bathing trunks, like shorts, with an itchy undershirt top. He wore a nautical-looking belt around his waist. In his hand he held two brightly colored beach pails. In a white linen suit playing schmaltzy Schumann on the piano the afternoon of her wedding. He wore the wrong tie, she remembered now, and she was late to the church while he changed. But she didn't mind even then because it was the last moment just between them as father and daughter. She belonged to him for those few remaining minutes.

And then she thought of him dead. It made her nauseous and she sang to remind herself that she was really happy, in a way, that it was over. "Tea for Two." "You Were Never Lovelier." "Night and Day." No good. She knew she was scared; she looked forward to the relief she would feel after she saw him and the private part would be over. And she knew from experience how death was nowhere near as debilitating, permanent, as grief. She was anxious to begin the hard part, because she was eager to get it over, but it would not spread any faster than it wanted. Grief took its own sweet time, its own goddam slow-motion time. And you could not cut it out.

"Ye Hielands and ye Lowlands." She sang a dirge. "O where for ha'e ye been. They ha'e slain the Earl o' Moray and lain him on the green. He was a braw gallant and he rade at the ring; and the bonnie Earl o' Moray he might ha'e been a king. O lang will his ladye love look frae the Castle Doune ere she see the Earl o' Moray come soundin' thro' the toun.' " Coming fast up the dirt road from the airport to the old house, she reached: "Onward, 'tis our country needs us, he is bravest, he who leads us . . ." when she saw the patrol car pulled up in front of the chicken coops.

She jammed on the brakes, dead in the middle of the road. Her heart choked her behind her teeth; her hands vibrated, clasped on the steering wheel. A policeman stepped off the veranda and walked toward her, big easy steps that made her left foot, with nothing to do, dance on its toes. She put her head down on the horn inadvertently as he approached. The honk brought her body back together. She rolled down the window.

"I'm Mr. Hughes's daughter."

He stood before her. "Mrs. Thomas? You made good time." He opened the door for her. "Would you like me to park the car for you?"

Alma stepped to the roadside clutching her purse. She waited, as if she didn't know what to do next.

"The coroner has just left. Your dad seems to have passed on in his sleep. Heart, probably."

"Probably," she said. Mind, she thought. He knew what he was up to.

Alma didn't move.

"The doctor is up at the farm with Mrs. Hughes now. When I got here she was sitting on the porch there by the new railing, hanging on. I think she was a bit upset. She couldn't walk. I drove her and the dog up."

He drew near Alma. "Well, now"—extending his arm—

"maybe I'd better take you up there, too. A cup of coffee would do you good."

"No," said Alma crossly. "I told you not to touch anything. I told you to leave him alone until I got here. He's mine, not yours, and you're not taking me anywhere."

"They'll be coming from the morgue. We have to get the body out of the house, you know."

She walked toward the kitchen door. Her step was firm, her body erect, her face absorbed as if she were completing a business transaction.

"You better let me come in with you, Mrs. Thomas. These things can be quite a shock. Not so pretty." He strode to catch up with her.

"Won't be the first time," she called back to him. He followed her. "Don't you come in," she ordered him. "This is between me and my father," and she stepped through the door to let the screen slam behind her.

Alma shut the door and leaned against it, her bravado crumpling up like an unstarched shirt front. The house was filled with him, but it already smelled dried out with death, only three or four hours. She looked right through the pantry into the TV room, across the kitchen to the table where she had so recently sat with him, and at last into the first parlor, the door of his bedroom ajar. The rooms felt eerie, and she reconsidered her promise to herself to spend his first hours of death with him.

I'm afraid to see him. But you'll never forgive yourself. Mary never cared about these things. You do. It's now or never. There's no second chance. Okay, you're right. And she passed quickly around the obstacle course of furniture, placed there now to halt her progress, pushed open the door and looked.

To her astonishment he lay backward in the bed, feet almost touching the headboard, his still shiny dome of a head pointed between the old pair of dirty green bedroom chairs where Thomas and Margaret had so often sat. The tubes and bags were pushed aside into a corner, but he must have pulled them all askew in his turning. The question would stay with her forever, and no one would know quite why he laid himself out this way. Alma could guess.

A thin blanket covered his whole body up to the neck, as if to keep him warm, the tiny, fragile form perfectly outlined beneath, arms at his sides to the waist, shoulders broad enough but tapering down to the lower torso of a young child. But he seemed longer lying down like this. He was not bent over. She dared now to look fully at his face. The ruddy color of his attack, not yet browned, gave his purple-white skin an unreal color, his beige lips a touch of pink, but she could stand it. It was not unattractive. His eyes were half-lid shut, as if they had refused the coroner's touch until she got to him, she thought. He knew she would come.

Why? How come he knew she would come? Alma stood over him, inspecting the old man's thought processes now that he had none, a judgmental exercise. Was she ready to believe herself, and him? Did he never recall the violation, the perfidy he suffered her, and in her own childhood bed? Had he ever remembered? With unspoken shame and guilt as he ought. If so then why again and again until the last time, when he was actually at her, closing her against his everything, she unrelenting in her entombment of him, alive, until time taught her to let him loose? Or was he, indeed, as heartless in his unlovely affection as she had so often believed, her anger at him freezing up her want?

Come on, Alma, this is no time to dredge up all that, he's trying to look up to you. You're wrong again, she answered herself back firmly. It's the only time. If there is anyone who knows why these two may not be joined in natural relationship, speak now or forever bite your tongue.

And then she passed the final sentencing, irrevocable, before he reached the grave.

He never remembered. He could not have faced himself or her.

He never knew.

She believed it as clearly as she could spy the longing still lingering in his unfocused eyes. She would have him die at last, and in peace. Carefully, the tips of her fingers numbed by her own boldness, she closed his eyes against the light of her gaze, then timidly drew back the cover down midway, where his small hands rested across his diaphragm. She reached out, pulled back, reached again and finally placed one in her palm. The warmth was gone, but the flesh was soft. She dropped it like a snake, repulsed. It fell uneven with the other, on the white hairs of his shrunken old chest.

"Oh, Daddy." She spoke quickly, softly, the love-worn familiarity escaping her as if released from a bottle of soda water. The sound of her own speech hovering in the silence that only she could break alarmed her, and she grabbed his shoulders roughly between her hands and swiftly kissed him on the forehead. Her lips were warm with fear, his tight-stretched skin cool like a polished stone. Covering him completely, she left him forever, closing the door behind her, and went to sit in the wing chair where James had stood last Friday.

"That's him dead," she said to the armchair that Mary had wanted. "He's dead," she repeated. "He's dead," she yelled, "and I want him back." She rose up, hurrying to the bedroom door. She could have him in death. Nobody else would want him. But she took her hand from the latch at last and walked into the front room.

Before the mirror, her mother's favorite, she looked to see her own middle-aged face, the blond hair a little faded, the cheeks dead white now, the lips blood red with life. "It's okay," she said, calm, "he's dead. He died. He's dead now. Maybe you can have him back." Alma saw beyond herself in the mirror, the dark splotches of wear here and there in lines and circles and free-form shapes as if shining spotted black through the antique glass to mar the gloss, imperfection grown accustomed to like muddy puddles of disappointment and lonesomeness across the surface of anyone's life. She thought first of her mother, then of her father. The idea seemed applicable to both, separately and now together. She didn't often think of them together. "Now that you know something about what he and she were about, maybe you can have the good parts of both of them, and leave the rest to die," she continued.

Startled by the ease with which she considered casting aside pieces of her parents as if they came apart like a picture puzzle, Alma looked back at herself, ready to scold. Distracted, she saw the morning sunlight through the side window reflected back at her. It fell directly on an eighteenth-century bronze candelabrum, four-branched, the stem the figure of a young maiden discreetly draped in twists of golden leaves. Her mother used to light the candles on special occasions—birthdays, Armistice, Twelfth Night. It had bored Alma as a girl and even in adulthood it was not her style. She had missed it in her previous inventory. But now the crystal drops hanging on wired pins from each bobêche threw rays of color into the room, the sharp edges of the prisms glowing purple, yellow, green, pink. The whole thing seemed to dance freely, irresponsibly, in the midst of life and death.

Alma laughed. "It's okay, Alma," she said to her own image, "it's over."

She left the mirror, the chairs and tables of her former life mixed in with some other. She left the body of her dead father, to be dealt with now so that she could take him home and set him in the ground where he belonged. She walked into the kitchen and picked up the telephone receiver to call James. As she dialed she looked at her watch. Only ten o'clock. 24. Monday. Four days. That's all it took, four days. And she thought purposefully on James. She knew her James. If he wasn't taking one of his secret showers, he'd be in the kitchen dripping egg yolk and bacon grease all over the burners of the stove. He was still on extended hols from her. Not for long.